THE
OTHER
NORMALS

THE
OTH
NORM

HER

MALS

NED VIZZINI

Balzer + Bray

An Imprint of HarperCollins*Publishers*

Balzer + Bray is an imprint of
HarperCollins Publishers.

Library of Congress Cataloging-in-Publication Data
Vizzini, Ned.
        The Other Normals / Ned Vizzini. — 1st ed.
               p.   cm.
        Summary: "A boy is sent to camp to become a man—but ends up
on a fantastical journey that will change his life forever"—Provided by
publisher.
        ISBN 978-0-06-207990-9 (hardcover bdg.)
        [1. Maturation (Psychology)—Fiction.   2. Fantasy.]   I. Title.
PZ7.V853Ot   2012   2012014341
[Fic]—dc23   CIP
                                                                AC

Typography by Torborg Davern
12 13 14 15 16   CG/RRDH   10 9 8 7 6 5 4 3 2 1

First Edition

TO MY FATHER—

who taught me that an adventure story must always "deliver the goods."

I love you.

THE
NOR
W

MAL
WORLD

1

THIS IS A STORY ABOUT BECOMING A MAN, so naturally it starts with me alone in a room playing with myself. Not *that* way—playing Creatures & Caverns, the popular role-playing game. *Popular* being a relative term. I guess if Creatures & Caverns were really popular, I would have other people to play with.

"Perry!" my brother, Jake, calls, knocking on the door. "Are you ready to go to your stupid store?"

"Hold on a second!" When my brother sees my gaming materials, his automatic response is to make fun of me, so I hide them in my backpack and put it on. My graph paper, manual, and mechanical pencils disappear quickly as he turns the knob and enters, smiling under his long hair, with his guitar slung over his shoulder.

"C'mon, I'm gonna be late for practice."

We head down the hall. Jake walks like he's carrying a tank in his pants and I try to imitate him, but my legs aren't long enough. Mom is in the living room having a conversation with her boyfriend, Horace. You can tell she's talking to Horace because her feet are up on the couch and she's twirling her fingers in the air as if there were a phone cord when there isn't. She's in lazy Sunday-afternoon mode, like I was until a few minutes ago.

"Perry? Oh, Perry's doing fine, you know. He's a late bloomer."

I squint at my mother. She doesn't even notice me. I wonder how that bizarre notion could enter her head. *Late bloomer?* I'm an RPG enthusiast. I'm an *intellectual.*

"Hey! You coming?" Jake calls. He's already at the front door. I follow him out—intentionally not saying "Bye, Mom!" because maybe that's what *late bloomers* say.

Jake and I walk to the subway through New York streets piled high with recycling bags awaiting Monday-morning pickup. It's a gorgeous spring day and the daffodils are out in small plots for trees, where dogs will be attracted to soil them. The late-ish bloomer-ish phrase bounces around in my head. As a fifteen-year-old you don't want to be compared to a flower. By your mother. And then have the flower be faulty. The daffodils make it worse: they bloom on the same damn day every year.

2

MY BROTHER AND I SIT ON THE SUBWAY.
Jake takes out a water bottle and sips it and turns his headphones
so loud that I hear them next to me. I always hated people who
did that, and now he does it—but I don't hate him, I worry about
his ears. He's listening to his own band, The Just Because, which
has a small reputation in New York for disrupting "battle of the
bands" competitions but is otherwise rightfully unknown.

We are the stoners (aah-ah!)
We built America (aah-ah!)
We built America (ah-ahhh)
Yes we did

"That's a stupid song," I tell Jake, even though it's catchy. I
wrinkle my nose. Somebody on this train smells like booze. I
check the car—there's a homeless guy lounging in the corner in
rumpled, stained clothes, taking up two seats.

"What?" My brother turns the music down.

"Nobody wants to hear songs about you smoking pot and
building America."

"I didn't write it. The singer wrote it. I don't smoke. Girls don't like it." He sips from his water bottle.

"Jake, what are you drinking?"

"Raspberry-infused vodka."

"What the—?" I pull out my phone. "It's *twelve*!"

"Exactly. Sunday-afternoon cocktail."

"Give me that!" I grab for the bottle. Jake uses his long arms to keep it out of reach. He stuffs it back into his guitar bag. "You can't start drinking in the middle of the day!"

He grabs my arm and squeezes, *hard*, like a mechanical claw. "Shut up, bro. Don't embarrass me. There are girls on this train."

He nods across from us at a beautiful woman with short blond hair and earbuds. I don't know how I missed her. I'm supposed to have laser focus for people like this. Maybe if I were blooming properly I would. She looks up from the book she's reading. *Jane Eyre.*

"Don't look at her," my brother tells me.

"I'm not."

"Then why are you looking at her?"

I look down.

"I'm a musician," he whispers. Vodka and raspberries hit my face. "It's my right and duty to stay buzzed whenever I can."

"No it's not. You're going to get in serious—"

"You have bigger things to worry about anyway: I heard you're going to summer camp."

"What?"

"Heard Horace tell Kimberley."

"No! Why?" So far, in life, I've managed to avoid summer camp by excelling at math enough to qualify for a program called Summer Scholars in the city.

"Dad wanted to send you to math camp, but Mom's making you go to real camp with public-school kids."

"I *am* a public-school kid!"

"You're a specialized-school kid."

"Why now? I'm too old to go to camp. Wouldn't I be a counselor?"

"Inflation. Horace told Kimberley that Mom can't afford to have you home all summer. You consume hundreds of dollars a week in food, although I don't know where you put it. With camp, for a few grand she doesn't have to feed you or do your laundry or anything. Maybe she'll send you for three or four weeks, but if she really wants to save cash, she'll send you for eight. She already gave you that bowl haircut; that'll last until September."

I touch my hair. Our parents, after entering their divorce proceedings eight years ago, each began dating their divorce lawyers. Dad's is named Kimberley; Mom dated a number of different lawyers until she found Horace. Due to their special relationships with my parents, Kimberley and Horace handle their cases pro bono.

"Kimberley says that Mom read an article about how boys who go to summer camp become more 'emotionally mature' men."

I stay quiet.

"And you're already having issues in that department if you're riding with me to buy Creatures and Caverns books."

"Like you're going anywhere important."

"Legendary Just Because band practices *are* important. And I don't understand why every time I give you a chance to go to one, you just want to play by yourself in your room. I don't make up the rules, Perry. Creatures and Caverns is a waste of time! There are certain things that are so uncool they're cool, but role-playing games isn't one of them."

The train screeches to a halt. Jake drinks more vodka. The *Jane Eyre* girl gets out.

"What's the name of the camp?"

"Some normal name. It's very traditional, I think, with canoeing and log splitting and bears and counselors who molest children. In New Jersey. It'll be good for you! What else you gonna do? You didn't make Summer Scholars this year, right, because you're a bitch?"

I ignore him, but it's true. It's a permanent blot on my math career. A month ago, on a qualifying exam, I did what I call a mutant paradigm shift: I filled in the answer for problem 15 in the bubble for problem 14 and then shifted every subsequent answer up by one question. Even though it was possible to see that I completely understood the questions, my score had to be counted with the incorrect answers. Mr. Getter, the Summer Scholars coach, told me he couldn't have such a sloppy performer on his squad. I tried to explain the situation to Mom and Dad directly *and* through their lawyers, but they wouldn't hear it. I was about to try and get into college, they said, and hadn't they told me that no matter how divorced they were, I had to get into a good college? Mistakes of inattention—*human fallibility*—were no longer to be coddled or explained away; that period of my life was over. I got the feeling that my parents wanted me to get a *job* this summer, but I didn't know where—a bookstore? The zoo?

"What were you going to do all summer? Play Creatures and Caverns by yourself?"

I don't say anything.

"Jeez, Perry."

"I like looking at the books! Is that so bad? It's perfectly normal to enjoy reading role-playing-game manuals and making up characters by yourself."

"It's normal for some people, not for normal people."

3

WE GET OFF AT EIGHTY-SIXTH STREET in Bensonhurst, Brooklyn. Jake heads to band practice while I go to Phantom Galaxy Comics, which is like a three-story nerd mother ship. The first floor has comics thumbtacked to the walls and ceiling in polystyrene bags; the third floor has Pokémon cards; the second floor is home base for me—warm, brown, and quiet like an English den. The role-playing-game floor.

Alone, allowing the door to close behind me with the *bing-bong* of the electronic bell, I climb the steps. I always close my eyes and picture the RPG floor before I reach it. It has walls plastered with huge rich posters of fantasy creatures and landscapes: a beautiful woman with a dragon on a leash, an elf looking into a reflecting pool and seeing a human reflection, the album *Led Zeppelin IV.* It smells woodsy and solid, not glossy and cheap like the comics downstairs. As I reach it, though, I stop. I have the feeling I'm being watched.

I've heard this feeling expressed before in movie scores through the use of rising violin noise. I've never experienced it, though. I'm stunned at how clear it feels. As if something hot is sitting on my neck.

I whirl around. Nothing. Then a *skritch*, like a pencil taking down a note . . . but in front of me is just a smiling gnome on a poster and a security camera.

4

AT THE CASH REGISTER, A MAN SITS
behind a glass case. Below him are cabinets full of pewter
miniatures—small metal figures like toy soldiers. When you
get really into Creatures & Caverns, you can buy them and
paint them to be like your characters.

"Interested in something?" the man asks. I've never seen
him here before. He occupies his chair in the rough shape of a
pyramid with a sweatshirt.

"A new Creatures and Caverns expansion."

"Looks like you have some minis you're interested in too.
Want to see any?"

I scan them. The small silver figures look ready to do battle
for the fate of the world: knights, dwarfs, skeletons, pikemen,
horsemen, wizards, and dragons pitched forward wielding
swords, axes, spears, halberds, war hammers, staffs, and
poisonous breath. An archer draws back a flaming arrow with a
thin ribbon of metal curling up for the smoke.

"Are you playing a campaign right now?" the guy asks.

"No, I just make up characters by myself. I don't have
anybody to play with."

"Who's your main character?"

"I don't have a main one."

"You don't? Here's mine."

He pulls one of the minis out of the glass case. The glass squeaks as he closes it. The figure is a tall, thin wizard with a staff, who looks like Gandalf . . . but to a degree, all wizards look like Gandalf. This one is younger, with a goatee.

"That's Roland of Cornwall. Twelfth-level illusionist in the Pax Pastorum expansion. Here's his sheet."

He slips me a laminated sheet of paper. It has a colored-pencil drawing of "Roland of Cornwall" with his game stats: Strength 42, Speed 37, Health 38, Intelligence 99, Wisdom 99, Personality 99, Honor 2.

"In the new edition of the game, they give you an Honor stat. Characters with low Honor are more inclined to steal things and lie and cheat. Characters with high Honor are more inclined to get killed."

"I know about the Honor stat. Why is your character named Roland of Cornwall?"

"After me. I'm Roland."

"Are you . . . from England? Cornwall is in England."

"Of course. I'm into England."

"But you're not *from* England."

"I'm *into* it. It's an interest of mine."

I stifle a laugh.

"What d'ya think is funny?" Roland snatches Roland of Cornwall away. "If you're gonna laugh at me, you can get outta here. Go laugh with your friends. First you'll have to find some."

"I'm sorry."

"What do you name your characters, if you're so smart?"

"I'm never good with the names." Names are a certain place my head doesn't go. "I get stuck trying to think up different ones. Usually I just forget it and move on to create another character."

"That's because a name has to mean something. What's *your* name?"

"Perry Eckert."

"What do people call you?"

What a strange question, I think, considering that people *do* call me something different; am I the sort of person who everyone knows has a nickname? That only works for people in sports, or superheroes . . . I realize an Indian raga is playing through the sound system in the store, drifting around me and Roland like a waterfall.

"There are people who call me . . . Mini Pecker."

"Really? How did that begin?"

I sigh. I've told this story many times to people who I wanted to be my friends. They never became my friends. The story entertains me, though, so I keep telling it. Is this a disorder?

"This guy Justin Racho. He ran up on me in first grade. I was at a urinal in the bathroom. He shoved me on it so I hit the cold white part. I sprayed pee all over myself, and he yelled, 'Perry Eckert, Mini Pecker!' A friend of his named Jacoby Myers heard it in a nearby stall. He started laughing.

Now they still call me that."

"Mini Pecker?"

"It doesn't help that I'm short. I'm a late bloomer."

Roland doesn't look more inclined to be my friend, but he does look more inclined to make money off me at Phantom Galaxy. "I've got the perfect name for you," he says. He writes on a scrap of paper:

Pekker Cland

"Pekker?"

"Like they make fun of you for, but you spell it differently, to reclaim it, like *queer*."

"What's a Cland?"

"Cland sounds like *clan*, so maybe with a character named Pekker Cland, you can attract a clan and not just play Creatures and Caverns by yourself."

I stare at the name. You know what? There's something to it. I wouldn't mess with a person named Pekker Cland.

"As for a C and C expansion, have you heard of the *Other Normal Edition*?"

Roland steps out from behind his glass case and leads me down an aisle. We aren't alone; there's a hidden customer who potentially just heard everything that transpired, including the Mini Pecker stuff—a skinny black kid, about my age, with a shaved head and oval glasses and big ears. He tosses a bag of glass beads up and down. As we approach him, he examines a book on the shelves—a thick hardcover with a genie laughing over a pirate ship on the cover. *Maybe*, I think, *he's the person I felt spying on me before.*

Roland grabs the book. It's the last copy. "Sorry, I have a *customer* interested in this."

"No, it's okay," I say, pushing the book away. "You take it," I say to the kid. He clearly wants it.

"No, *you* take it," Roland says, "because he's here all the time and he never buys anything."

The kid pitches his bag of beads on the floor. "Fuck you, Roland. I don't even want it." He stalks away down the aisle.

"Drama!" Roland calls. "Outta here!" He picks up the beads.

"Do you know him?"

"That's just Sam. Don't worry about him. Check the book out. It's an alternate-universe thing they're doing based on *Arabian Nights*."

As I open the *Creatures & Caverns Rule Book: Other Normal Edition*, the raga climaxes.

5

SOMETIMES WHEN YOU OPEN A BOOK, time stops. I know this is supposed to happen with great novels, but to me it happens more with role-playing-game manuals. Honestly, I can't tell you how long I spend looking at the *Other Normal Edition* because I am immediately lost in the game world, which is called Enthral Moor and is centered in the folklore of classical Baghdad. I find a chart with sixty-four different types of scimitar on it. Sixty-four—2^6! An old friend, sixty-four. I look at the book's authors.

"'Gerard Hendricks and Fayid Ahmed. Special Consultant: Mortin Enaw.' What kind of a name is Mortin Enaw?" I ask Roland.

"Don't ask me. Very gifted people write these books."

"I'll take it."

"You want to buy a mini, too?"

I shake my head. Figures like Roland of Cornwall are expensive. Besides the free legal advice, another thing that keeps my parents' divorce going is that they're both very cheap, so they keep finding new things to fight over. They keep me on a tight leash. Financial requests have to go through the lawyers.

If I get a job this summer (computer programmer? cashier?), I'll be able to afford one of the figures, but I know this is the last summer before the summers that *really* count for college, and the idea of getting the *Other Normal Edition* and reading it every day alone and stopping time is beautiful to me. I'll wake up when the light comes into my room(s) and track the angles, reading the book in a sunbeam, understanding the sun the way the ancients did, leaving the house(s) just once to get on the subway because at least with divorced parents I have a reason to get on the subway anytime, to be "going home," and then . . . maybe I'll spot the *Jane Eyre* girl again! Only when I see her next, I'm going to ignore her and do something with my body that attracts her—blow hair across my brow or smile so that wrinkles crinkle at the sides of my eyes . . . something that works like it does in the movies.

6

I DECIDE TO MAKE MY NEW CHARACTER, Pekker Cland, reflect me as much as possible. It isn't a pretty picture. In Creatures & Caverns, a strength of 99 means that you can lift boulders and bend iron bars; I figure I'm a 2. A speed of 99 means you can outrun a cheetah; I figure I'm a 7. The only stats I think might be high are my intelligence, which I peg at 65, and my honor, which I figure is 50.

I'm going to make Pekker Cland human—until I read in the book that besides the usual options of human, elf, and dwarf, I can make him a *ferrule*. Ferrules are like humans except they have red skin, yellow hair, and tails. They are highly intelligent, live underground, and are impervious to fire. After I make Pekker Cland one, I have to find a profession for him, but based on my stats the only thing he's qualified to be is an artisan.

> *The* artisan *is a master of fine craft. Renowned for his/her skill at the forge, he/she creates weapons and armor and understands the principles of runecraft. An artisan may not fight in battle, but through his/her handiwork, a certain artfulness is always present in the blood that dots the land of Enthral Moor.*

I think, *Epic*. I'm not sure if Gerard Hendricks, Fayid Ahmed, and Mortin Enaw went to writing school, but as far as I'm concerned they're better than anybody that teachers make me read. The book says things like "the tempestuous force of high-level magicks" and "the fickle bodies of maidens in the chambers of slavering warlords." Though it starts out glossy and smelling like wax, as I read it in bed and get crumbs in the spine and dog-ear the pages and underline the important parts, it blooms into a danker, older smell.

7

"WHY AREN'T YOU ASLEEP?" MY BROTHER asks from the top bunk. The clock reads 3:35.

"I'm reading my *Rule Book*. Learning about lock picking."

"Uh-huh."

"Do you know about lock picking?"

"I'm sure it's like sex."

"I'm sure it's not like sex."

"How would you know? Everything's like sex. It's the universal metaphor. To pick a lock, let me guess, you have to go slow at first, but then you have to pull off some fancy moves, and you have to stay concentrated, and you have to stick something in something, right?"

"Jake, stop. What are you doing up anyway? Drinking schnapps?"

He climbs down and wrestles my flashlight from me. "Only pussies drink schnapps!"

He kicks me out of our room, so I have to go read the *Rule Book* in the bathroom. I get so into it that my legs fall asleep on the toilet. When I get up, I collapse on the floor. All this happens in Mom's house in Manhattan, where the neighbor's bathroom is six inches from our bathroom, and as I lie on the floor unable to move my legs, the neighbor's cat perches in the window and mews at me. Then Horace, who was busy sleeping with my mom, decides he has to use the bathroom, so he shoves open the door, whapping my skull to crinkle my neck into an unhealthy position. "Ow!"

Horace closes the door and goes back down the hall as if nothing happened. He doesn't like to stay in places where he might be liable for things. I sleep on the bathroom floor curled around my book and wake up with bruises.

8

AT SCHOOL, MR. GETTER CORNERS ME AFTER
an Intro to Logic class. "Perry, um, we need someone, um, for
the meet this weekend."

"I'm not on math team anymore, Mr. Getter. You kicked
me out when I failed to qualify for Summer Scholars."

"You're still a, um, reserve member."

"Like an understudy? Since when?"

"Michael Imperio is, um, sick, understand?"

"Michael Imperio is never too sick to do math."

Behind me, the students have all left and gone home or to
a ninth-period class or to a club or to a sports team because it's
2:55 and they have better places to be than talking to a teacher
who says "um" every other word. I think about camp. Will it be
like being sent to a 2,048th-period class?

"All right, um, he's not sick, he has an, um, issue with
qualifying for this meet."

"You mean like not having a green card?"

Michael Imperio comes from a country in South America
that doesn't have good diplomatic relations with the US.
Despite his lack of proper American entry protocol, he was

accepted into my school, Simmons Leadership Academy, due to his math skills, which are the sort of skills that might help steer the future of America.

"Um," Mr. Getter says.

"Yeah, fine, I'll sub for you. Where's the meet?"

9

I WILL PROBABLY NOT DO WELL. I WILL probably be humiliated by a greasy student next to me with a boil; this has happened. One math whiz from Cambodia via Bronx High School of Science has a boil on his forehead, right of center; when I sat next to him at a meet I began wondering about the way a particular drop of sweat was likely to run down the surface of the boil and lost my train of mathematical thought.

I walk into the classroom where we're having the meet with my face buried in my *Other Normal Edition*. Although it's at a different school, the room is as familiar as the role-playing-game floor of Phantom Galaxy Comics, as comfortingly sealed from the outside world and climate-controlled, even if it is a tropical sweatbox climate. The boil Cambodian is nowhere in sight. I set my cell phone to "off" and sit. I look up, shocked—I'm right next to the kid I saw in Phantom Galaxy. Sam.

"Hey," he says. "What's your name?"

He seems a lot calmer than he was in the store when he threw down his bag of beads. He's at the back row of desks; he's an understudy like me. I put my *Other Normal Edition* away.

"You been playing?" he continues. "My name's Sam."

"I know, Roland said—"

"Screw Roland. Fat bastard."

"Why are you here?"

"I got accepted to my school's math team. You have a problem with that?"

"You're not following me?"

"Why would I follow you? Why would *anyone* follow you?"

"You could be planning on ridiculing me in some elaborate way."

"Get over yourself. You been playing the *Other Normal Edition*?"

"Just by myself."

"What do you mean?"

"I just read the book and make up characters by myself."

"What, you think you get points for being sad?"

"No, I'm just telling you the truth—"

"Where do you play?"

"Everywhere. Mom's house, Dad's house, school . . ."

"What school?"

"Simmons." I know his school from the blackboard at the front of the room: Xavier in Brooklyn.

"I hang out near Simmons. You want to play sometime?"

"Really?"

"Yeah. I can't find that book anywhere."

"Why?"

"Look it up on the internet. Try A-Plus Comics in Flatbush. Prison Planet. It's nowhere."

"Why not? It's a great expansion."

"It's sold out. How spoiled are you? You never heard of something being sold out? Where do you play in Simmons?"

"At the bottom of the fire stairs by the science labs."

"Perfect."

"Excuse me? Mr. . . . *Eek-er?*" the proctor says.

"Eckert."

"Mr. Eckert, can you please come to the front of the room with your answer sheet?"

"I didn't get an answer sheet yet. We haven't started."

"This will serve as your answer sheet," she says. She's a prim woman with skin that's wrinkled and tight at the same time. She writes *Disqualified for speaking* on a piece of paper and passes it to my team captain, the assiduous and silent girl Min, who is so brilliant that she has rendered herself asexual (and whom I always feel guilty about characterizing this way).

"If your group has no other team members to take your place, you'll have to forfeit the match," the proctor says.

"I, uh—"

Mr. Getter steps into the room; he was outside pacing by a bench with the other math coaches.

"We have one, we have one!" he says, and produces Michael Imperio, who produces a Police Athletic League card. I've been told that these are get-out-of-jail-free cards if you ever get busted for pot or jumping turnstiles in New York. Apparently they work at math meets too. Michael Imperio takes my seat. I wave good-bye to Sam, who's now sitting with such attentiveness and rectitude that apparently he can't be disqualified for speaking.

10

I HAVE A GOOD THING GOING ON THE fire stairs. No one messes with me; I can set up my dice and my *Other Normal Edition* and my graph paper and mechanical pencils and create characters to my heart's content. A few times since I got the book I had the feeling I was being watched again; once I heard the *skritch-skritch* pencil noise like in Phantom Galaxy . . . but it was probably just me making the character sheets.

As I'm setting up my area a week after the disastrous meet (Mr. Getter isn't talking to me at all now, not even a single "um"), Sam opens the gray metal fire door. "What's up?" he asks.

"What are you doing here? Aren't you supposed to be in school?"

"School ended."

"Five minutes ago! Your school is in Brooklyn, I thought!"

"I cut some classes, calm down. I've been looking for you."

"You must be really obsessed with this book."

He pulls a pack of cigarettes out of his hoodie. "You want?"

"What? To smoke it?"

He scowls and creaks open the door he just entered. This door has an angry red bar on it that says EMERGENCY—ALARM WILL SOUND, but now Sam has opened it twice, from inside and outside. Why did I never try?

Sam blows smoke out the door. I watch it curl away into the spring air. He looks nervous while he smokes, but then he looks very relaxed. He asks, "You chill here, but you don't smoke? You could sell *drugs* in this piece."

"People do that. And there's a couple that comes here to make out some days, and yesterday the girl told the guy she was pregnant."

"So? Is it your baby?"

"No!"

"Then how come it's your business? I don't want people to know I play C and C. If you're the kind of person who spies on people and talks crap about them, I don't want to even start this."

"Sorry."

"All right." He shakes my hand, still smoking. "Now, what kind of character do you play?"

"Artisan. Named Pekker Cland."

"*Artisan?* What's wrong with you?" For a minute I think he's going to ask, "You gay?"—but he doesn't and I like him for it. "You got no business playing RPGs unless you're a magic user." His glasses slide down his nose. He motions for the *Other Normal Edition*. He turns to the runecraft section.

"You know what the best spell is? There's one that makes

people fall in love with rocks. You cast it on them, and they'll fixate on the next big rock they see, and they'll think that rock is a beautiful man or woman, and they'll marry it and give up everything that they have going in life, and they'll stop fighting if they're in the middle of a battle, just to be with the rock. It's an eleventh-level runecraft. Rock Spouse."

"Do you play a certain character?"

"I got a bunch. One of them's a mystagogue. She's like a fortune-teller with the skills of a highly trained assassin."

"What level?"

"Thirteenth."

"Wow!"

"I got another who's a seventh-level thief. But the best is a fifteenth-level barbarian I got. Peter Powers."

Sam reaches into his hoodie and takes out a black velvet drawstring bag. He opens it to reveal a perfect pewter miniature: a bald giant with a huge beard standing in a pile of snow, snorting in the cold air, holding a mace high, about to bring it down on an enemy.

"How'd they sculpt his *breath*?" I peer in fascination.

"I don't know." Sam puts him back. "Maybe if you look at it too hard, it'll go away."

"Sorry. Where do you get the money to buy figures like that?"

"What'd I tell you about being nosy?"

"Sorry."

"You just told me sorry three times, and we haven't even

talked for two minutes. What, you think if you say it enough, the Candyman is gonna come?"

"Candyman?"

He tosses his cigarette out the door. "Let's start playing an Enthral Moor campaign. I'll run the games." Sam sits down—and it turns out he can stop time just as well as the book.

11

SAM MAKES UP A LOT OF RULES AS WE
go along. Role-playing games are meant to be played with
more than two people, so to help me out, he invents a character
to accompany Pekker Cland on his adventures: a beautiful
woman named Ariane who's escaped from prison.

In our first game, Ariane accosts Pekker while he kneels
at his forge trying to make a scarab-shaped cigarette holder in
the market in town. (Sam tells me that ornate cigarette holders
are big sellers and if I don't want my character to be poor, I'd
better make them.) Ariane has long dark hair and a robe that
reveals more of her to those with more honor. Innocent men
see her naked; hardened criminals see her in a full dress and
veil. Since Pekker has a 50 honor, he sees her in Leia's slave
outfit from *Return of the Jedi*.

"That's hot," I admit.

"In Los Angeles you can get your cars washed by girls
dressed in that costume," Sam says, and we branch out from
there to the far reaches of nerd culture. Not the things that
women like too, but the things that only boys secretly enjoy
when we're boys without shame, like Warhammer and Magic

cards. The things that are so uncool they're uncool.

Back in-game, Ariane tells Pekker/me that if I can get her out of the city she'll reward me with treasure from her land of P'Sai. We sneak out of the market. Sam keeps offering dishonorable opportunities: swords that are easy to steal, free drinks. . . . I have to roll dice against my 50 honor; if I make a bad roll and fail to be honorable, Ariane's slave outfit expands to cover more of her.

We find a magic lamp. It's lying in the desert under a cactus. When I rub it, a genie comes out. He punches me in the face and ties me up. Ariane attacks him but gets torched by his Breathe Fire ability. He starts gagging my mouth.

"What are you doing?" I ask.

"For a thousand years, I lay trapped," the genie says. Sam does all the voices himself. "And I promised myself, 'Whosoever frees me, I shall grant three wishes,' but then this morning I finally got frustrated and decided, 'A thousand years, fuck it, whosoever frees me is getting robbed.' And here you go and release me. Who am I to tempt the gods?"

"Please, genie," I say. "Let me get home so I don't starve like a common rat."

"Home to who? Your family?"

"I have no family."

"Then who but the desert rats will care if you starve?"

And the genie steals everything I have but leaves my canteen filled with fresh water, so I can wander back to the market. End of game.

12

"WHERE DO YOU GET THIS STUFF?" I ASK
Sam. (Our first game takes two weeks.) He shows me a book:
*The Arabian Nights: The Marvels and Wonders of the Thousand
and One Nights,* from the Brooklyn Public Library. "All the
best stuff is from original sources," he says, and points to the
story "The Fisherman and the Jinnee." Then he shows me the
Pyramid Texts of Saqqara, in a book called *Ancient Egyptian
Literature.* The stuff found in Unas's tomb sounds just like the
magic spells that people yell in *Lord of the Rings*:

> *If he wishes you to die, you will die,*
> *If he wishes you to live, you will live!*

The difference is that Unas *did* live, 4,400 years ago.

"People used to be more in touch with actual magic," Sam
says.

"You believe in magic?"

"I believe in *something*. Whatever else I do during the day,
I always make sure to remember, 'Nobody knows how the
pyramids were built.' You know? You go through life worrying

about your little assignments from school, trying to be smart, playing the game, and meanwhile nobody can explain how the pyramids exist. Two-point-five to fifteen tons, each block. Five thousand years ago."

"Who do you think built them? Aliens?"

"It doesn't matter. Aliens, magic . . . Until someone explains the pyramids to me, how'm I gonna take life serious? You want to start a new game?"

13

I WANT, MORE THAN ANYTHING, FOR THE world of Enthral Moor to be real. I pray at night that I'll wake up *as* Pekker Cland, a full-grown artisan/magic-user ferrule, with red skin, a tail, and a taste for danger, adventuring with Sam. I've never prayed for anything before and I feel guilty about it. I'm not even sure how to pray; I say, "God, life is too boring for me to live anymore, so can I please wake up in the morning in a more exciting place? Not that I want to be a whiner."

I say these prayers at the end of the night, after fighting boredom by reading the *Rule Book,* which I now read in lieu of homework. Sometimes I say them as Jake sneaks in, drunk, and lies in bed blabbing to me: "You know what's amazing about girls' nipples?" "Man, don't ever do sake bombs after you've had Mexican food." "If you say anything to Mom and Dad or the lawyers, I'm gonna kill you." Once he passes out and I hear that he's breathing okay, I turn out my light and fall asleep, but not before checking if there's been any action in my personal area in terms of hair growth. There hasn't.

I begin testing what Sam does every day—cutting class. I

start with English, where we've been assigned *David Copper-field* and the first chapter is "I Am Born" and I think it must be a joke. I cut a chemistry class and find that the laws still work; I cut Spanish class and find that I still can't understand Spanish. During the extra time I play Creatures & Caverns with Sam or read one of the books he brings me from the library. I never smoke any of his cigarettes; I never try to drink with him; he never brings up pot; our transgressions are wholly childish and so we hide them as if they're sexual.

When I come home, to Mom's or Dad's, I'm astounded that my parents and their lawyers have no idea what I'm doing. I start to feel like I can get away with it, like I've been a fool to ever attend school, like the real reason the outlaws and movers and shakers of the world didn't need school was because they had friends: Steve Jobs had Steve Wozniak, and Bill Gates had Paul Allen, and I have Sam.

14

I COME HOME TO DAD'S HOUSE IN Brooklyn and find Kimberley, Dad's lawyer, waiting at the rounded edge of the kitchen counter. When I stay with my father, we sometimes eat cereal here, both standing as if we're on a packed subway; I'm always careful not to let any milk drops splash him. Dad oversees computer programmers at an enterprise-solutions provider and travels a lot. When he sees me, he always taps his bald head and says, "Kiddo, I'm jealous." And I want to hit him because bowl haircuts are stupid.

"Perry, we need to discuss a few issues." Kimberly says *issues*; I hear *problems.*

"Issues with me personally or issues with my father with you acting as legal counsel?"

"Both."

Kimberley opens a briefcase. I see what Dad sees in her. Jake does too. She's buttoned-down, but the lines of her skirts and suits suggest a wildness beneath. She has dyed blond hair, streaked with her natural brown, that frames her face in a huntress's bob.

"Good," I say. "I want to talk about some issues with my

father too. I made a new friend. I'd like to invite him over for dinner. You may have heard from Horace about the incident a few weeks back, where I was alone on Mom's bathroom floor with no circulation in my legs, clutching a role-playing-game manual. I've changed since then."

"We know," says a voice behind me. Horace walks into the kitchen. Hawk-nosed and widow's-peaked, never in anything but black.

"Both lawyers in the same place? What an occasion!"

"Your mother is concerned about you, Pecker," Horace says.

"Don't call me that."

"Isn't 'Pecker' how you identify yourself in your game?" Kimberley asks.

"That's different—how do you know about that? Have you been spying on me?" They don't answer. Kimberley hands me a sheet of paper with *Simmons Leadership Academy* at the top and a signature from Student Affairs at the bottom and a complete list of all the classes I've cut in the last month in the middle.

"This, really, I can explain."

"How?"

"Technical error."

"A technical error for two dozen classes?"

"Mutant paradigm shift. Error in the system. Happens every year. Massive lawsuits are filed against the College Board for errors in the SATs—"

"It wasn't a technical error."

"Personal vendetta."

"Against you? Why would anyone care?"

"I . . . because . . ." But I can't think up a reason. I'm not important enough to have vendettas against, I admit it. The person who probably has the biggest vendetta against me is me.

My mother and father walk into the kitchen. Crap. My mother is short and feisty. My father is tall and lanky. They used to play Frisbee together—it was the craziest thing, in Central Park, with smiles on their faces, in love in a way that made people sick . . . but I was about five when this was true, and it could have been in a movie or commercial.

"Dad, Mom, I can explain."

"Explain what? Where have you been going during the day?" Mom asks.

"We can tell from your pale skin that you've been indoors," Dad says.

"I was playing Creatures and Caverns with Sam, okay? By the fire stairs, okay? But look—you know how college works? You only have to go to class once every three days, and then you do the work on your own. I'm, like, doing free college prep."

I wait for them to accept this brilliant answer.

"Perry, you aren't progressing socially," Mom says. She always looks like she could be holding a rolling pin. "You don't have any friends."

"I just asked Kimberley to let me invite my friend over!"

"You aren't maturing," Dad says. "We feel like you're in a state of suspended animation—"

"That's not my fault! That's biology!"

"It's not *all* biology," Mom insists. "You're using this 'Caves and Critters' game to shut out the real world and avoid the tough choices that face you as a young man."

"So we've decided to send you to summer camp," Dad says.

"Toldja!" Jake bursts in, grinning sloppily.

"No! This is outrageous! *I'm* not the one with the problems! Look at him! He's—"

Jake narrows his face into a sledgehammer of doom.

"It's not about Jake, it's about you," Mom says. "We feel you'd grow more as a person—as a man—by going to summer camp this year."

"Eight weeks," Dad says. "We've spoken to our counsel."

The lawyers nod. Mom hands me a brochure:

CAMP

WASH

HISKA
LAKE

15

SIX WEEKS LATER I'M STILL LOOKING AT
the thing. The brochure is crinkled and rumpled from my
obsessive analysis of it. I'm in Mom's SUV with my mother,
father, brother, and the lawyers, driving through the
surprisingly secluded woods of northwestern New Jersey.

"'Camp Washiska Lake and Conference Center: a
nonreligious, activity-centered recreational community for
boys and girls ages ten to fifteen.' It doesn't sound so bad,
right?" I ask the car.

"Shut *up*," Jake groans. "You keep *reading* that. Like we
care." He's got a headache and he's wearing sunglasses and
drinking actual water for once. The Just Because played last
night, and he sneaked into our bedroom at five a.m. I look at
the SUV's hybrid energy gauge, which says we're getting 99
mpg and then flips to 0.01 mpg.

"Look, we're here!" Mom says.

I snap my head back and forth from the brochure to
real life. The cover of the brochure shows a happy bunch of
racially mixed kids waving under an ornate carved wooden
sign: CAMP WASHISKA LAKE. In real life, the sign is chipped

white paint on nailed-together two-by-fours hanging from a wizened tree.

"Stop the car! What is this?"

Mom ignores me and keeps driving. Horace explains, "That entire brochure is clip art. If it were for legal services, they would have to say 'paid spokespeople.' But to advertise a summer camp, you can use whatever clip art you want."

I put the brochure away and pull out my Pekker Cland character sheet. That usually calms me down. Jake snatches it.

"Hey!"

"Shut up a minute, I want to see this. What's this say? 'Honor fifty?' Is that out of a hundred?"

"Gimme that!"

"I thought you were good at this game. Didn't you read the *Odyssey*? The people with honor die quickest."

"Perry, I don't know if you're going to be able to bring your gaming materials to camp," Dad says.

"We'll just deal with that when we have to, okay?"

"What would you do if I ripped this up?" Jake asks. He tugs at the corners of the sheet.

"No!" I grab it from him, moving a lot faster than I thought I could with Speed 7. I put the character sheet in my backpack. Jake, for a moment, looks impressed. I know someone else who would be impressed. I pull out my phone and send Sam a message: *wish you were here.*

16

"I ADVISE YOU TO PULL OVER," KIMBERLEY
tells my mother. She pulls over. A sign is posted at a crossroads
in the woods:

NO LAWYERS BEYOND THIS POINT

The sign is terra-cotta with white lettering; it looks more
official than the camp sign. "I advise you to let us out," Horace
says. Mom nods; Kimberley and Horace exit.

"What are they doing?" I ask. The lawyers dust themselves
off. Jake is as astonished as I am. I don't want them to go.
They're annoying, but they serve as a nice buffer between me
and the nuclear Eckert family unit. I don't like that unit. There's
something wrong with it. We could never even be happy at
McDonald's.

"They're obeying posted notices," Mom says.

"We'll wait here until you pick us up," Horace says. He sits
on a log with Kimberley.

As we drive away, I ask, "What is this evil place you're
bringing me to?"

"Moments like this, without the lawyers, make you think about the importance of real conversation," Dad says.

"Do you have any questions you want to ask us before we drop you off at camp?" Mom asks.

"Questions about women, specifically, Perry. You know this is a coed camp."

"Dad!" I want to tell him, *Yes.* I want to tell him, *A woman appears late at night before my dreams begin behind three sets of horizontally bisected saloon doors. In the first set, the bottom door is open, showing her naked hips and legs; in the second, the top is open, showing her breasts and head and neck; in the third, both doors are open, showing her in full bloom, but try as I might, I can never make the same staccato shuffling noises as Jake does in his bunk.* Instead of saying that, I pull out Pekker Cland's character sheet. Dad grabs it this time.

"We're concerned about you, kiddo. This game. Can you make a career out of it? Play it for money?"

"No—give that back!"

"Listen. When you were growing up, we always told you that you could do whatever you wanted with your life. It's time to drop that lie. As you get to be an adult, you have to *dial down* your dreams into practicalities. If you were very into the stock market, say, or being a doctor, it would be one thing. But you're doing badly at school and spending all your time on something that never had any social value when I was young"—Mom nods—"and I'm sure still doesn't." Jake nods.

"Dad, if you don't give me back my character sheet—"

"I'll put it in your bag. I don't want you looking at it until you meet your fellow campers."

"Deal."

We crest a hill and see the lake. Although the camp is called Camp Washiska Lake, the lake is called Lake Henderson, in one of those weird Americanisms that doesn't make sense. It's six miles long and a half mile across. I check it against the brochure. In the brochure, the lake is filled with diverse teens in polo shirts sailing over a logo for "Hideaway Village," the name for my age group—the fifteen-year-olds, who are old enough to be treated like men. We're paired with "Oasis Villa," the girls' section that corresponds in age.

Sure enough, Oasis Villa is on the other side of the lake—I see a glint of white cabins in the woods, like a magical commune for virgins—but the lake itself is drained. There's a puddle's worth of black water in it.

"What happened?" I ask.

We descend back into the woods. No one answers. Sam would answer—he'd help me look the lake up on our phones; maybe it's controlled by a hydroelectric dam—but he hasn't responded to my text. I can't count on Sam up here.

17

MOM PULLS INTO A DUSTY PARKING LOT IN front of a big building that looks like an airplane hangar. A sign says DINING HALL, but I don't believe it. This is in the brochure too. The picture shows a group of kids in a crystalline cafeteria like something out of a Frank Lloyd Wright catalog. This is a huge slab of concrete with occasional streaked windows.

"Looks great!" Dad says.

Next to the dining hall, in the parking lot, stand dozens of boys. They lounge on trunks, shoulder duffel bags and backpacks, and hug their parents and legal guardians embarrassedly while establishing social status with the boys around them. I can't hear them, but from their body language I know what they're talking about: comedy bits they've seen, rap lyrics they've memorized, and women they've allegedly been with. I will probably have to make up a woman I've been with.

"They look friendly," Mom says.

No they don't. They look like a skyline: there are kids who've had the Growth Spurt and kids who haven't; jutting Adam's apples and child-sized clothes . . . but no potential friends. No one with my bowl haircut. Two of the bigger boys drum up dust with a basketball, spinning, showing off their long limbs, and I track from them to two boys unloading a trunk, to two boys comparing logo-ed caps, and I realize: *I'm the only white kid.* I see Hispanic, black, and Asian in equal amounts. I'm the asterisk.

I power down my window. The group's buzz of gruff speech hits me. I recognize that I've never *been* in the racial minority before. It feels different. It feels scary.

18

JAKE, DAD, AND I HAUL MY TRUNK OUT
of the SUV and carry it to the center of the gathered campers.
A counselor—a big, good-looking guy named Travis—checks
me off a list.

"Eckert? Can I see your backpack?"

"Why?"

"It has to be inspected."

I hand it to him. Inside, besides my character sheet, are my
Rule Book, my dice, and my mechanical pencils. Travis tosses
the bag into a bin on wheels, like something used to haul trash
away from a demolition site. "We have to check for drugs,
alcohol, and candy."

"There's no candy in there! That's mine! Give it back!"

"'Give it *back*!'" my brother mocks. "'I need it *back*!'"

"Stop it, Jake!"

"Can you open your trunk, please?"

I unlock it. Travis pokes around my tighty-whities
while checking things off his list. I watch the bin that holds
my backpack. Another counselor wheels it to a picnic table,
where more counselors remove comic books and DVD players

from the bags within.

"All clear," Travis says. He leaves me with my dad and brother.

"You're never getting that back," Jake says.

"Shut up!" I shove him, pushing with two hands on his chest. He doesn't move an inch (I guess I really am Strength 2) and he shoves me back (I would put him at Strength 28), targeting my kidney. I fall into Dad. It hurts more than Jake could know—I woke up with a nasty bruise on that area this morning. I can't explain it; it's a kidney-shaped bruise over my actual kidney. I guess I sleepwalked into something. Ever since I fell asleep on the bathroom floor, I've been waking up with strange bruises.

"*What's going on?*" Mom shrieks, hustling toward us. The boys go quiet except for embarrassing comments:

"*Oooooo*, snap."

"Here she comes."

"Watch this crazy white woman."

"I leave you three alone to have male-bonding time for two minutes, and you start shoving each other? This is why you're going to summer camp, Perry: *antisocial behavior.*"

"I'll handle this," my father says. He kneels in front of me. "Perry, you have to let them take your game if that's what they think is best for you. It isn't real. It's kid stuff. And you're not a kid anymore. You're putting off real life. I know real life is hard"—he quiets down—"I was married to your mother. But you have to face it. In your own way, you're as bad as Jake."

"Hey! Fuck you." Jake spits in the dirt. "There's nothing wrong with me." He stomps back to the car.

"What are you gonna do with *him* while I'm at camp?"

Dad sighs. "We're taking him to rehab."

"About time!"

"We're trying to get him into a good college. It'll make his profile more interesting. Don't worry about him, kiddo. Worry about you. Make friends. Meet girls. Okay?" I don't respond in any way, but Dad hugs me and walks back to the car like he really got through to me.

"Here," Mom says. She hands me a shopping bag with something hard inside. The bag is much bigger than the item, which is cool and angled. I slip it into my pocket, surprised. "Be safe," she says. As she hugs me, I see a bald kid's head behind her.

"Sam!" I cup my mouth so the exclamation doesn't escape. I don't need Sam seeing me with Mom. He's probably seen me already and is avoiding me because of the volatile nature of my family.

"What?" Mom asks.

"Nothing, it's fine. You can go. There's somebody here I know!"

"Where?"

"*Don't look!* Just go. Please, Mom, don't ruin this and introduce us, please."

"Thank you for your text message," she says. She holds up her phone: *wish you were here.*

"I was . . ." I start trying to explain that I was trying to send that to *Sam*, that I have so few people in my phone that I must have sent it to "Mom" instead of "Sam" . . . but then I think better of it. "You're welcome, Mom." I almost tell her I love her, but what would be the point?

"Enjoy what I got you." She looks strangely beautiful for a moment before going back to the car; thirty seconds later they're gone.

19

SAM STANDS WITH A GROUP OF THREE
kids. One is short; the other two are the tall ones who were
dribbling the basketball. Why didn't he tell me he was coming
here? I blurt, "Hey, Sam!"

He turns around quickly without being able to control
himself, the way you do when you hear your name. He sees me.
His face drops. He looks away. The smaller kid with him has a
flat nose and pointy ears like an evil imp. The taller two could
be twins, with dreadlocks, except one is much darker-skinned
than the other. I get it: these are Sam's *old* friends, older than
me, and he's going to need time to catch up with them. He'll
talk to me later.

I pull the plastic bag out of my pocket and reach inside,
making sure no counselors see. It's a pewter miniature.

Mom! How'd you know? It's as big as Sam's miniature
of Peter Powers. It shows a young man crouched by a forge,
looking up, and you can see both the heat in the forge and
the scorching heat of his eyes. It's Pekker Cland! He has a war
hammer at his side, and I instantly decide that Pekker Cland
will specialize in war hammers. I can picture his red skin and

yellow hair. I wrap my hand around him. With Pekker, I'll be okay. I'll have to write Mom a thank-you note—

"Yo, let me see that," a voice says behind me.

I turn. It's someone I've never seen before: an Asian kid, about my height, with flashing black eyes and a cocky snarl.

"What is it? A doll? Let me see it, yo." He sticks out his hand.

"Do I know you?"

"My name's Ryu. Let me see the doll."

"Ryu like . . . from the video game?"

"Yeah, *exactly* like from the video game. Now let me see your doll, *faggot*."

With that word, as if it's a command, two henchmen appear at his side: one big Asian guy and one medium-sized one with hair that drapes over his eyes in two small tails.

"It's not a doll, it's a pewter miniature," I say. "And it's mine."

"I didn't say whether it was *yours* or not. I said I wanna see it."

"Why?"

"Because you look like a bitch and I wanna see it." He snatches at it. I pull it away. He claws at it again—I flail my arm and *crack* him in the temple.

"*Agh!*" Ryu takes his hand away from his ear to reveal a thin red cut. The sun catches his blood against his skin.

"I'm sorry, I didn't mean to, I just—"

"*Hey!*" The counselor, Travis, runs toward us, but I feel strong arms grab me from both sides: Ryu's henchmen. Ryu steps forward. He pushes a small tight fist right at my head.

20

WHEN I COME TO, I SEE A BRIGHT WHITE light, very close. . . . Am I *dead*? Have I died without having sex? Won't that mean I'm in heaven? I reach up to check my face—

"Ah! Ah! Stop right there!"

A nurse tilts into view. She's young and pretty. She blocks the light. "How're you feeling?"

"Pain . . ."

She pulls the light away from my face. I'm in a dentist's chair in the middle of a woodsy room. It must be the nurse's office, with dirty windows and bins of Band-Aids and itch cream, and posters telling me how to identify poison ivy. I have an ice pack in my limp hand. "Silly! Press that against your eye. Keep holding it."

A man enters the room. He's tall and sturdy, with a ponytail and a wide, dark mustache; he looks like an environmentalist trucker.

"Peregrine Eckert," he says. "I'm Dale Blaswell, Washiska Lake camp director. The head honcho here, buddy."

"My name's not Peregrine. It's Perry."

"Says here 'Peregrine.'"

"Peregrine's my birth name. My mom wanted to try something natural. They legally changed it when I was six."

"You're Peregrine on my forms, so you're Peregrine to me. Your head hurt?"

"Yeah."

"That's because you were punched in the face. You care to get litigious about it, or can you read signs?"

"What is this place? Nothing here is like the brochure—"

"You can't learn about life from a brochure!" Dale comes close. "At Camp Washiska Lake, we live in pods. And Hideaway Village is your pod. That's your unit. Your clan. Your brothers. And one of the things you don't do with members of your pod is *fight* them, understand? When we fight, everyone loses. See?"

He points to a motivational poster in the room with two dogs snarling at one another. It says, WHEN WE FIGHT, EVERYONE LOSES.

"I didn't start it, though."

"That's not what I hear. What I hear is, you whacked Eric Chin in the head with a metal doll—"

"The miniature! Where is it?"

"We took it along with the rest of your gaming materials, Peregrine. You're not here to bury your nose in books."

"No, no, please, I need those back. I'm stuck here for eight weeks!"

"*Stuck* here? You're *lucky* to be here. What you need to do is continue to ice your eye, and we'll see you tonight at the

Village-Villa square dance."

"What? I can't dance!"

"It's not a dance, it's a square dance. An introductory social event to meet the girls from Oasis Villa. They come from all the way across the lake."

"Good for them."

"You have a problem with girls?"

I don't answer.

"With that kind of attitude, no wonder. I'll tell you what you won't have a problem with, though: fighting. If you do it again—"

And then Dale's mouth keeps moving but no words come out. I just hear silence—not even the tone of the room—a whoosh of *nothing* like a glitch in the universe—

"—*Peregrine.*"

Dale leaves with his ponytail swinging. Sound is back like normal. Maybe I got hit harder than I thought. I shake my head. The nurse raises a finger. "How many fingers am I holding up? Do you know who the president is?"

"May I please have a piece of paper?"

"Why?"

"Just something to write on and a pencil. Please."

She gives me a handout about acne. I write on a pockmarked face with a camp-issue pencil: *Ryu = Eric Chin.*

"You're lucky we've been icing your eye, otherwise it would be a huge red lump right now, and tomorrow it would be a shiny bruise," she says.

I put the acne handout in my pocket. I get up. "Where do they put the things they confiscate?"

"Those would be in Dale's cabin; I wouldn't worry about them."

"I don't think you understand. I'm getting my miniature and my backpack and I'm going home. I don't know what this place is, whether you've been feeding me medication or hypnosis treatments or what, but you've got an empty lake and a welcoming committee of kids who punch you in the face and people who come with a mute button. I'm outta here. And I'm taking my friend Sam with me."

I open the door and rush out of the room.

21

A GIRL SITS ON A BENCH IN THE WAITING area, knitting, in a baggy sweater and jeans. I'm still pissed off at the nurse but when I see her, I jump behind a fire extinguisher to hide until I can figure out what to say to her.

"Hey! Is someone back there?"

Shoot. She puts her knitting aside; she's making tiny mittens. She has beige skin and black hair. I can't guess what wondrous combination of ethnicities has produced her. I step out holding the fire extinguisher.

"What are you holding that for?"

A response comes to mind, a response so perfect I think this whole situation must have been set up by a reality-TV camera crew. That would explain Camp Washiska Lake, actually: the signs for the lawyers, the random encounters and villains, the confusing audiovisual stimuli . . . maybe this is a reality show!

"I need this because you're so hot," I say, brandishing the fire extinguisher.

22

I'D LIKE TO SAY THERE'S A SLIVER OF TIME between when I offer my line and when she responds—some pregnant period when there's the possibility that she might laugh, or come back with a complementary phrase ("I *am*"), but all she says is, "Do I *know* you?"

"Sorry." I put the fire extinguisher back. "I guess I could try and play it off like I was trying to be funny, but that was actually the best thing I could think to say."

"Who are you?"

"I'm Perry; pleased to meet you." I stick out my hand.

"Are you the guy who got in the fight with Ryu?"

"How'd you know that?"

"I hear he knocked you out with one punch."

"Word travels fast."

I leave my hand out. She looks at it. I have gone beyond the point where I can pretend that I was sticking it out for any other reason than a failed handshake. I grit my teeth and look at my palm. Will. Not. Fail.

"Do you want me to shake that?"

"Yes."

She shakes it with the tiny mitten she's working on.

"I'm Anna."

I laugh at the mitten. It's soft. "Who's that for?"

"My sister."

"But it's summer."

"By the time I'm done, it'll be fall. Knitting teaches you patience."

"Aren't you supposed to be on the other side of the lake?"

"I've been here before. I have something I leave in the nurse's office every year and I'm here to get it before I get settled."

"Is it weird to shake hands?"

"No, it's formal. It's normal, I think."

"Cool! I mean, cool. So . . . are you gonna be at the square dance tonight?"

"If I decide to make an appearance." She narrows her dark eyes. "Will you?"

"I was . . . sort of . . . planning on leaving the whole camp. But now I—"

"How old are you?"

Late bloomer. Inside those two words are all the questions of childhood.

"Fifteen."

"You just turned fifteen?"

I blink. When did I turn fifteen? Basic mathematical machinery is breaking down. Under Anna's influence, time hiccups between moments and I cannot speak—

"I hear fourteen to fifteen is big for boys. Fifteen to sixteen is big for girls. And twelve to thirteen."

"Nine months ago," I blurt.

"O-kay . . ."

"And it's not big. Fourteen to fifteen. It's not a big deal. It's cool."

"So you still feel like you did when you were fourteen?"

"No, I feel bigger."

She gives me a look like, *You used to be smaller?* How is she painting me into these corners?

"When's *your* birthday?" I ask. That's it. Turn it back on her. Take the offensive.

"January twenty-sixth."

"Aquarius." Now we're in my territory. "The Water Bearer."

"I was never into signs."

"Aquarius! The only human. All the other signs, animals; but Aquarius, a simple man. Human. Man-slash-woman, you know."

"What about Gemini? That's two humans."

"They're demigods."

"I always thought it was dumb that there wasn't a sign that was, like, a car."

"The ancient Romans didn't have cars."

"They could have a chariot or something, no? I gotta see the nurse. See you, Perry."

She nods. I notice how full her lips are. She walks past me, but I don't want her to go. I want to say something to keep her here. Anything.

"Anna?"

"Yeah?"

"It's because I play Creatures and Caverns. That's why I know so much astrology and why I got into the fight with Ryu." I grab the fire extinguisher to represent Ryu. "He tried to steal this pewter miniature my mom gave me. So I swung it at him, and . . ."

I trail off. There's nothing else I can do, watching her face. Her smile has evaporated. In its place is disbelief and pity.

"Oh. You're one of *those* guys."

"Sorry. What? No. What do you mean?"

She opens the door to the nurse's office.

"Didn't you know I was one of those guys when I came up to you with a fire extinguisher? Hello?"

Even from behind, something about her radiates newfound disgust with and dismissal toward me. The door to the nurse's office swings back and forth on its two-way hinge, giving me strobe-like vision of her from behind as she speaks with the nurse: "Is Dale here?"

Behind me, a rough voice says, "*Idiot!*"

23

I SPIN AROUND AND LOOK DOWN THE
hallway, but there's no one, just a watercooler and a poster
about Lyme disease.

"Hello?"

I have the same feeling I had in Phantom Galaxy Comics
and at school—the feeling I'm being watched. Only this time,
whoever it is got too close. Down the hall, a door slams. The
bathroom.

I run to it. The room is clean and orderly, ready for a
summer of use. There's no one in either of the stalls, but above
the second one, a small window is open, letting in a light breeze.
I climb up onto the toilet—

And see a ferrule running across a field away from me.

I blink. Then I squint very hard, but when I open my eyes,
the person still looks the same: bright red skin, yellow hair, and a
tail. Just like the ferrules in the *Other Normal Edition*—and just
like Pekker Cland! His tail sticks out of the back of his pants;
maybe he's wearing them backward. It's red with a bushy orange
tuft at the end. Something is attached to it—something wooden
like a wrist-mounted crossbow.

"Hey!" I yell. The ferrule turns. I get a glimpse of a sharp red face—like the devil, but I never pictured the devil looking scared. He keeps running.

I can't say I'm unprepared for this moment. I have been praying for this moment. A lot of people probably would stop at this point and doubt themselves or wonder what they were *really* seeing or come up with some alternate explanation for a red man with a tail running away from them, but not me. I hoist myself into the bathroom window.

"Hey!" I try to get through, cursing my Strength 2, but the truth is, if I were larger I probably wouldn't have made it. I scrape my shoulders across the windowsill. The ferrule is almost at the trees across the field. I squeeze forward, grunting—

And fall out the window. I flip in the air and land on my ankle. *"Agh!"* It twists on the grass. Pain like fire shoots up me. I try to stand. "Hey! Please! Stop! My ankle—"

On the word *ankle*, he stops. He turns and comes back to me, running as fast as he was running the other way. I don't want him running at me like that. I back toward the nurse's office, on my butt on the ground, streaking grass against my pants, the way I would if I were trying to keep away from a ferocious animal—

He arrives. He doesn't attack me. He looks me over. I focus on his face: small ears, rounded nose, all red. Yellow, messy hair. Not blond—yellow like a highlighter. He does wear jeans—backward—and a black T-shirt. I look around: no one else in the field. No witnesses. A hallucination?

"Of course it's gotta be the ankle," he says.

A hallucination with visual and audio components?

He sweeps me up in his thick, stubby red arms.

A hallucination with visual, audio, and somatic components?

"What are you doing? Put me down!"

"Shh." He tosses me over his shoulder. For a minute, I think both of us actually don't know what to say to each other.

24

I HUG THE FERRULE'S BACK. HE SMELLS like iron. His body is stocky and barrelesque. By the time we get to the trees, I'm squeezing him tight, pressing my cheek against him and grinning.

"Stop that! Off!"

I shake my head, feeling his shirt bunch against my cheek. I look at his tail with the wooden trellis attached to the end. "You're real!" It's the iron smell that convinces me. No hallucination could smell like that. "I mean, look, I can be practical about this. A real ferrule here at camp. But you gotta give me like five minutes to just *appreciate* you or whatever—"

"Off!" He kneels. I hiss as my foot touches the forest floor. I hop to a tree. "Sorry."

"Don't be sorry, just be reasonable! How's your ankle?"

I pull off my sneaker and peel down my sock. My right ankle is swollen fat and round.

"Not good. Who are you, sir?" I ask.

"We'll get to that. First, I want you to think: if you hadn't heard me call you an idiot—which you shouldn't have—and followed me—which you shouldn't have—and climbed out that window—which you *know* was a bad idea—is it possible that you could have injured your ankle some other way today? It's important for me to know how out of the ordinary this is for you."

"Meeting ferrules is *very* out of the ordinary."

"Don't call me that. And don't be smart. That's how you lost Anna."

"How do you know about Anna? Who are you? Are you the real Pekker Cland?"

"You made up Pekker Cland. My name is Mortin Enaw."

"Mortin Enaw? You're the guy who did special consulting on the *Other Normal Edition*!"

"*Pfff.* Those guys put me in that as a joke. Don't read into it too much."

"Are you from the real world of Enthral Moor? Do you have a scimitar?"

"*Stop.*" He goes silent. I hear the birds and bugs around us. The dirt parking lot and nurse's office and Ryu and Anna seem very far away, and I miss my brother—briefly, in a flash, his shaggy hair and teeth. Fear creeps into the air between me and Mortin Enaw.

"I know it's hard for you to believe, but I have my own problems." He reaches into his backward jeans and pulls out a pipe. It has an inverted U in the middle; it looks as if it was carved from a single piece of black stone. He picks up a few pebbles from the ground—just ordinary pebbles—and puts them into the pipe. He pinches it in his mouth and scrapes his tail against the ground. The back of the tail flares up. The thing attached to it is a *lighter*, I see, and after it strikes, a lick of flame burns steadily as he waves it over his pipe. He inhales, holds it in, and blows out . . . pebble dust, I guess.

"*Ahhh,* that's the stuff." He closes his eyes in a quick reverie and then turns to me with utmost seriousness.

"We're working on an information discrepancy," he says. "I know more about the multiverse than you do, so naturally you look at me with wonder, and you don't think to yourself, *Hey, this guy might have problems too.* But I do. And my problems center around *you*, Perry Eckert. What I need you to do, the sooner the better, is find a way to have a decent romantic kiss with Anna, who you met back there."

"Why? Is this a TV show?"

"No!"

"Is it part of a live-action role-playing game?"

"No! Do I look like a player? I'm a professional. I'm a consultant. And I'm telling you that if you can kiss Anna, just one decent romantic kiss, *you're going to save an entire world from certain destruction*!"

"What world? *The* world?"

Mortin puffs. "My world."

"Is your world . . . Enthral Moor? The world I've been playing with Sam?"

"Come with me. It's easier to show you."

"Where?"

He taps out his pipe and offers me a walking stick. "To an

inconvenient place, to go and to say. It has a name that can't be conceptualized by human thought. You remember how Prince changed his name to a symbol?"

"The musician?"

"Right, and you know how he changed his name for a while to a symbol you can't pronounce?"

"No."

"He did. And my home is like that. The name can't be pronounced, written, or conceptualized by the human brain."

I remember Dale Blaswell's words turning into silence as they streamed out of his head. I remember all the small times in life when I have heard things wrong, or turned around because someone called my name but no one was there, or woken up with a strange bruise. . . . It's all standard, right? There are ragged edges around everyone's life, things that can't be remembered or explained. Even the most normal people see ghosts, hear voices. . . .

"What am I supposed to call your home?" I ask.

"People have called it different things over the years. I grew up calling Earth the World of the Other Normals, because you people here are sort of normal, but you're a bit ridiculous. So you can call my home the World of the Other Normals and it'll be fair."

"Okay."

"And you can call me Mortin Enaw, or just Mortin, correspondence consultant. I'm based out of Subbenia, with the Sulice Corporation."

"And I'm Perry. Which you seem to know. I'm a student . . . ah . . . based out of Manhattan or Brooklyn, depending on whether I'm with my dad or my mom, with no corporation. And no friends. I had one friend, Sam, but he doesn't seem to like me anymore."

"Don't say that. I'm your friend."

"Really?"

"Yes, and don't complain to me. You have nothing to complain about, with your mind and your rich parents."

"My parents aren't rich!"

"No? What are they?"

"Upper middle class."

"Yeah, like you're a public-school student. I just got fired. How's that for something to complain about?"

"I thought you said you were with the Sulice Corporation."

"I was. That's how it's supposed to be. With them for life. I don't know when I'm going to stop saying it."

"What'd you get fired for?"

"Having *big ideas.*"

"How are you speaking to me in English?"

"What are you, racist?"

25

MORTIN ENAW LEADS ME FARTHER INTO the woods, transforming in five minutes from a mystical creature whose existence astounds me to a loopy companion who likes to smoke pebbles and talk. He seems happy and grateful that the pebbles are everywhere, just waiting for him to stuff into his pipe. When he dumps them out, they look about the same as when they go in, so I'm not sure what he gets out of them, but he likes the ones with quartz and emphasizes to me that quartz is "the stuff."

"So your home that you can't pronounce, did anybody ever try and pronounce it 'Middle-earth'? Or 'Narnia'?" I ask, keeping weight off my ankle with my walking stick.

"Tolkien said the climate reminded him of being a baby in South Africa," Mortin says, pronouncing J. R. R. Tolkien's name "Tol-*kine,*" which I know is wrong. He pushes aside a branch for me.

"You knew Tolkien?" I'm geeking out. I pronounce it the right way.

"Not me. A colleague, almost a century ago."

"Is your world where Tolkien got his ideas for Middle-earth?"

"No, he made up Middle-earth." Mortin stops. "You ever notice how nobody's ever *broke* in Middle-earth?" He grimaces on *broke* and scrunches his face. "Sure, they've got no possessions because they're all on an adventure, but have you ever seen somebody deal with a *bill* in Middle-earth? Or with, say, a punk punching them in the kidney because they owed him money for earthpebbles?"

"No," I say. I hang back.

"What?"

"I'm staying here. You look like you're going to get violent."

"I just get frustrated. There's a lot of repetition in my line of work. That's why I need the pebbles to stay relaxed. You're not the first person to ask about Tolkien, I'll put it that way."

"Tol-*keen*," I insist. "He wasn't Jewish."

Mortin Enaw looks embarrassed. "That's how you say it?"

"Yeah."

"I've been mispronouncing it all this time?"

"Don't worry. I'm sorry."

"Don't apologize! I've been doing that for years!"

"It's an honest mistake."

"You know, one of the most insidious things you can do to a friend is hear them mispronounce a word and not correct it." Mortin seems to recall a specific incident: "That guarantees the friend will mispronounce the word later in front of somebody important."

74

"Well, you pronounced my name right."

"You pronounced my name right too. Thanks."

"We should shake hands," I say, and we do, in the woods, before moving forward to wherever he's taking me.

26

CRACK—I STEP ON A BRANCH. THE SOUND scatters through the trees. My ankle flares up. Mortin shakes his head. "You've never walked in the woods before, have you?"

"No. The park?"

"Walk on roots, okay? Roots and rocks. That keeps you from leaving a trail—or a sound. What if you have to meet Anna at a secret location late at night?"

"Where are we going, Mortin?"

"We're looking for an old car battery."

"There?" I point.

"Good eye."

We head over. The battery sits in front of a tree. It looks like a normal car battery—black paint, scratched up, rusty—with the air of something abandoned without premeditation. "Is it like Narnia? Is this a special battery instead of a wardrobe that's going to lead us to the World of the Other Normals?"

Mortin Enaw takes a deep breath and shakes out his pipe. "This battery, you can tell me where it is, specifically, in space, right? With numbers?"

"Yes."

"Well, not everything's like that."

"Of course it is. Everything can be described with numbers. That's why they're numbers."

"Try electrons. They decide where they're going to be when you measure them. What are the numbers behind that?"

"Quantum physics." I can keep up with Mortin. Who does he think he is? "So you're from another dimension, like . . . *Star Trek*. And this camp is like a special pen for human children where they're brought for experimentation by people from your dimension if their parents are cheap enough to want them away for a summer—"

"You're part of one universe in a multiverse. And it's your consciousness that chooses, not the electron, because consciousnesses choose things and electrons don't. Your American scientist Hugh Everett published the truth in the 1950s. Then he went to work on top-secret military projects and never published another paper. He knew the secret behind this battery."

Mortin unscrews the caps. Upon closer inspection, the brand is "Logo Spermatikoi," which I've never heard of and which definitely does not sound focus-tested.

The sun gleams off the battery leads. Mortin eyes me, and I think for a moment about God. *This*—meeting Mortin—is the first experience I've had that makes me think, *God exists*, and it's pure madness! Where's the sense in that? God needs to be doing more crazy things to prove himself.

"Do you have . . . access to the other universes?" I ask.

"Why?"

"Is there a universe you could take me where, like, I'm bigger? Or my parents are . . . not crazy?"

"They exist. They all exist. Every time something happens, a universe is created where it happens a different way, so universes are constantly branching off to infinity; that's the multiverse. But I can't take you to them all. I can only take you to mine. If you want to be bigger, I suggest you exercise, fix your posture, and eat chicken breast."

"You don't have a pencil, do you?" I pull my acne handout out of my pocket.

"No, I don't have a pencil, and you've got to leave that here, so you better put it aside. You can't bring anything over."

"Is your universe safe? Does it have an oxygen-and-nitrogen-based atmosphere?"

"Please touch the battery right there." Mortin points at the lead marked *negative*.

"I don't want to be 'negative.' Is there running water? Is it ninety-three million miles from a star similar in nuclear composition to the sun? Is this going to hurt?"

"Stop whining. See that clump of mushrooms?"

I don't see them until he points them out: a piddling cluster next to some ferns beside the battery. They don't look special. "You're going to touch those when the time is right, while holding the negative lead."

Mortin takes the lighter off his tail and leaves it by the tree, along with his pipe. Then he takes off his clothes, matter-of-factly, the way old people do in locker rooms at pools.

"I'm going first. You come after. Give me thirty seconds to make sure everything is safe on the other side."

"Do I have to get naked?" I avoid looking at Mortin's genitals, although they seem normal in my peripheral vision.

"You better."

"I'd rather not. I don't like being naked. I haven't really had the Growth Spurt yet, you know what I mean?"

"Perry, I thought I knew about you from studying you, but I didn't realize that at any given moment your brain is either scared, apologetic, or *thinking* about something. You need to make more room in there for *direct action*." He points at my head. "Count to thirty and follow me. And remember, when you touch the mushroom, *don't* think about me, okay? Whatever you do, don't picture me."

27

MORTIN TOUCHES THE MUSHROOM WHILE holding the negative lead. As soon as his finger hits it—one finger on the battery, one on the mushroom, crouched in the forest, stark naked, his tail curled behind him in a big S—his body begins to shake. It's as if a great electrical current is running though him. He chitters, letting out clicking pops like a bug zapper being swung through a cloud of mosquitoes, as two halos of light shoot out from his bare feet.

I throw my arm over my eyes and peek through my fingers. I expect heat, but there's just bright, clear light. The halos move up to Mortin's ankles—and below them, his feet are gone. Zapped. Dematerialized.

I discern a *pattern* in the chittering, like rapid Morse code—*pop, pop, poppoppop*—as the halos move up his legs. When they reach his crotch, they join and become such an intense burst that my eyes can't handle it; I squeeze them shut and see black spots and hear violent snaps until I open them again—and Mortin is gone.

I hear something loud and realize it's my breathing. I blink. The animals know something's up. The woods are quiet. If it's all been a hallucination, this should've been the violent brain-cleansing incident that knocked me out of it. I pinch myself, but I'm still in the same spot, a long way from the nurse's office.

"No way," I say. It's time to go back. Not for me, no thanks. Interesting, but I've had enough adventure for one day; I prefer my fantasy life compartmentalized in books, without any nudity—

I hear a growl. In front of me, crouched, shoulders up, head down, is a gray wolf. I guess it could be a coyote—I've been reading that coyotes are more common in the tri-state area these days—but something in the lowness of its growl says *wolf*. It twitches its lips and shows its incisors.

I back toward the car battery. *Wolves?* No lawyers, no white kids, and *wolves?* What kind of a place is Camp Washiska Lake? I review my attributes as I had them figured for Pekker Cland: Intelligence 65? Might be more like 10.

I touch the negative lead of the battery, peering over my shoulder at the wolf. I brush my finger ever so lightly against one of the mushrooms.

What did Mortin tell me not to think about? Himself, that's right. I try not to think about him, so of course I do, and with the image of his legs scrolling out of existence firmly in mind, I enter

THE
WO
OF THE
NOR

RLD
OTHER
MALS

28

IT'S LIKE HAVING A SEIZURE—LIKE HAVING
one seizure followed by another followed by two more, at ever
tightening intervals. My body spasms and my teeth clench.
The trees in front of me shake back and forth, and then they
shake up and down, and then they shake in a direction I never
noticed before and can't describe: it's a bit like a diagonal, but it
also has something to do with *time,* because the leaves alternate
between reds and yellows and summer greens, faster and faster,
like they're aging and getting younger, and the sound goes with
them, warping in and out as if someone's detuning me on a big
radio dial, and I chitter: *pop, pop, poppoppop.* . . .

My feet crackle and glow. Electricity runs through me. I'm
not sure if it hurts or if my body is experiencing new things and
the only way it can register them is as pain, but I scream. I try
to pull my fingers away from the battery and the mushroom,
but they're suddenly, inexplicably far from me.

"*Yaaaa—!*"

The halos shoot out from me and move up. My feet shimmer
and disappear below my ankles. The pain ascends my spine as
the ring eats my stomach, and then I feel my stomach *isn't there,*

as if it fell asleep the way my legs did on the toilet reading the *Other Normal Edition.*

The ring moves up my chest—my chest disappears. It takes my neck and my face. The forest explodes in light, brighter than the sun. The light comes from me, from my eyes.

My mouth doesn't exist, so I can't scream anymore except in my head, but that does the job—*Yaaaaaaaaaagh!*—bridging the moment between when everything explodes to the moment after, when I realize I'm somewhere different, somewhere with a roof.

"Aaaaaagh!"

I am in the center of a chamber, on the floor. My body is back, but it's naked.

29

A CIRCULAR ROOM. DARK WOODEN WALLS. No windows. Barrels and crates are stacked around the perimeter, along with shelves holding folded sheets of burlap and small sacks that look like ice packs. A few smooth-worn, bone-colored levers stick out of the wall. Fat white candles in simple metal sconces provide light; the smoke leaves through a dainty chute in the center of the ceiling. It reminds me of a submarine, or a witches' den.

Mortin stands in front of me, wearing a brown loincloth. He has good musculature. He's rubbing something under his eye, like sunscreen. He turns away to finish up, as if he's hiding something from me, and then I notice a girl standing next to him.

She seems about my age, with pale skin and bright blue hair. My brain registers two things: First, she's beautiful. Second, I'm naked. Women allegedly like naked men, but I've never seen this confirmed. I cover myself on the floor.

"Hey!" Mortin says, whirling around. His face looks fine; I don't know what he was doing to it. "You made it!"

"Where the hell are my clothes?"

"What did I tell you? You didn't take them off?"

"No! There was a . . . where'd they go?" I lower my voice. "And who's *she*?"

"Don't worry about it."

"How'm I not supposed to worry about it? Where am I? That hurt!"

"Don't whine. Does it still hurt? Is it starting to itch?"

"What do you—"

It starts in my feet, the way the halos did, but then it blooms: the most ferocious itching I've ever experienced. It creeps up my legs and around my sides. My stomach itches. My spine itches. My eardrums itch. As the itching burrows deep into my body, it gets stronger, and I wonder if an itch can get worse and worse indefinitely. With pain, at some point you black out, but with itching, what happens? I send my fingernails into my naked skin, clawing—

"*Stop!*" Mortin yells. "Here!" He grabs an ice-pack-like sack from a shelf and tosses it to me. "Press that against your chest!"

It has green liquid inside with a brand name on the front. The text is some weird language, but it's red and yellow, which is how I know it's a brand name. I press the sack to my chest. It has an immediate miraculous effect. It crackles and sparks where it touches my skin. Rays of comfort and joy flood my body. The itching rushes to the bag and leaves.

"God . . . phew . . . okay," I say. I feel like a new man. I feel like a man! I pull the sack away and inspect it.

"Ugh!" Inside, tiny green tadpoles swim around, agitated.

They seem to notice me, turning to attack the inside of the bag.

"What do they want, to get in my body?"

"Did they solve the itching or not?"

"What are they? Giant green sperms?"

"Hepatodes." The girl speaks up. "They sense discomfort and eat the electrical signals that cause it. But you've gotta keep them in the bag; otherwise they'll paralyze you."

"You're welcome," Mortin says.

"It's better than hurting you to make you forget you're itching, which is the only other way to handle it," the girl says. "Itching is a side effect of transit. Would you like some clothes?"

The girl hands me a folded piece of burlap from a nearby shelf. It's a loincloth, like Mortin's wearing. I put it on quickly. I remember Anna, who Mortin told me I was supposed to kiss; it seems odd that I would meet two women in the space of an hour and have them both be willing to speak to me. It almost seems odder than meeting a fantasy creature and being "transited" into another world, which is where I suppose I am. I heard somewhere that the way it works with women is that one minute you have two and the next you have none (and this always frustrated me because I thought, *How do I get to two?*), but apparently it works the other way: zero women can become two without warning.

"What happened to *my* clothes?" I ask Mortin, looking at my legs in the loincloth. They're too skinny.

"You can ask me," the girl says. "You don't have to pretend I'm not here, and you don't have to be scared."

"Trust me, he's scared."

"No I'm not!"

"Your clothes have been eaten by the multiverse," the girl explains. "Everybody comes through naked. You're wearing a *getma* now, don't worry."

"What about my keys and wallet and cell phone? They were in my pockets."

"Your getma fits you. Consider yourself lucky."

"I've gotta report my phone missing? Jeez."

"I told you to get naked," Mortin says, affixing a different lighter to his tail. "We're born naked and, if we're lucky, we die naked."

I wiggle my toes. I'm on springy, forgiving dirt. I didn't notice before: although a wooden floor runs around the circumference of this room, the center is a bare dirt pit. I look into the dirt and see a web of tiny white threads that spread and pirouette as they dive into the ground. The threads form a close-knit honeycomb; they remind me of pictures I've seen of neurons in the human brain, drooping in empty space and connected in the most complicated way imaginable.

"What am I standing on?" I ask the girl, to show I'm not scared. Her ears are high and light, with pointed tips. She has deep eyes and full lips. She wears a getma, too, with a belt and what I can only describe as a stylish animal-hide fanny pack. Her top, which hangs from her shoulders on two wide straps, drapes over her body so that I think I might be able to see her belly button, but it could just be a shadow—or maybe she doesn't *have* a belly button. Why do I find this attractive? I picture running my hand over her stomach. . . .

"Why do you look at me that way?" she asks.

I stumble. I'm not sure how to play this, but then I make a decision: she's too beautiful ever to be interested in me. It'll be counterproductive to think of her that way. Plus, she's seen me naked, so she knows my deep and hairless secrets.

"No reason. We should do this properly. I'm Perry. Pleased to meet you." I stick out my hand. Businesslike.

"I'm Ada Ember," she says. "Mortin's intern."

We shake: strict, cordial, nothing romantic about it. I like Ada's handshake. It's better than Anna's, where I just shook a mitten.

"You know what my mother would ask if I told her you had an internship? She'd ask if it was paid." I chuckle.

"It's not," Mortin says.

"Your parents are fascinating specimens," Ada says. "We've been studying them. Did your mother give you the pewter—"

"Ah! Ada!" Mortin interrupts. "Let's keep some things under wraps! We need to prepare Perry for analysis and orbitoclasty—"

"He's not going to remember this, so why can't we talk about what we want?"

"What am I not going to remember? I'm going to remember this for sure."

"*You maintain the correspondents' sense of free will,*" Mortin hisses, ignoring me. "If they realize what's happening to them, their heads explode."

"Hello? If my head were going to explode, it would've happened already. Guys? What's this thing I'm standing on that looks like white plant roots?"

"A *thakerak*," Ada says, before Mortin can stop her. "It's biologically analogous to a fungus's hyphae, which are the parts of a mushroom that you don't see, that perform all the functions besides sex."

"It's alive?" I smack the ground.

"Stop!" Ada grabs me. The threads under the dirt pop and rustle. "Don't hit it!" She pulls me aside. "Is that the first thing you do when you see something new—hit it?"

"Sometimes, yeah," I admit.

"Are we all being civil in here?" a voice calls from across the room.

30

A DOOR, CARVED SURREPTITIOUSLY INTO the wall, has opened a crack. A man pokes his head in. It's a bald, pugnacious head.

"Everything's fine, Gamary," Mortin says, rushing to close the door. The person outside, Gamary, pushes back. "Who's *that*?" he asks. He gives me a stern look. His head is very high off the ground.

"I'm just . . . Perry Eckert; pleased to meet you." I stick my hand out.

"Mortin!"

Gamary shoves the door open and knocks Mortin over. He steps into the chamber, and I see why his head is so far off the ground: it's attached to a short torso that turns into a large potbelly that turns into light-brown fur on top of *four hoofed legs*.

"Centaur!" I blurt, like a kid yelling out the name of a dinosaur at a museum.

"Mortin, I told you, no more tweaks!"

Gamary kneels on his two front legs and starts punching Mortin. Mortin scrambles away and reaches behind a barrel.

He pulls out a short, unadorned sword and tosses it from one hand to another.

"Don't touch me, okay? I paid for this space."

"No illegal transits!" Gamary reaches for a saddle mounted on his own back and pulls out an ax. Crap. I back up, flabbergasted, but as animal fear kicks in, some analytical part of me notices that he's too small to be a real centaur. His lower half is six feet long, not ten like a full-grown horse. He looks more like a man on top of a deer, with horizontal stripes on his forelegs and backward-pointing knees.

Gamary and Mortin circle each other. Mortin jabs with his sword. Gamary easily blocks with his ax. Sparks sprinkle toward the ground and the thakerak buzzes as if in answer. I can't tell if they're just playing or if they're really trying to hurt each other. They're very talkative.

"My father rented thakeraks from your father, and you won't even give me the courtesy of a little privacy?" Mortin slaps Gamary's leg with the flat of his sword.

"Your father wasn't a degenerate pebble addict like you are!" Gamary brings his ax down a centimeter from Mortin's foot.

"That's my medicine! Don't talk about my medicine!" Mortin slashes at Gamary's hand.

"You brought over some scared human child who's going to soil himself on my property!"

"Hey! I'm not gonna soil anything!"

In sync: "Shut up!"

"Stop it, both of you!" Ada rushes between Gamary and

Mortin. Gamary holds his ax over his shoulder. "This boy is the one we were telling you about," she says. "The one who has to do with the princess."

"Princess?" I ask.

"Ada! Quiet!"

"Him?" Gamary inspects me.

"What princess?" I want to know more. The word *princess* has a seminal place in my head. But instead of giving me answers, Gamary stands over me, putting me in a shadow of candlelight. "You sure you got the right one? He seems a little small. And dumb. He called me a centaur."

"I know you're not a centaur," I say. "You're too small."

"Excuse me?" He raises his ax. "You want to go home in two pieces, princess boy?"

"Gamary!" Mortin shoulder-checks him. He drops the ax. Ada grabs it and locks the door. Mortin raises his sword and holds it against Gamary's neck. *"Don't touch him."*

"What do you want me to do? If the authorities find him"— *me*—"they're gonna have me arrested!" Gamary twitches his tail. "My daughter's sick, Mortin. The bad fever. As soon as I can, I'm taking her to Laurentia for medicine. I can't do that if I'm rotting in a cell, you understand?"

Mortin puts his sword down.

"So you're gonna send him back, right? So long as you send him back, it's no problem."

"Yes, we'll send him back."

"When?"

"A few minutes."

"Back where?" I ask. "Back to *camp*? No way!"

"He doesn't sound like he wants to go back."

"Don't worry. He's quite timid."

"Hey!"

Gamary picks up his ax and heads for the door. "I'm sending one of my interns to look after you. Just in case."

"Who? Your punk kid?"

"He's a good kid."

Before he leaves, Gamary has final words for me: "Princess boy, I'm not a centaur. I'm an *okapicentaur*." He puffs his chest out. "That's part man, part okapi, like the African ungulate. What are you, racist?"

I can't think of a good answer in time, so he leaves shaking his head. I don't think I've earned his respect.

31

"I'M NOT GOING BACK TO CAMP, OKAY?
I'd like to make that clear. I'd also like a full explanation of
what's happening," I tell Mortin and Ada.

"No problem. Get up here," Mortin says, hitting a lever.
A wooden table swings out of the wall and chunks into place.
He pats it like doctors do when they want you to sit for an
examination. As I consider heading over versus making a run
for it, the door reopens and a new visitor enters.

He's a guy, not a centaur, but not quite human. He looks
like Ada: light-blue hair, pointy ears. He seems about my age, in
a leather vest with a getma over his crotch. He has streamlined
muscles, pale arms full of spiral tattoos, and a lip ring. I always
hated lip rings. His sneer is familiar; I've seen it on the faces of
people who make fun of me in school, all the way back to Justin
Racho and Jacoby Myers. It's the sneer of a bully. Ada glares at
him. Mortin scowls at him. I see that neither of them trust him,
but under Ada's dislike I suspect an appreciation of his triceps.

"Don't mind me; I'm just here to make sure you all observe
protocol."

"Ryu, good to see you," Mortin says.

"Ryu? Hold up. Ryu like at camp?"

"Excuse me? Don't speak to me, tweak."

"What's a tweak? That's rude. Do you have to be rude?"

"You *are* a tweak. It's not my fault you don't know it. I can call you whatever I want."

"No, you can call me Perry. Pleased to meet you." I stick out my hand. I've been shaking a lot of people's hands lately. "I'm from New York. Brooklyn. Well. My parents are divorced—"

Ryu ignores my hand but perks up at the word *Brooklyn*.

"Do you know the Beastie Boys?" he asks.

"Uh . . . I know some of their videos."

"You don't know them personally?"

"No."

"Then what do I need you for? You two carry on; send him back."

"On the table," Mortin reminds me.

"No, wait, stop!" I stand my ground. "How am I meeting two people named Ryu in one day? That's not normal."

"You're still concerned about normal?" Mortin asks.

"You got a problem with my name?" Ryu presses.

"Look: I get punched in the head by a kid at camp named Ryu, and now there's a Ryu here with blue hair? That's not a coincidence. Dreams are used to store memories. Is *that* what's happening right now? I don't want this to be a dream because it's a lot better than my real life, but I need one of you to start explaining. If my parents find out I've been kidnapped to the 'World of the Other Normals,' they're going to find their lawyers—"

"Didn't your parents leave their lawyers in the woods?" Ada asks.

"How do you know that? I assume they picked them up—"

"Perry," Mortin says. "All we want to do is check out your ankle. How does it feel?"

I touch it—after all the itching and subsequent excitement, I forgot about it, but now it throbs. "Hurts."

"Good. Where there's pain, there's life."

Mortin pulls another lever on the wall. A system of pulleys squeaks to life, and the room's ceiling slides back like a mechanical football dome. It reveals a gargantuan pool of water above, held in by clear glass. I shield my eyes. The water stretches up far enough to erase any chance of gauging its depth. Light pours in from the top. It's bright and blue and clear, with no fish or plants of any kind. As soon as I see it, I hear a quiet, pleasant hum. The thakerak likes the water.

"We're underwater?" I ask in awe.

"We're at the bottom of the Great Beniss Basin," Mortin says. I stare up at scaleless blue as Ada offers me her arm and leads me to the table. She moves lightly. I feel bumbling and stupid, my elbow in hers, as I hobble on my bad ankle. It's the first time a girl has ever touched my arm. Her hand is warm and smooth.

I lie down. Mortin stands at my head. Ada stands at my feet. Ryu watches everything with his arms crossed, making me feel small and inadequate, even though he isn't taller than me, like the Ryu at camp wasn't. It's his attitude that makes him tall. What a trick!

Ada pulls a rope down from the ceiling and puts it around my ankle.

"Ow! Not too tight!"

Ryu laughs. Ada raises her eyebrows at me.

"Fine. Make it tight."

She pulls the rope taut. It grips my ankle like a claw. I wince but hold the pain in. The rope leads to the glass above me, where it attaches to a hook. Above the hook, on the other side of the glass, a thin metal rod sticks into the Great Beniss Basin. I shake my foot. The rope moves; the hook and rod move with it. It's like I'm attached to a car antenna. It's fun. I kick my foot aside and accidentally clip Mortin.

"Ow!"

"Stop him!" Ryu says. "Keep him still!"

"Don't move," Ada whispers, grabbing me.

Mortin holds his side. "Are you okay?" I ask. "I didn't kick you that hard."

"It's fine. I just—I've got a bruise there," Mortin says, shaking it off.

Ada holds me still. "Gamary will go nuts if you interfere with the Basin. Just relax your foot while we take the reading."

"But *what* are you reading? How does it work?"

"Mortin? Permission to do a formal introduction?"

He nods and waves her on, still holding his side.

"Yes." Ada pumps her fist. It's wonderful to see. Ryu sighs like we're wasting his time. Ada flits back around the room, carefully avoiding the thakerak, and returns with a notebook full of the strange writing that I saw on the bag of hepatodes.

It's a leather-bound notebook with a thick cover, alien but familiar—a school notebook. I'd know a school notebook no matter what language it was in. When she opens it, I see doodles in pencil on the side.

"This is my first introduction," she says. "It's a big honor. I've been preparing."

"Like a test?"

"Yeah."

"You're doing great."

She clears her throat. "Peregrine Eckert—"

"Perry. Perry's fine."

"I like Peregrine."

"But I really—"

Ada blinks. Her eyes are blue like her hair. When she blinks, I think maybe she doesn't find me so shrimpy and untouchable.

"Peregrine's fine," I agree.

"Thank you. Peregrine Eckert, I'd like to welcome you to the World of the Other Normals!"

32

THERE'S A MOMENT WHEN IT FEELS LIKE
people should clap, but no one claps, so I clap.

"Hold still!" Mortin orders.

"I have a question: what do *you* guys call it? When you're talking to each other. You must call it something else. Some real name."

Ada looks to Mortin. "Show him," he says. He slides a panel aside in the wall. Behind it is an array of buttons, dials, and wheels. He focuses on these while eyeing the rod in the water, which jitters as my ankle moves with my breathing and circulation.

"It's called—" Ada starts, and then her mouth moves but her voice cuts off, just like Dale Blaswell's did back in the nurse's office.

"What?"

Ryu laughs. Ada explains, "The true name can't be understood by your mind. When you hear it, it doesn't register."

"That's ridiculous. I have to call this place something. 'World of the Other Normals' is too long. What about 'Anormalia?' No, that sounds like a disease."

"Hurry it up," Ryu says.

"Freaking Americans." Mortin adjusts dials and levers. "They have such problems with names. I bring somebody over from Nepal, they understand that certain things can't be expressed in words. But Americans need names."

"Continuing!" Ada says. "Peregrine, our universe split from yours six hundred million years ago."

"So it's Earth? This is like Earth?"

"It's a planet like Earth, in a solar system like Earth's, but a lot of things change in six hundred million years. When the split happened, shelled animals were just starting to appear. On Earth, you got dinosaurs and birds and humans. Here, we got other normals, like Mortin and me and Ryu."

Ryu smiles. "Baby, you could teach me a class any day."

Ada glares at him, but then he adjusts his lip ring with his tongue and cocks one eyebrow. She blushes. No way. That's unfair. I can't cock one eyebrow like that. I thought people could only do that in cartoons. I always move both eyebrows and it just looks like I'm surprised. *Focus, Perry!*

"What about Gamary, the okapicentaur? Is he an 'other normal'?"

"Yes, we come in several varieties. There are highborn other normals, like all of us in this room, and ingresses— hybrid creatures—like Gamary. All part of our evolutionary tree. Mortin, how's the reading coming?"

"Good." Mortin looks at the thakerak as my ankle twitches in midair. The white threads click and buzz in reaction to the small disturbances I produce in the water. It's like an organic MRI.

"Then—and I want you to relax, Peregrine—in the year twelve hundred fifty-eight ADD—"

"A*D*," Ryu corrects. "ADD is a different thing."

"Oh." Ada takes a note. "Do you know a lot about Earth, Ryu?"

"I got a dream, to go to Earth and make movies."

"Like a director?" I ask.

"A *writer*-director, like Quentin Tarantino or David Lynch. Or a rock star. That's my backup plan."

"Have you ever been to Earth, though?"

"No."

"Oh." I can't help but feel superior. "Too bad."

"You wanna get punched?"

"*Anyway*, boys, in twelve hundred fifty-eight A*D*, our two universes came back together."

"How?"

"That year, on Earth, the Bayt al-Hikmah was destroyed. It was a library in Baghdad, the greatest of its time."

"I should know this. . . . I play an RPG based on *Arabian Nights*."

"Yes, that's very impressive. When the Mongols destroyed the Bayt al-Hikmah, they threw so many books into the Tigris River that it ran black with ink for six months. It was the greatest single loss of information ever in the history of Earth, and it happened to correspond with a great loss of information in our world, too. At that moment, the thakeraks here connected with fungi on Earth. So much knowledge was lost that it was possible for our universes to be, for an instant, together again. Ignorance as bliss. We started making trips."

"That's impossible," I say. "We would know. You couldn't just have mystical beings going to Earth without people finding out—"

"I'm not a mystical being, I'm a consultant," Mortin says, making adjustments at the wall.

"We were shocked at first, but we're disciplined people," Ada says. "The Appointees, when they learned about the connection, strictly regulated trips."

"Who are the Appointees?"

"Our leaders," Ryu grunts.

"A bit like your president," Ada says, "except the Appointees are appointed for life, and they appoint new Appointees before they pass away. They keep us safe; they keep us organized—"

Mortin huffs.

"What's that?" Ryu asks. "You have something seditious to say?"

"And they're vitally important for everyone's *safety*," Ada continues in an everybody-stay-calm tone. "The Appointees controlled exploration of your universe as we found out about the correspondences between your world and ours. But now, the princess, daughter of the Lead Appointee, has been kidnapped by a terrible monster named Ophisa. Our world has been thrown out of balance. War and sickness are spreading through the land. The Appointees are detaining anyone suspected of working with Ophisa. These are dark times."

"Sounds like you need a hero," I say, thinking, *You're lucky this is my territory.* "What's Ophisa like? Serpent? Humanoid?"

"He's a horrific mutant beast that combines the insectoid and reptilian, with a hundred ten eyes and poison fangs, as tall as a tree," Ada says.

"All right!" Mortin steps back from the wall. "Perry, you're fine. You can get up now."

"What?"

"Reading's done. Ada has proven sufficiently distracting—"

"But it was just getting good—"

"Your ankle's okay. It's not going to cause any problems for your correspondent—"

"Who is that? What did you do?"

"Explanation time is over, Perry. I'm taking a quick smoke break, and then we're sending you back to camp." Mortin grabs some pebbles from behind a barrel.

"Hey!" Ryu says. "What do you think you're doing?"

"Calm down, pipsqueak." Mortin lights up. "Get your boss in here if you need someone to yell at me. I'm not gonna be lectured by a kid with a cheap lip ring who's got a crush on my intern."

"Excuse me?"

Mortin blows a smoke ring at Ryu. The pebbles don't make him calm the way cigarettes make Sam calm; they make him giddy and, I think, they convince him that whatever he's doing is cute. "Pretty soon people are gonna be tripping all over themselves to give me my job back for saving the princess! Ophisa's gonna be a thing of the past, all thanks to me and Perry here, and some attenuate errand boy is going to tell me how to live my life? I don't think so. Get out!"

I expect a reaction from Ryu—verbal if not physical— but he takes the suggestion. He blows a kiss at Ada, sneers at Mortin, ignores me, and leaves the room. Just like that.

33

ADA BANGS HER FIST ON MORTIN'S CHEST. "What is wrong with you? You can't smoke here! He's going to get Gamary!"

"So? The old joker's just trying to look tough. I'm not going to let him push me around."

The door slams back open. Ryu and Gamary enter.

"Look at that!" Mortin says. "Just talking about you two. Sorry, I know no smoking. Putting it out now. Got a little carried away." He dumps the pebbles on the ground and smiles, but Gamary just points at him, a deep distance in his expression. "That's him, Officer."

Three monsters enter the room.

They're all hybrid other normals—*ingresses*, I remember from Ada's introduction. The front two are men from the waist down, or at least from where their legs come out of their getmas, and *fish creatures* above, with scaly chests, spindly arms, fins sticking out of their backs, purple bulbous eyes, and jagged teeth. They wear belts with handcuffs hanging off. Their stench hits me—like rotting fish and beached seaweed—as they stand at attention with spears. The best I can say for them is that at least they're *up front* about being monsters.

The third one is more subtle. He's a human from the waist up—if he held your gaze, you'd think he was just a dour man with a thick, dark mustache—but his lower half is composed of thick, slimy octopus tentacles. He makes puckered sucking noises against the wood as he approaches. He's the leader; the other two stand still as he moves. He's shirtless, wearing a long burlap skirt (*kilt*, I correct myself), underneath which his tentacles bloom. He has a lantern-jawed face, brown hair, and controlling eyes. He rotates his palm on the hilt of a conspicuously large sword in a jeweled scabbard as he looks at Mortin, Ada, and me.

"Mortin Enaw, you and your associates are under arrest."

34

I'M READY TO RESIST. I SIT UP, BRING MY fists to my face, and, even though I'm facing two fish-men and one octopus-man (and even though my ankle is still tied to a rope), move my hands in little circles like a boxer. I figure I'll wiggle out, jump at the octopus-man, push him into the thakerak, and hit it so it sparks up again. With luck it'll zap him back to Camp Washiska Lake, where counselors or a SWAT team will deal with him. Then Mortin and Ada and I will handle the others. As I play through this scenario, I realize I'm not treating the World of the Other Normals like a hallucination, or a dream, or even real life; I'm treating it like a game. Games prepared me for it. And it has something to win—the princess, whoever she is, or Ada, who is a princess as far as I'm concerned.

Ada mouths at me, "Don't move." I put my hands down.

"You're suspected of performing unlicensed tweaks, Mortin," the octopus-man says, "and considering *him*"—me, as indicated by tentacle—"I've got ample evidence to bring you in. Plus Ryu tells me you've spoken with questionable tone about the Appointees."

"I'm trying to *help* the Appointees! I'm trying to get the princess *back*!"

"Mortin . . . such a sad, delusional case. You used to be one of the brightest minds in correspondence, one of Sulice's youngest field operatives, and here you are, descended into madness at the hands of that most plebeian substance, earthpebbles."

"Shut up!" Mortin lunges forward before Ada can stop him. In a blur, the octopus-man shoots out a tentacle and wraps it around his wrist, twisting him off balance. He lands on his tail; with a quiet *crick*, his lighter cracks apart.

"No! That's vintage!"

The octopus-man restrains Mortin's wrists with one tentacle and his ankles with another. He pulls out his sword with one of his buff human arms and points it at Mortin's neck while the fish-men aim their spears at his chest.

"All right," Mortin says. "I surrender. But don't hurt the boy; it's vital that he return to Earth to complete a mission."

"Nobody's returning anywhere! Handcuff this criminal and get him out of here!"

The fish-men advance on Mortin, kneel down, and babble at each other in a rotten, wet language. They snap cuffs on his wrists and ankles. One of them throws him over his shoulder. Mortin looks desperately at me and Ada as he's carried off. "Ada, get him back to Earth! Explain about the princess!"

The door slams. Mortin's gone. The tentacled man steps

toward me. With one tug, he undoes the rope around my ankle. It flops on the table. "Ow!" I curse myself for saying something so wimpy in front of Ada and Ryu, who's smiling at me in a way that demands a girder be pushed at his face.

"You'll be getting further explanations from *me*," the octopus-man says. I grit my teeth. Jake taught me once how to deal with cops: first, treat them as deferentially as possible; second, lie about everything.

"My name's Officer Tendrile," he says. "What's yours?"

"John . . . Johnson," I say. Will it work? In Creatures & Caverns, the determining statistic for whether someone believes your lies is Personality. Pekker Cland is Personality 5.

Officer Tendrile wraps a tentacle around my left wrist, snaps it over to my right, and squeezes both. He feels cold, damp, and strong. Where his suckers bite into my skin, a sharp burn, like sandpaper, runs up my arms. Blood escapes from under his tentacle.

"Aaagh!"

"Listen to me." He moves close. His big pecs twitch. Behind him, Gamary looks guilty. "I've never had a problem with humans. I don't like running spears lengthwise through their digestive cavities, or feeding them to sand sharks, or just plain eating them, like my servant here." Next to him, the remaining fish creature gnashes his teeth, revealing a forked black tongue. "But if you start lying to me, things will get very unpleasant for you very quickly."

"Don't hurt him!" Ada says. "He's sensitive!"

"I don't need to be lectured by an *attey*!" Officer Tendrile snaps. "You witches think everybody's so sensitive. He looks fine to me. Guard! How's that blood taste?"

I stand stock-still as the fish creature comes up to my wrists, bends down, and licks the blood seeping out from under Officer Tendrile's coiled tentacle. He nods and grins.

"Strong blood, strong body," Officer Tendrile says. "Don't listen to these conjurer scum. You're just fine, Mr. . . ."

"Eckert. Perry Eckert."

"That's better. Guard?"

The fish creature cuffs my hands behind my back. My blood clings to the cool metal. *Do something, Perry!* Pekker Cland wouldn't give up in this situation! He'd bust out with a pep talk from Sam. But now the fish creature is cuffing my ankles. "No, wait, I'm—*ow!*" I stagger and fall. I land on my shoulder next to the destroyed remnants of Mortin's lighter. "My ankle's injured!"

"Suck it up," Officer Tendrile says. "What's the matter with you?" He puts a tentacle under Ada's face. "And *you*. What a well-formed piece of equipment! You could be making big money dancing Upper."

Ada moves her lips around like she's thinking of a witty comeback. I glance at the splintered lighter behind me—a small scatter of wood and metal slivers. I roll my cuffs against it. Some pieces get picked up by the blood that's congealing on me and stick to my skin. I don't know why I do it. Maybe I'll be able to help Mortin put the lighter back together later.

Ada unleashes her comeback—but it isn't words. It's spit. *Splat.*

"Cuff 'er!" Officer Tendrile wipes off his mustache. The fish creature secures Ada's wrists behind her back and kicks her notebook across the room. He has tawny human feet.

"Hey!"

"Get them out of here! Let's go!"

"What are we being arrested for?" I insist.

"For being yourself."

The fish creature wraps his scaly arms under my armpits and flings me onto Gamary's back. I cough into his coarse okapi hair. Ada is next, but she gets tossed on in the opposite direction, so that all I see are her shackled feet. She has normal feet—everyone in this world seems to go barefoot—but her toenails are silver, with small glittering sparkles.

"I like your toenail polish," I say. I know it's good to give girls compliments.

"Shut up!" Officer Tendrile says. He slaps me across the face with a tentacle. "Move!"

Gamary lopes forward. Ryu stays at the thakerak. "Well done," Officer Tendrile tells him. "Have a good time checking out New York, and I wish you luck with your movie-making rock-star career."

"Cool, Officer."

Punk, I think.

"It's not polish," Ada says quietly. "I'm an attenuate other normal. Our nails are like that."

She wiggles her toes. The light that shines through the water glints off them. Despite myself, despite the situation, I blush, and I'm glad she can't see as Officer Tendrile leads us out of the thakerak chamber into

SUBB

ENIA

35

MOST OF THE TRAVEL THAT TAKES PLACE
between Earth and the World of the Other Normals happens
in Subbenia, centrally located, where Mortin brought me when
he took me over. The city stretches from under the Great Beniss
Basin to its shores to the mountains that surround it, and, as
is true in New York, cities that are economically dependent
on travel and free enterprise are homes for disease, crime,
adventure, and very odd smells, which smack me in the face as
Gamary carries me down the passage from his thakerak-for-rent
to the central market of Penner. Penner is a giant subterranean
chamber, two hundred feet tall and several city blocks long,
filled with bickering, chattering, otherworldly creatures in an
open-air flea market.

"Jeez," I say, straining to take it in between coughing fits
into Gamary's hair. It looks like the farmers' market in Union
Square, except instead of just having beards and tribal earlobe
inserts, the people are monsters—strange variants of the things
I've read about in Creatures & Caverns.

Some look like Mortin, with red skin, yellow hair, and
tails—and there are many who smoke pipes like him (although

I don't see any with tail lighters; maybe that *was* vintage). Some look like Ada and Ryu ("attenuates"?), with pale skin, blue hair, pointed ears, spindly bodies, and twinkling fingernails and toenails. Some are aqua blue with throbbing gill slits on their necks in large glass collars full of water.

Then there are the ingresses, the hybrids. Each is part human and part something else. I see okapicentaurs like Gamary; fish-men like the guard who strides beside me (who, although he looks fishy, seems fine breathing air); octopus-men like Officer Tendrile (who all appear to be cops); proper horse-bottom centaurs, who look tall and regal and (I admit) sexy; fauns with goat legs and human bodies; men with dog heads that slobber and bark at one another; and men with large, bumpy, moist-looking frog heads.

The ceiling, like the inside of the thakerak chamber, is a giant glass sheet under bright blue water, which makes the chamber feel like a bizarre aquarium where the creatures have escaped and decided to sell things. Different stands offer pottery, rugs, books, fruit, jewelry, weapons, and medicine. Everyone wears getmas or kilts or robes. I see no women. I see no shoes.

Creatures crowd Ada and me as we're paraded through, smoking, spitting, blabbing in different languages, mostly English. *Why English?* I assumed before that everyone spoke English because this was happening in my head, or because it was a setup for a cruel psychological experiment, but no psychological experiment would involve construction of a set this elaborate, and when it comes to dreams . . . I was never this successful with women in my dreams. I know I haven't succeeded with Ada in any way that a healthy heterosexual male would count, but she *has* looked at me, and I *have* given her a compliment, and she has touched my arm, and this is better than I usually do, even in my dreams.

Let's assume that what Ada says is true: I'm in an alternate universe that split off from Earth and then reconnected after millions of years. Did the creatures learn English from *us*? Maybe they just like English. I wish they weren't speaking it, though, because I can understand what they're saying about Ada:

"—look at the little one—"

"—she'd fetch a good price—"

"—it's tight like that—"

"—Officer Tendrile, let me sketch you, sir, twenty *di*—"

I hear this word *di*- a lot in the rattling conversation of the market. It's the beginning of one of the words my brain can't conceptualize, so every time I hear it, it remains an untended prefix, but it's easy to tell from the context what it means.

"Dumplings! Fresh dumplings here! Two *di*-!"

"Taxes! Getchyer taxes done here! Don't let the Appointees take your *di*-! *Hai hillai!*"

Among the many stalls in the market, the ones with the longest lines advertise, in plain English, "correspondence services." I'm not sure what it means, but as the crowd mobs us, we slow down, and I find myself hanging next to two creatures on line. The first is an aqua man with neck gills under a glass collar; he has a row of gold and silver rings on each gill slit. The second has a frog head.

"*Riggity buggle*," the frog-man says.

"We're trying one more," his companion says. "But if we can't hack it, you're going to have to settle the case."

"*Buggle!*" the frog-man says.

"Whose fault is it, huh? Did I try and lick someone inappropriately?"

"Mr. . . . ah . . . Officer Tendrile?" I call out. "How come everyone's speaking English?"

I'm hoping the question will flatter him. A certain type of cruel intelligence is flattered by questions. I'm right; he lights up. "The Appointees assigned English two hundred years ago. I never liked it. Dirty language. Too many words."

"People just took it up?"

"We listen to the Appointees here. Who do you think makes this a males-only marketplace? That's how you keep a society strong."

"Where are you taking us?"

He smiles and *slucks* away. We pass coopers, tailors, and blacksmiths. One person reminds me of Pekker Cland—a red-skinned smith with a semicircle of axes spread out in front of him, negotiating with a dog-head. The dog-head sniffs at me as I pass; I sniff back. There's a lot to smell, especially when we pass the food stalls, which sell a plethora of variations of meat on a stick. There's meat on a stick dusted with pepper powder, meat on a stick drizzled with orange sauce, meat on a stick fried golden brown and contorted into long looping shapes. . . . The odors hit me in waves: barbecue, cardamom, cinnamon, onion, char. . . . Among them are smells I've never dealt with before: nasty impossible smells like peanut-butter shrimp and sautéed sour milk clump.

We come to the end of the market chamber. Gamary stops. I've gotten used to his harsh hair; my neck hurts from craning it to see everything. In front of us, I spy a gigantic wooden door.

"Pleasure doing business with you," Officer Tendrile says to Gamary. His guard hoists me and Ada off the okapicentaur's back and flings us on the ground, which is coated with the grunge of innumerable bare feet.

"Sorry," Gamary says to me and Ada. "My daughter."

"*Shhh*," Officer Tendrile says. "Go." He hands Gamary a pile of golden coins. Gamary heads back into the market with a regretful lope.

36

THE GIGANTIC WOODEN DOOR SWINGS
open from the inside. An octopus-man nods at Officer Tendrile.
Tendrile's guard pulls Ada and me through the doorway. The
door shuts with a hollow, echoing thud. The sounds of the
market disappear.

In front of us, the ceiling dips precipitously and the
passageway gets narrower and turns to the right, to a chamber
filled with jail cells cut into opposing rock walls. Officer
Tendrile leads us to it. Lanterns hang in the dank air. Octopus-
men sit on stools drinking what smells like regular old coffee
in clay cups. Fish creatures pace back and forth holding spears.
Pleading faces—some dog-heads, some frog-heads, some
centaurs—look out from the jail cells. Dirty hands grip the
bars.

We're pulled into an empty cell at the end of the chamber. The
fish creature holds a bowl of water to my lips. It smells pondish
but I sip some. Ada drinks it too, and I briefly recognize this as
an intimate moment: sharing a drink with a girl. Officer Tendrile
points at a trough on the floor behind us.

"When you need to relieve yourself, go there. This is one of the things I love about our world. Mr. Eckert, on Earth, you have pants, yes? Pants aren't allowed here. The Appointees haven't approved them. So people wear getmas, and I can leave my prisoners handcuffed, and they can still relieve themselves no problem!"

He secures the door with a lock as large as my head. It clangs against the bars. He steps out of view, leaving me alone with Ada. I sigh. I'm about to apologize for getting us into this mess, but then I remember Mortin and Sam telling me I apologize too much, so I shut up, and Ada speaks.

"Gamary. What a spineless bum. And that little snitch Ryu. I'm gonna kill them both."

"You can take Gamary, but leave Ryu to me," I say, trying to sound badass. "I have a beef against a different Ryu, and there has to be a connection."

"There could be a correspondence."

"What's that? And what are correspondence services? I saw those in the market."

"People in your world are connected to people here. The populations are identical. It has something to do with the way our universes came back together. Everyone in your world has a single correspondent here, and by doing something to a person's correspondent in this world, you can affect them in your world. And vice versa."

"So Ryu here corresponds to Ryu at camp?"

"Maybe. Sometimes people who have the same name don't

correspond. Understanding it all is very complicated. That's why it's a high-paying job."

"Which was what Mortin had."

"Exactly: a correspondence consultant. But I want to go back to something. How would you 'handle' Ryu? You're not skilled in physical violence, Peregrine."

"Uh . . ." I think I've just been called a pussy. I decide to change the subject. "I'm glad they put us together."

"It's a sign of disrespect. They think we're too stupid to figure a way out of here."

"Are we?" I think we might be. Our hands are cuffed behind our backs. What're we supposed to do? I never thought I was stupid, but now that I know this whole world exists, I do feel pretty dumb. . . . I need to learn more. In Creatures & Caverns, the more you read the books, the better you're able to deal. "What were all those creatures out there?" I ask.

"Full of questions, are we?" Ada shuffles around the cell on her butt, looking at the walls and ceiling, scanning for weak points. "The highborn other normals come in three varieties: attenuate, like me and Ryu; saturate, the ones with the gill slits—you probably won't see much of them; and ferrous, like Mortin Enaw."

"Like ferrules in the game."

"Yes, but don't tell Mortin that; he'll get insulted. He thinks that game is a hack job. Besides the highborns, you saw members of the seven ingress races: the okapicentaurs, the centaurs, the fauns, the hequets, the cynos, the celates, and the batracians."

"The what and the *what*?"

"The hequets are the frog-heads; the cynos are the dog-heads; the celates have the tentacles like our friend Officer Tendrile; the batracians are the fish-men. The fauns—"

"I know what a faun is!"

"Well, clearly I can't make assumptions. Didn't you take biology?"

"Yes."

"Then you should be able to figure out the word *batracian*."

"I have specialized knowledge, okay?"

"Like what?"

"Creatures and Caverns."

"Right, then, here you go! You're in a certified cavern guarded by creatures. This is perfect."

"No, it's . . . in C and C you've got a party of adventurers, and weapons, and armor . . . and spells! Magic! Do you know magic?"

Ada shakes her head.

"Runecrafts? Special escape magic?"

"There's no such thing as magic."

"Well, crap. Where did they take Mortin?"

"Mortin's got a record, so they took him to Granger. It's a high-security prison on the other side of Penner." She gives me a quick-and-dirty geography primer. "We are five hundred helms, or a quarter mile, underground. Penner is one market chamber out of dozens that make up Subbenia's lower portion, which is full of prisons, brothels, bars, restaurants, criminals, adventure seekers, and earthpebble addicts. Most chambers are men only; some are women only; a few are coed. Up above is the Great Beniss Basin, which is as long as the Red Sea but totally devoid of life due to its unique chemical composition. It's enclosed by mountains on either side. To the south is Laurentia, the capital, where the Appointees live."

"Can't we go plead our case to the Appointees? Like a trial?"

"Trial? What a cute Earth idea."

"Maybe they haven't been introduced to it. I can explain to them. I can be eloquent. I'll say I was minding my business at camp. . . ."

Ada shakes her head. "There's no way out of this." She turns her shoulders in. I recognize the posture. I do it in quiet moments of clarity when I realize my own worthlessness.

"Hey," I tell her. "It's okay. Don't worry." I shuffle on my butt next to her.

"You don't understand," she whispers. "They'll hang Mortin, rape me, and kill you."

"The Appointees?"

"Anyone who's suspected of disagreeing with them can be branded a friend of Ophisa and . . . disappeared."

"Because Ophisa captured the princess."

"Yes. The crime of the century."

"So she's like the president's daughter?"

"Imagine if your president were the president of the *world*, and *his* daughter got kidnapped. She's like that."

"What's her name?"

"Princess Anemone Naru."

"Really? Is she, like, part anemone?"

"No!" Ada laughs. She wipes a tear off on her shoulder. "She's a highborn attenuate other normal like me. Beautiful, kind, and just. I have . . ." Ada tilts her hip toward me. "Inside the pack there I have something that will show you what she's like. Can you open it?"

Ada is referring to the thing that I previously identified as her "animal-hide fanny pack." Officer Tendrile really must think we're stupid because he let us keep everything. I bend over and use my teeth to undo the button that holds the pack closed. Ada tells me to ignore a few personal items inside (that look like makeup) as I get my teeth around something cold and metal and fish out—

"Uh pewtuh mini!" I say with my mouth full.

I place the pewter miniature on the ground. It's as good as the one of Pekker Cland—or Sam's figure of Peter Powers. It shows a gorgeous, strong girl holding a torch—a bit like the Statue of Liberty, but this girl is younger, maybe Ada's age, and instead of wearing robes she has a draped top that ends over her stomach. She herself ends not much farther below, where her hips turn into ragged unfinished metal. She has no legs.

"Pewter? Excuse me? That's *silver*," Ada corrects.

"Sorry—I mean, how was I supposed to know?"

"Because I'm not the kind of girl who carries around pewter."

"What happened to her lower half?"

"Nothing. My mother gave this to me when I was a child."

"So you broke it?"

"No! All depictions of the princess are like this. It's improper to show her lower half. She's the great figure of our time. She stands for truth and peace and fealty to the Appointees."

I look at the figure's silver eyes. They're proud but scared. *Save me, Perry*, they say.

"How was she kidnapped?" I ask Ada.

"Ophisa stormed the Appointees' palace and took her while she slept."

"How'd he get in? Isn't it guarded?"

"It's not for human minds to comprehend the horror of Ophisa. No one who has seen him has lived, except for his perverted servants. He can see into the thoughts of anyone he turns his hundred-and-ten-eye gaze on, speaking to their deepest fears."

"Where is he now?"

"He took the princess to the Badlands with his rebel hordes, where he holds her for ransom. He's demanded that the Appointees step down and the world answer to *his* command."

"And where are the Badlands?"

"South and *ouest* of Laurentia."

"You mean south and *west*?"

"We say *ouest*. It's French. It caught on."

I like it. "But why did Mortin say *I* have something to do with the princess?"

"That's our gambit, Peregrine. It's why we've been watching you. Mortin did an analysis and determined that our princess"—Ada nods at the figure—"corresponds to a girl in your summer camp, Anna Margolis. He further deduced that if you kiss Anna, the princess will be freed."

"*What?* Why? Ophisa will just let her go?"

"Maybe she'll escape; maybe Ophisa will have a mutiny among his men; maybe we'll all wake up tomorrow and it'll never have happened. That's how correspondences work—they're fuzzy. But trust me: if you kiss Anna, the princess *will* go free—Mortin determined it, and he's the best. But when he told his bosses about the connection, they fired him, and now somebody's sent the authorities after us. Someone wants to make sure his plan fails." She looks at the ground. "Poor Mortin. Off in Granger, without me, without his lighter . . ."

"Hey," I say. *"Hey!"* It's the mention of the lighter that does it. It sets off a chain reaction in my brain, a batch of thoughts that for once, instead of curving around to nowhere, shoot straight out to form a *plan*. There's more, too: Ada's face, and her story, and the princess at the mercy of this unspeakable monster in somewhere bad enough to actually be called "the Badlands"—it's a situation that requires direct action.

"We're getting out of here," I say.

"How? Magic?"

I tap my handcuffs against the ground behind me. The pieces of Mortin's lighter, which were stuck to my skin with dried blood, fall off. I peek around to see: two of them are metal slivers, about a half inch long, that look great for picking locks.

37

ADA RAISES HER EYEBROWS AT ME.
A shadow passes by the door to the cell. I stop moving. A
fish creature—a batracian—looks in at us for a few terrifying
moments, then moves on. I nod for Ada to give me her hands.
With our backs to each other, using the tips of my fingers,
working blind, I lift a metal sliver and ease it into the keyhole
on her handcuffs.

I remember Jake's words: *Everything's like sex.* I close my
eyes. I have a Creatures & Caverns book with pages and pages
on lock picking. I can do this. In a game I would roll dice. In
real life I just have to do it.

I press the metal sliver against the inside of the lock and try to
turn it. This will be my tension wrench. To pick a lock, you have
to first apply tension to it and then push the individual pins up
one by one until the lock clicks and turns. I'll have to hold one
piece of metal steady while I explore with the other. The good
thing is that, even though my wrists are shackled, I can freely
move my fingers; I just can't see them. I pinch the tension wrench
against the lock while I insert the other piece: my pick.

I feel one of the pins. It sits in the shaft of the lock. I push it up with the pick as I turn with the tension wrench. *Click.* The pin settles on top of the turning shaft.

"Holy crap!"

"*Shh!* Did you get it?"

"Not yet."

"Well, hurry up!"

I feel for the next pin. As I do, my fingers slip, the tension wrench comes out, and I have to start over. *No!* This has to work. Eventually I'm going to need to use the bathroom, and I'm not doing it in a trough in front of Ada.

I get the first pin clicked again. Then the second. The third one I have to push up very far, the fourth only a little. The world inside the lock magnifies in an exploded view behind my closed eyes; my tiniest motions take on great significance, like when you play with your mouth when you have a cold sore. The last pin won't move, so I pull the pick out, turn around, spit on it, and stick it back in. *Click.* Ada's cuffs spread open and slip onto the stone floor.

"*Yes!*" she whispers. She rubs her hands. "Now I'll do you." She picks my cuffs in about a tenth of the time. "These local locks—cheap. We're lucky."

"I thought I was good."

"No." She smiles. "You're good. Now don't start moving your hands. They might see us. Stay calm and follow me into that corner." We shuffle over. Ada picks the locks on both our feet. "Now you need to get ready to run. Can you do that?"

I test my ankle. "I think so. Can I bring the princess figure?"

"Yes, Peregrine, get the princess figure."

I slip it into the side of my getma, nestled against my hip bone. "I feel like it's calling to me."

"It is. You just have to kiss Anna at your camp and you'll do what it wants you to do."

"What about you?"

"Excuse me?"

"Can I kiss you? Before we try to get out of here. Just in case."

"*What?*"

"Like, what if we get caught? I've never kissed a girl. I don't want to die without doing it. I—"

"No, you can't kiss me, Peregrine. Anna's the one you need to kiss. Didn't anybody ever explain to you that you shouldn't *ask* to kiss girls?"

"No. I thought it would—"

"If you want to kiss someone, you just have to *do it*."

"Right. Okay."

I pucker my lips and lean forward. Ada pulls aside. "Not me, Peregrine!"

I wipe my lips on my shoulder and pretend that that's what I meant to do all along. Normally this kind of social failure would make me want to die via implosion, but right now there are too many other things to worry about. "It's cool," I say. "Honestly."

"Humans," she says. Then she adds, "*Boys*," and then she calls for a guard.

38

A FISH CREATURE COMES TO THE DOOR, mottled and smelly. I can't tell if he's the same one who threw us in the cell, but for some reason I picture him playing baseball—getting ready in the batter's box—and it makes me smile. I'm not handcuffed. God, life is good when you're not handcuffed.

The batracian hisses at us, "Whatthyou want?"

"I'm sick," Ada says. "I need to see a nurse."

"Whathh sickkk on you?"

"It's private. You wouldn't understand."

The fish creature grumbles and unlocks the door. Ada grabs my wrist; as soon as the door is fully open, she squeezes. I guess she forgot that Officer Tendrile scraped me up with his tentacle in that exact spot; I yelp as I jump and run behind her for the door.

The batracian snarls at our unshackled legs and reaches for his spear, but Ada whirls her decuffed handcuffs and thwacks him in the eye. He shrieks. He grabs at her, but he's too slow. I run out the door after her—right into the passageway between the cells, which is full of batracian guards.

"What do we do?"

Six of the guards point spears and hiss. From the cells on either side, excited prisoners scramble to watch. Ada holds up the cuffs she whacked the guard with and jangles them. They're dull black metal, and the light from the overhanging lanterns is dim orange, but the guards are as fascinated as if they're seeing diamonds. They blink their purple eyes. They try to focus on us, but they can't stop looking at the twitching cuffs. Ada sways them back and forth.

"What are you doing?"

"Distracting them with shiny objects!"

"That works?"

"Of course it works! Haven't you ever gone fishing?"

"It's still the first day of camp; I haven't had a chance!"

I think part of the magic lies in Ada's hands, which are so finely put together, with subtle curves ending in glittering fingertips. I'm momentarily distracted too. Then I notice one guard, directly in front of me, aiming his spear harmlessly toward the ground. *You have Speed 7*, I remind myself. *You shouldn't do anything drastic.* But really, if any moment calls for something drastic, this does.

I grab the spear. The guard falls forward and smacks the ground. The prisoners cheer.

"Good job, little human!"

"Now stab him! Stab him!"

I examine my new weapon. It's several feet longer than me. I've never stabbed anyone in real life; I'm not particularly good at stabbing people in video games; once I cut myself on a plastic butter knife while eating fish sticks . . . but I *have* stabbed people in C&C with Sam. I lunge forward and plunge the spear into the batracian's shoulder. It goes in with surprising ease—like stabbing nothing. The creature howls. Ada leaps over him and runs back toward the market.

"Wait for me!" I leave the spear in his body and follow. The guards snap out of their trance and hurl their weapons at us. One of them grazes my side, tearing a whispered rip above my pelvic bone, but the princess figure stays safe, and by then, honestly, I think you could have clonked me with a microwave and I'd still be moving.

Ada and I run toward the giant doors. I steal a glance behind me: two of the guards are tending to their injured comrade; the other three are in pursuit.

"Can we—*huff*—open the doors?" I manage.

"We've got to! We need to get you back to the thakerak chamber!"

But that isn't going to be easy. Two octopus-men—celates—are guarding the doors. They drink coffee on stools. One is Officer Tendrile. He stands and says, "Look at this! Mr. John Johnson Perry Eckert, come back to play." The other officer steps up behind him, but Officer Tendrile shakes him off and pulls his long sword: *ssssing!* "Do you believe in God, Mr. Eckert?"

He's ten feet away. "I . . . uh . . ." I back against Ada. "My mother used to make me go to Episcopalian church. . . . I never really believed in it, but I liked the community. . . ."

"You're not supposed to answer," Officer Tendrile says, furrowing his considerable brow. "That's just something I ask humans before I kill them."

"You're not killing me," I manage, "so it makes sense that you would get a different answer."

"What are you doing?" Ada hisses. "We're not getting through there!"

"Fire door," I say. I grab her wrist and run to the right.

39

OFFICER TENDRILE SWINGS AT ME, BUT I
suck in my chest to avoid the tip of his blade. I've spotted a
passageway that leads along the rock wall next to the giant
doors. The other celate, seeing my speed (maybe I'm more than
7! I've never really tested myself) spills his coffee and yelps. I
know we have a few seconds before he's not-burned enough to
kill us.

The rock is cool and dry under my feet. The seam that leads
away from the doors is big enough for me and Ada. . . . I hope
it's too tight for Officer Tendrile. Tentacle noises behind me
destroy that notion. He's closing in. The only chance we have is
to reach a door I don't know is there.

"What are you *doing*?" Ada gasps.

"Whenever there's a big door, there's a small door." I hope
I'm not a liar. I'm looking for a service entrance, something
like the fire door at school that Sam could open and close so
freely.

"If you stop now, I'll kill you quick!" Officer Tendrile yells.
I turn back—his tentacles pump on the floor and walls beside
him, propelling him through the passage like a tumescent

insect. His sword is out. He'll be on us in seconds—

There. A door cut into the wall on the left. Small and gray with a red bar across it. *Emergency.*

"'Alarm Will Sound,'" I tell Ada, and shove it open.

40

A RAUCOUS CLANG HERALDS OUR TUMBLING into the Penner marketplace. Opening the door pulled a string to set off an array of bells. People stop their selling and haggling and cursing and spitting and eating smelly meat on sticks to point at us.

"Othersider!"

"Human!"

"Female!"

Officer Tendrile powers out the door, a mass of tentacles and torso, and swings at me. His blade glints and the glint speaks to me—*duck!*—and I grab Ada and crouch as the sword decapitates the air above me. I pull Ada away and trip into a meat stand, upsetting a sizzling grill, knocking it into a bewildered frog-head. I apologize and pick up some meat on a stick and throw it at Officer Tendrile. He catches it in his mouth and chews as he advances. He doesn't just chew the meat; he chews the stick.

"What you do? What you do? You destroy my stand!" the frog-head yells. Ada and I are surrounded by peppers and broken plates and utensils and spices and gawking creatures, and the alarm is still sounding and I think, *Really, if this is a dream or a hallucination, now is the time for it to stop, when the bad guy is coming forward munching on the last thing I've tried to use as a weapon against him.*

"This kind of property damage, you realize it comes out of my paycheck?" Officer Tendrile smiles.

"I . . . I'm sorry."

Ada holds my arm. I don't think she's holding it because she likes me; I think she's holding it because she wants to be holding on to something warm when we die. But it's still there and it still counts for something. I grab her hand and hold it tight. What with the failed kiss in the jail cell, this is officially the farthest I've been with a girl. Holding hands might not count for a lot of people, but it counts a hell of a lot for me. I'm not letting anybody hurt Ada. Not a blue hair on her head. And I'm not letting the princess down. I'm going to be a man about this.

"No," I declare. "No, I'm not sorry, Officer Tendrile. You can cut me open if you like, but I want everyone here to know that I'm *not* sorry! I haven't done a thing wrong and I'm not apologizing to you"—I point at the hair above his lip—"or your stupid Mark-Twain-in-a-synth-pop-band mustache."

"*Oooooo!*"

"Snap!"

"Listen to the othersider!"

Officer Tendrile roars. He jabs his sword at me like a fencer. I take a deep breath, my last—I will meet the point of his blade with an expanding chest—and suddenly I hear a jarring clang. An ax cuts through the air and knocks Officer Tendrile's sword aside.

"Gamary!"

The okapicentaur steps into view. He doesn't look like anything having to do with an ungulate—he looks like a full-on war machine with a bald angry head not about to take shit from anyone, snorting and brandishing his ax. Officer Tendrile retrieves his sword, his arm still vibrating from the force of the blow. Gamary flings a handful of gold coins at him. "Take your dirty *di-* back! I won't have any part of killing children."

"You came back!" Ada yells.

"Get on!" he orders. He kneels as marketplace gawkers swarm over Officer Tendrile, snatching up the coins. Tendrile has to slash at them, and by the time he has a clear shot at me and Ada, we're on Gamary's back, clinging to him as he gallops through the market.

"I wanted to kill you, you bald-headed fool! I was telling Peregrine all about it!"

"She was!"

"I wanted to kill me too—*huff*—couldn't bear the thought of you two—*huff*—not your fault Mortin brought you into this madness."

"What about your daughter?" I ask.

"Misfortune is no excuse for cruelty."

I cling to the pumping sides of his body as he barrels through guards who try to slow us down. He's faster than any of the octopus- or fish-men and he has the added advantage of righteousness. He's like an out-of-control carnival ride, unregulated—*real*—and I feel my heart beating through his flesh. Powerful juice seeps through my body. I've heard of adrenaline but all I knew about it was the sweep of a good book or movie or roller coaster. Now I understand: real adrenaline is insanity juice. Real adrenaline is magic.

"Out of the way!" Gamary yells. Shoppers cheer the spectacle as guards try in vain to keep up with his pumping hooves. Centaurs, perhaps, would catch us, but the centaurs are as amused as everyone else, watching with the same detached glee that people do when there's a fire in Manhattan or a car accident or a homeless person yelling at a rich woman for no reason.

Gamary approaches the end of Penner, where we left his thakerak chamber an hour before. I have to give us credit for a quick jailbreak.

A contingent of batracian guards awaits us. They hold their spears at the ready.

"What do I do?" Gamary panics.

"Stop!" Ada yells.

He brings his gallop to an abrupt end, digging his hooves into the rocky scree of the market floor, and Ada leaps off him like a cannonball, pulling her knees up and her shoulders in and landing in front of the guards, tumbling over herself and under one of them.

Damn, she's awesome. She springs up and punches a guard

in the groin. He doubles over. I cheer. She grabs his spear, parries another guard who stabs at her, and puts the spear through his neck. He squelches against the wall behind him. Gamary advances. Guards attack him, but he whacks them away with his ax. Ada tosses a spear to me, still on Gamary's back; I catch it, heft it, and jab it at the guards who circle us. They gibber and spit with their forked tongues but they can't get close enough to me, not in my dominant position. I'm a knight! A knight on a white horse! The horse isn't white and isn't a horse, but that's okay . . . you get a weapon bonus in Creatures & Caverns for being mounted, and now I see why—I'm like a king!

"*Agh!*" Ada yells. A batracian guard grins as he digs a spear into her shoulder.

"No! Get her!" I kick Gamary like he's any old horse, which he probably doesn't appreciate, and he surges forward, smashing through the remaining guards and the door that leads to the corridor to the thakerak chamber. The wood explodes around us as he grabs Ada and runs down the hall.

"Are you okay?" I ask her.

"It's nothing—Tendrile and the celates will be here any second—let's do this!"

"Off!" Gamary says. We're at the door to his chamber. Other business owners stare at us in wonder.

I slide off him, streaking against wet patches on his hide. "You're hurt!"

"Don't worry. Just get in there and go home. You never should've been caught up in this."

I enter Gamary's thakerak chamber, noticing that my ankle still hurts. I laugh—it's nothing now, a pittance, the concern of a lesser person.

Inside, blue-haired Ryu sits reading.

41

"WHAT ARE YOU DOING HERE?" HE ASKS. He drops his book. It's handwritten in that odd language from the sacks of hepatodes and it has pencil illustrations instead of glossy photos, but I see what it is: a New York City guidebook.

"What do you care?" Gamary locks the door behind us. Ada grabs a strip of burlap and wraps it around her injured shoulder. Her blood is red, like mine.

"You two should be in jail! Or dead! I'll call the authorities—"

Someone pounds on the door. It buckles, but Gamary puts his bulk against it and it holds. "They're here, but they're not getting in, and you're not getting out."

"What's wrong with you? You got paid."

"I've given it back."

"An attack of conscience from a thaklord? Will wonders never cease."

"Step aside, Ryu. We have business to take care of."

"No, *I* have business to take care of, and you should already *be* taken care of!"

147

"What have you been doing all this time?" Ada asks.

"I know." I approach Ryu. The thakerak in the dirt buzzes and clicks like it recognizes me. "You've been sitting here getting ready to go to Earth, reading that guidebook to make sure you've got everything straight."

"That's not—"

"Don't lie. You're scared. You're trying to prepare for the unknown. So you read the book. You sit here, testing yourself, sweating, doubting, unable to make the final leap. I know. It's a hard leap to make. I couldn't have done it myself if weren't for the wolf."

"Wolf?" Ada asks. Gamary shrugs.

"But now you've waited too long. Now you're not gonna get to New York and be a movie-making rock star. It's sad but it happens. People fail. You failed."

"Shut up!" Ryu says. He whips out a knife, a curved blade that reflects an electrical pop of the thakerak.

"Open this door!" someone yells outside. More banging, and then a metallic squeal. They're trying to pick the lock.

Ryu charges at me. The knife is his focus and mine. I see the arc it will tear through the air and through my body. I edge to the side. He stumbles and hits the wall. I have nothing else to throw at him so I use the princess figure. I miss, badly; the silver clatters on the floor.

"Hey!" Ada yells.

"Sorry!"

Ryu comes at me again. I pick up Ada's notebook, still

on the ground, and hold it out blindly. The knife stutter-steps off the cover, and I feel the zinging recoil travel up Ryu's arm.

"Hey *again!*"

"Well! Do you want to help me?"

"You've got it under control."

Ryu slashes at me; I block with the book. The time-slowing power of adrenaline lets me see all his muscles and tattoos and . . . his lip ring! Right there at the end of his sneering face—

I grab it and pull. Down and to the left.

Ryu screams as he jerks like a hooked fish. I jump back—I didn't mean to do that. I mean, I *did*, but I didn't anticipate the blood, or the tearing sound, or the inhuman rancorous gurgle that comes from him as he throws his knife at me, desperate to do something to me—*me,* who would want to stab *me*? All of a sudden everyone does.

The knife flies past my ear. I feel my temple and realize a critical portion of my bowl haircut is gone. A thin cut brings to mind the trickle of blood I left on the other Ryu, today, at camp, hours ago, centuries ago.

"*Die!*" Ryu snarls as Gamary and Ada restrain him.

"I thought I had it under control," I tell her.

"Not anymore!"

I note the symmetry: Ryu's friends at camp grabbed me, and now my friends are grabbing Ryu. I cut Ryu with Pekker Cland, and now Ryu has cut me in the same place. Ryu knocked me out, so I know what I have to do. It's almost like I'm not in control of myself, like I'm a different person, and not necessarily a better one, as I swing Ada's notebook at him. He crumples to the ground.

42

"ALL RIGHT," ADA SAYS, "I WANT YOU TO listen very carefully." She moves around the room with the confidence of an ER doctor, opening panels on the walls, setting dials. The thakerak hums and purrs.

"Whoa!" Gamary yells as a sword jabs through the door.

"Open up!" a voice orders. The sword jerks up and down but, lodged in the wood, it can't get far. From the size of it I know it's Officer Tendrile's.

"Hurry up!" Gamary pleads.

"Peregrine." Ada takes my hand. "You have to go back to camp and kiss Anna Margolis, do you understand? We'll find Mortin in Granger Prison."

"How? You're trapped here."

"I have a service exit," Gamary says, "if you two don't get us killed by dawdling."

"If you don't kiss her, you won't free the princess, and the dark shroud of violence that you see will continue to befall us." She holds up the silver figure. I look into the princess's eyes. The thakerak sparks, and I swear, for a second, the princess winks at me.

"Why can't we free her here?"

"Excuse me?"

"Open up!"

"Ophisa—he's in the Badlands, right? We'll get an adventuring party together and defeat him. Me, you, Gamary . . . plus we can rescue Mortin and bring him. I've demonstrated my worth as a warrior, right? We'll kill the monster, free the princess, and all live happily ever after."

"You're saying you would rather travel to the Badlands, infiltrate Ophisa's lair, try to avoid the poison that he spits from his unblinking eyes, run under him with a sword, and plunge it into his dark and distended heart . . . *than kiss a girl in your summer camp?*"

"Yes! That's exactly what I'm saying!"

The door splinters and bends. "Hurry!" Gamary says.

"You have bowels, Peregrine, I'll give you that, but—"

"Excuse me?"

"You're brave. Bowels."

"Oh. Uh . . ." I'm embarrassed to correct her, and we *are* in a time-sensitive situation, but I remember what Mortin said: you should always correct a friend who mispronounces something.

"You're thinking of a different term, Ada. It's *balls.*"

"Like *male human testicles?*"

"Yes. Well. Yes."

"That's not fair. What do you say for a woman, then?"

"I never thought about it."

"Open this door!"

"Remember, for Anna," Ada says, "*don't* talk about Creatures and Caverns. Instead, compliment her. Don't think of her as a magical, unattainable creature. Think of her as a *person*, like you, like me. After you've talked to her for a maximum of three minutes, propose that you meet in a romantic location to continue your conversation. Once there, go for the kiss. Okay?"

"What if I don't want to kiss Anna? What if I want to kiss you?"

"What did I tell you about asking that? I'm not even human."

"Are you a magical, unattainable creature?"

She blushes.

"Hurry!"

"One final thing: *don't* think about the tree and car battery where you first traveled to our world. Can you do that?"

"What?" As soon as she says it, of course, I picture the scene: the mushroom patch, the Logo Spermatikoi battery, the woods. . . .

Ada shoves me into the center of the room. I trip and land on the thakerak. It pops happily around me. The halos shoot out of my feet. Gamary pushes a shelf aside, and a second door rotates out of the wall. The main door bursts open in a shower of wooden shrapnel as Officer Tendrile and his guards plunge in. Ada and Gamary hustle away (Ada clutching the princess figure). My bodyless head meets Officer Tendrile's fierce glare as I transit back to

CAMP

WASH

HISKA
LAKE

43

I MATERIALIZE NEXT TO THE CAR BATTERY
and clump of mushrooms, exactly where I'd left, just as I
pictured. The trees shoot out at me in bleached high contrast
and settle into their normal positions. Before I even have my
whole body back, I'm running.

I'm convinced that Officer Tendrile and his men are on my
tail! I figure they'll be coming after me at any moment, ready to
cut a bloody swath through camp. It'll be all over the news . . .
but maybe nothing here ever makes the news. Maybe that's
what "No Lawyers Beyond This Point" means.

I stop. I'm naked. No one's coming after me, but the wolf
stands in front of me.

I forgot about the wolf. "Are you kidding me?" I ask out
loud. I guess I returned at the same time I left, or maybe the
wolf likes to hang out here. It growls, but I hear fear in its growl.
I've been through way too much to be scared of a wolf. I shoo it
away like I would a cat—and the itching starts.

It begins in my feet and spreads up my legs and arms. I
collapse on the forest floor. It infests every inch of me. I don't
have any hepatode bags to help; I writhe on the ground and

plunge my nails into myself and scratch at my chest, arms, and legs. I have to do something. What did Ada say? If you can't get rid of the itching with pleasure, you have to . . .

I *slam* my hand on a rock next to me.

"Aaaaagh!"

That does it. The pain spreads out and numbs the itching. I lie on the ground as my body settles. I take a deep breath. The sun shines through the leaves at an afternoon angle. A bird calls. The insects start up. Earth. It smells like Earth; it looks like Earth; it's a North American deciduous forest in summer, and everything's where it belongs. I need some clothes.

Mortin's clothes are in the pile where he left them when we traveled together. His lighter too. It's real. As real as Earth. Could both Earth and the World of the Other Normals be real? I look down my nude body as if the answer is there.

A *hair*!

44

IT STICKS OUT BETWEEN MY LEGS LIKE
an intrepid explorer reaching for the stars. I stare at it and think
about the component words of *late bloomer*: the first one is *late*,
and that's bad, but the second is *bloomer*, and the blooming
really does happen.

"I did it!"

I skip, trip over a root, and hit the ground hard, but I can't
stop laughing and examining myself. Have my adventures made
me hit puberty? Must be! I hop in circles to celebrate, but that
only lasts a few seconds, until I check the side of my head—the
cut from Ryu's knife has traveled back to camp with me. The
blood is congealing into a bumpy wall against the elements. My
ankle's still tender, too, and my hand still hurts from smashing
it on the rock to stop the itching, and my wrists have tentacle
sucker marks on them. I have a lot of explaining to do.

I put on Mortin's clothes. They're too big but they're better
than nothing—I'm not *that* proud of the hair.

45

MY NAVIGATION SKILLS HAVE IMPROVED;
I might have higher Intelligence now. I use the sun. I remember
from the brochure that the nurse's office is near the southern
end of camp, and the sun has crested in the west, so if I keep it
to my right, I'll be fine. I never thought to use the sun before;
in New York it's easier to find a watch than the sun.

I wonder if I did a specific thing in the World of the Other
Normals to make myself get the hair, or if my "correspondent"
did. Ada said everyone has a correspondent: Who's mine? Is it
Wizard of Oz–style? Did mine do something brave to make me
level up?

I step on roots and rocks so as not to leave footprints, but
I also snap the lowest snappable branch of every tenth tree. It
makes a clear path back to the transit point, a path only I would
notice.

After ten minutes I reach the edge of the woods. In front of
me is the field I ran across with Mortin so many eons before.
I step out, holding my pants up. Was I gone for an hour, or a
second? Does time work the same way here that it does there?
It certainly seems like the same afternoon I left, but what if
it's been *years*? What if the nurse's office is abandoned? Maybe

mice are nesting in the cabinets, and spiders have taken over the motivational posters. . . .

The nurse who tended to me stands outside, smoking. She looks at the sky as the smoke whiffs away.

"Ah . . . excuse me?"

She whirls around, flinging her cigarette down and crushing it in one guilty motion.

"Holy—what happened to you? You were just here!"

"Ah . . . I started wandering in the woods and I got a little confused and I seem to have lost my clothes and I also found these clothes and I have some injuries I can't explain." I try to sound calm. "Do you have clothes from the Lost and Found to fit me?"

"Get inside! Jesus! Let me see your head!"

She holds open the door for me. I've figured out how to jut my hands into my pockets and press them against my hips to hold up Mortin's pants, so I hope I look natural, but I don't think I quite pull it off.

"Thanks for your help. And hey, I didn't get a black eye, huh? That ice pack must have worked."

"Excuse me?"

"Remember? When I was here? You gave me an ice pack?"

"You didn't need any ice pack. You were fine when you came in. I don't know what happened to you *since,* but—"

"If I was fine, what was I here for?"

"You were here to talk with Dale Blaswell after you knocked out poor Eric Chin! You don't remember?"

46

THE NURSE GIVES ME KHAKI PANTS AND
a bright pink T-shirt from the Lost and Found. I don't think
the clothes are "lost"—I think they were wisely jettisoned by
previous campers. I change in the bathroom where I climbed
through the window after Mortin Enaw. I put Mortin's clothes
in a shopping bag; I figure he might want them later. I picture
him coming through to Camp Washiska Lake and not finding
them and being very mad at me. At least I left his lighter.

I check myself in the bathroom mirror—my hair is ridiculous and asymmetrical, but isn't asymmetrical hair popular
these days? This is the face I have to work with. Everybody gets
one face, and there's no point hating it. I used to think mine
looked doughy and needy, but now I'm just glad it's *attached to
my body.*

When I go back to the nurse, she's on the phone at her desk
in the examination room.

"Yeah, he just wandered out of the woods. He seems con—"
I press the button on the phone cradle.
"What—"
What would Ada do? She'd be smart, like when she told the

guard she needed a doctor. She'd find leverage.

"I don't think it's appropriate for you to be smoking cigarettes in front of campers, do you agree?"

"Excuse me? I was on the phone!"

"I know, but I'm saying, maybe it's best that you not tell anybody about me coming out of the woods."

"Who do you think you are?"

"Perry—" I start, but then I decide to try something different. "*Peregrine.* Peregrine Eckert, of New York. And I'm not trying to be unreasonable. Smoking isn't permitted at Camp Washiska Lake; I read that in the brochure. So let's just hide our secrets together and both be cool. Cool?"

She puts the phone in its cradle and nods.

"I think I'm ready to join the other campers now."

"Head down the road to the right. Follow the signs for Hideaway Village. They should be getting ready for dinner. The square dance is after. And whatever happened to you"— she leans forward—"if you need to talk, I'm here. I'm a licensed behavioral therapist."

47

I WALK ALONE DOWN THE BADLY PAVED
road that bisects the boys' side of Camp Washiska Lake. The
shoes I found in the Lost and Found are flip-flops that cut
into the skin between my big and second toes, so I take them
off and find myself more comfortable barefoot, World of the
Other Normals–style. The asphalt is warm and cracked. The
streaming light around me feels safe. I never realized before:
it's a *luxury* to be safe, to walk around without fear of serious
imminent bodily harm. It's rare, and it's recent.

It's also boring. The adrenaline is gone. Time goes at its
normal pace, and all the old thoughts come back: *I'm not big
enough I'm not good enough I'll never make it it's too late I'm dis-
appointing someone somewhere right now people hate me I deserve
to be hated palsy fever acne blister bone drench fluid burst.* . . . I
wonder how my brain can be such a clear and beautiful machine
in mortal danger and such a tedious drag when I'm safe.

I come to a bend in the road and see a sign tacked to a tree:
HIDEAWAY VILLAGE. I proceed up a wide, well-worn path and
bump into a burly male adult of the hip-hop persuasion coming
the other way.

"What the hell is wrong with you?" He wears a tight stretch top like people who go to the gym. He has a big neck and short blond hair. It seems the only other white people at this camp are adults. "Are you Perry Eckert?"

"Peregrine."

"Who gives a shit? Where you been?"

"I was going to Hideaway Village."

"I'm your counselor. Ken. You were supposed to be here an hour ago. What happened?"

"I was in a fight and I got injured. See?" I show him my head.

"Fight? You look like you got a drive-by haircut. I know about the fight. You'll be happy to know the kid you beat up is in the same yurt as you. Right now we're doing a cookout, and nobody from my yurt can eat until my campers are accounted for, so come on."

I don't ask what a yurt is. I know from the brochure. I'm not eager to see one in person.

48

PICTURE A SMALL CIRCULAR CABIN WHERE
you sleep on the floor. That's a yurt. Nomads in Tibet live
in them. For some reason Hideaway Village campers do too.
When Ken and I reach ours, though, I'm comforted: it looks
like Gamary's thakerak chamber. It's round and compact with
wooden walls, a flimsy screen door, and no windows. In front
of it is a campfire pit. Around it, sitting on logs, are five angry
campers.

"Can we eat now?" one asks. He's the darker of the two guys
who were playing basketball in the parking lot before. Next to
him is the guy he was playing with.

"Everyone," Ken says, in an adult-summarizing-things tone,
"this is Perry, the seventh member of Hideaway Village yurt four.
Please welcome him. You can start cooking your hot dogs now."

"Peregrine," I correct. No one welcomes me. Ken lights the
fire. I think of Ada. What's she doing now? Is she rescuing
Mortin with Gamary? Is Mortin *alive*? It feels wrong not to
know . . . and for what? So I can rot with these fellow humans?
The basketball duo snap open a cooler and hand hot dogs to
everybody.

"Eckert," Ken says, "meet Kolby and Jaxson." He nods at the pair. They ignore me. Next to them sits a small guy with a pushed-in nose and angry, beady eyes. He was hanging out with Sam in the parking lot too. He sneers as he puts his hot dog on a stick.

"You get in a fight and keep us all from eating, what's wrong with you, bitch?"

"This is BJ. BJ, please be respectful."

"*JB*, son, *JB*," he says. "If you mess it up again, I'm'a punch you."

Ken tightens his fists and flexes his chest at JB; JB backs off. Ken gestures to the next guy, a portly Hispanic kid. "George."

George ignores me. He's totally focused on his hot dog, as if by looking at it he could make it cook faster.

"And you know Ryu."

There he is: the original Earth Ryu. He has to correspond to the one I hit with Ada's notebook. Not just because of the name. He looks different now, far removed from the confident, predatory character I encountered at the start of camp. He has a bruise under his lip and a cut on his temple. I guess because I defeated the other Ryu, I did a reverse-history thing and beat up this one as well. He looks like he has vengeance on his mind.

"Hey, ah, it's okay." I sit next to him. "Whatever we were fighting about, I'm sure I'm cool with it now."

"I don't care if you're 'cool' with it, I'm not 'cool' with it."

"Hey!" Ken says. "You two: one wrong move, and neither of you gets your hot dog."

Ryu mouths, *I'm going to kill you.* I slide away from him.

"Ken, you said there were seven people in our yurt? Who's the last one?"

Ken nods behind him. Coming toward us, pushing his glasses up his nose, is a person I was worried I'd never see again. "Damn, this place has some off-brand bathrooms. What's up with you putting the bathrooms ten minutes from where we gotta sleep?"

"Sam!"

49

SAM IGNORES ME, WALKS TO THE COOLER,
and gets a hot dog.

"Sam? We're friends, right?" I hope I haven't effected some
kind of correspondence change where Sam and I no longer know
each other. I can't survive the next eight weeks without Sam.

"Yeah, we're friends," he says, sticking his hot dog over
the fire. That's it. He clams up. I get a hot dog. I sit next to
Sam and cook it. At least he doesn't move away. After many
uncomfortable moments, I build up the courage to speak in
the quietest voice I can.

"What's wrong?"

"Why are you *here*?"

"Why didn't you tell me *you'd* be here?"

"Not your business. I don't need people knowing what a
ghetto camp I go to."

"It's not so bad."

"Tell me that in a week. There was a nerdy white kid here last
year, couldn't make it to Visiting Day. Ran away."

"My parents thought it would be good for me."

"Real people, huh? They want you to be with real people
instead of geniuses."

"I'm not a genius."

"*I* know that, Perry."

"Call me Peregrine."

"*Peregrine?*"

"Yeah."

"Who do you think you are, an MC? I'm not gonna start calling you some stupid-ass name."

"Sam . . . I'm different. Some weird things happened to me."

"What?"

"I thought you might be able to tell me. I came in today and . . . I got in a fight, right?"

"What, do you have amnesia?"

"Just tell me what you remember."

"You came in like it was prison, where you're supposed to fight the first person you see. You picked on Ryu. I don't know why you did it. I just sat back and watched you deck him. I couldn't believe it. Counselors broke it up. You went to the nurse's office. Now you're here."

"Who started the fight? I did?"

"Didn't see."

"Was he trying to take my miniature? I got this amazing new miniature for Pekker Cland, and—"

"What you two faggots talking about?" JB asks.

I start to answer, but Sam expertly pokes me in the thigh with the end of his hot-dog stick.

"Nothing."

He slides down the log and leaves me alone, watching the skin of my hot dog turn black and puff out into nasty wide blisters.

50

FOLLOWING OUR COOKOUT, THE REST
of which I spend sitting by myself trying to simultaneously
ignore people and overhear their conversations, we have a
"Hideaway Village powwow" chaired by camp director Dale
Blaswell. All forty Hideaway Villagers gather at a set of picnic
benches in a clearing central to the yurts. Behind us are the
bathroom and showers, housed in a building that looks like a
zoo shed meant to hold electrical equipment. Dale is all smiles,
but something underneath looks reptilian and untrustworthy.

"Welcome, everyone, to Camp Washiska Lake!"

My fellow campers *mmm* dismissively.

"Let's try that again. Welcome to Camp Washiska *Lake*!"

We cheer, obeying the rule of repeated crowd exhortation
by adults.

"That's better. That's the kind of enthusiasm this place
deserves." Dale smooths out his mustache in two strokes like a
villain in a western. "Camp Washiska Lake is one of the world's
special places. You may not realize it, but you are all about to
embark on a journey that will introduce you to special places"—
yes, he says *special places* twice—"and special people. I'm lucky;
I get to be here every year. But unless you end up working here,

you have a limited time to experience all that we have to offer. Now, rule number one at our camp is *respect.* . . ."

I'm already gone. I can't take seriously anyone's offer to show me a *special place* now that I've really been to one. I'm probably ruined for life with special places. What if, when I get home, I win a trip to Ibiza? I won't even care. And Ibiza is the resort destination where people go to have dance-floor sex with European girls. I read about it on the internet. It really is special for Earth.

I look at my fellow campers, trying to figure out how to survive the next eight weeks. There have to be vulnerabilities; there have to be friends. Ada wouldn't want me to just be a loser until August. All I see, though, are kids bubbling in their own groups, snickering (at me?), whispering (about me?), and smiling (at my expense?).

Three of them are Ryu and his henchmen, the big Asian guy and the medium-sized one. They sit at the end of a picnic bench and eye me with death stares. It annoys me that my actions in the World of the Other Normals have earned me an enemy instead of a friend.

"Do they always give this talk?" I ask George, the big Hispanic kid in my yurt, as Dale drones on.

"Every year the same, yeah: respect, no drugs, no candy."

"Where are you from?" Success! He's talking to me!

"Sunset Park. I dunno when he's gonna shut up so we can get to the dance."

"What's the dance like?"

"It's when you get to see who's gonna hook up with who for camp."

"You know this girl Anna Margolis?"

"*Pfff.* What about her? She's stuck-up."

"I talked to her. She's, well . . . I won't say she's stuck-up, but she's anti-role-playing-game. It's important that I kiss her, though."

"It's important *what*? You a weird little dude, you know that? What's wrong with your hair? Don't talk to me."

George slides away. I sit stock-still. I breathe quickly. I hope no one notices, but they probably all notice—how could they not? I talk to a person and they move away, simple as that. George says something to JB. They both laugh while looking at me. I thought these people would see that I was *different*, that I'd done something amazing, something perhaps no human had ever done. No such luck. They see my face, my size . . . they certainly don't care about my single pubic hair . . . they see a weak animal and they hurt the weak animal and how can I blame them for doing what comes naturally?

"Peregrine?" Dale Blaswell asks.

"What?"

"Are you paying attention?"

"Respect," I say. "Respect, no drugs, no candy. Right?"

"Peregrine. I asked what people are most excited for at camp, so we can share our journeys later."

"Uh . . . the dance," I say. "I'm excited for the dance."

"Good," Dale says. He rubs his mustache and furrows his

brow over his beady eyes, making them even beadier. I feel like he knows what I almost said: *I'm excited to go back to the World of the Other Normals.*

Because it's the only thing I'm excited about. I left that path in the woods for a reason. I'll suffer through tonight, and maybe tomorrow, but as soon as I can, I'm going back to the place where people talk to me even if they're trying to kill me.

51

CAMP WASHISKA LAKE DOESN'T HAVE A
lot of facilities; the best place the camp organizers could think
to hold the Hideaway Village–Oasis Villa square dance is the
dining hall, with its generous square footage and roof. After our
powwow, we're given time to change; in the yurt, I stand over
my trunk, which was brought over by a very bitter Ken while
I was indisposed, and watch my fellow campers transform
from outdoorsy boys into nightlife-primed young men in dark
jeans, collared shirts, cuff links, dress shoes, and cologne. I can't
believe it: they took my C&C books but left people cologne. I
look grievingly at my own options: corduroys, cargo pants, and
T-shirts that either my brother gave me after vomiting on or my
dad picked up at trade shows.

"Clothing crisis?" Sam asks.

I don't look at him. "Are you sure it's okay to talk? I'm not
hurting you socially?"

"Don't be that way." He pulls a striped collared shirt out of his
own trunk. I've never seen him wear anything like it. "I don't hate
you. But man, you show up and start a fight, and it's like, I *know*
these people. From way back. You—"

"I'm just some guy you play RPGs with."

"Don't say that. You know I want to keep that under wraps."

Counselor Ken maintains order as our yurtmates try on outfits, show off dance moves that I've never seen or considered the horror of performing, and talk about girls—what they're going to be like this year, which ones will be hot, who will give it up, who will have big breasts. They're distracted enough that Sam and I speak without them noticing.

"Did you sneak in any books?" I ask. "Can we play?"

"No, they confiscate that here. They think it's like gambling."

"They've got bigger things to—forget it." I catch myself.

"What?"

"Nothing. I can't tell you."

"Why not?"

"You know how you tell me not to be nosy? Now you don't be nosy."

"Fine. Just keep it to yourself. That's healthy. Here." Sam hands me black jeans and a black T-shirt. "When you don't know what to do with clothes, wear black, get it? Makes you seem badass."

"These are too big for me."

"That's the baggy look, don't question."

I change into Sam's outfit, wrapping myself in a towel to remove the pants I'm wearing so that no one will see my underwear.

"I know you're wearing tighty-whities too. You need boxers."

"Understood."

52

THE SUN IS SETTING AS WE LEAVE THE
yurt for the dance. My heart thunders in my chest. We travel
as one: a mini army of teen boys, most clustered in groups,
reassuring one another how awesome this night is going to be;
some walking next to counselors, giving them an opportunity
to be men. I move alone, picking up sticks, breaking them
apart, wishing I were somewhere else. I watch Sam from a
distance—he walks with Jaxson, Kolby, and JB. We have a tacit
pact, I now understand: when he's with his friends, I am to stay
back and not interfere; when we're alone, or something like it,
he can be the kind of friend he is on the fire stairs at school.
He's a shape-shifter.

We hear the girls long before we reach them. I thought I
was scared when I first heard the male Washiska Lake campers outside the dining hall. This is worse: the girls are excited,
and their excitement comes through in tweeting sonic bursts. I
know that most people—normal people—would hear a group
of teenage girls laughing and chatting in a parking lot and
think, *That sounds like a good time*, but in its own way it's as
scary as Officer Tendrile. The sound of women is the sound of

challenge and the unknown.

I grit my teeth and pat my heart under Sam's oversize T-shirt. I have to remember that I'm not doing this for myself. I'm doing it for the princess—whose beautiful silver face I can still recall perfectly, winking at me (but of course that was just a trick of the light)—and for Mortin, and for Ada.

53

ACROSS THE ENTRANCE TO THE DINING
hall is a banner: WELCOME TO CAMP WASHISKA LAKE! Dale
Blaswell stops under it and turns to face us as I blink at the
girls of Oasis Villa. I can only imagine the zany machinations
they went through to get into the outfits they now sport. I see
hoop earrings and dresses and glitter and tube tops and tank
tops. Some of the girls are opening their bags (they have *bags*)
and pulling out shoes that they couldn't wear on the journey
over. *Dancing shoes*, I think. We are expected to go inside this
building and dance with these women in a way that affirms
our status as healthy young Americans without getting too
sexual.

I look at my own dancing shoes: beat-up sneakers. I'd rather
be barefoot.

"Men of Hideaway Village!" Dale announces. "Here are the
lovely ladies of Oasis Villa, who have traveled all the way across
the lake to be here tonight! Let's show proper respect like we
discussed!"

He bows. I can't believe it, but the boys of Hideaway Village
bow too, smiling, and I bow with them. The girls laugh, curtsy,

and blow kisses. An invisible line runs across the parking lot, keeping the sexes separated; Dale stands in the middle of it.

"I'd like to introduce you to Miss K, Oasis Villa head counselor," Dale continues. A middle-aged human of indeterminate gender stands next to him. "We're going to watch you very carefully tonight! Now let's go inside and have the best square dance ever!"

Everyone cheers. Even people who are reluctant to cheer, like me, cheer once we see people cheering around us. I look for Anna among the girls but can't see her. I also can't see anyone who is lithe and pale with blue hair and sparkling toenails.

We enter the dining hall under the WELCOME TO CAMP WASHISKA LAKE! banner. The letters are all in different colors with excited stars and lightning bolts around them. The girls must have made it. Fifteen-year-old boys would never make something like that. We would just rearrange the letters into *A Wassle Kaka Chimp* and walk away.

Inside the hall, circular tables have been folded up and stacked against the wall along with phalanxes of plastic chairs. Purple and silver streamers hang from the rafters. A disco ball dangles, spinning slowly and reflecting a spotlight set up in a corner. A DJ booth stands by a door I assume leads to the kitchen. An old man holds court in the DJ booth, grinning in a ten-gallon hat.

"Everyone, meet DJ Cowboy Pete!" Dale calls. The old man tips his hat and hits a button. Speakers mounted in each corner of the two-hundred-person-capacity room (according to the fire sign) blast a famous dance tune. The crowd whoops and splits into two groups: the ones who migrate to the center of the floor and the ones who stay back, petrified by light, noise, and shame.

"Isn't this supposed to be a square dance?" I ask counselor Ken, since none of my fellow campers will speak to me.

"They get to the square part later. If they don't play some jams at first, all the kids go crazy."

In the middle of the room, girls and boys move in self-segregated clusters. The girls face one another and dance *at* each other, shaking their bodies and throwing their shoulders up in instant fashion-snapshot poses. The boys don't face one another; they form loose lines and circle the girls like an enemy army, moving their arms and hips but not dancing, not really, just waving back and forth in a cool way that makes it seem like they might *start* dancing.

DJ Cowboy Pete grabs the mic. "How many of y'all are excited for *summer?*" The girls shriek. The boys cheer. I back away from Ken—literally, my arms reaching behind me to feel for a solid surface—until I hit a wall. The wall is home base. The wall won't move. If I stand at the wall, I won't be expected to move. This is what it means to be a *wallflower.* Now I understand.

I'm not the only person not dancing; some boys and a few girls stand clustered at other walls, although each lonely girl only lasts until an enterprising Hideaway Village lad pulls her onto the dance floor. In the back, by the DJ booth, is a table set up with punch. I can make it to the punch. I have picked a lock in prison and escaped from a man with an octopus posterior; I can get to the punch.

I start across the floor. I can't take the most direct route because it will put me right in the middle of the bodies. Don't these people realize how dumb they look? Curling back at weird angles, pretending to raise the roof, jutting their lips out and posing for breaks in the music . . . they look like idiots, until I glimpse my own feet and see that I'm the real idiot, walking across a dance floor like a waiter, unable even to shake my hips.

"Screw this," I say. I stop. I listen. The music is simple: bumping noises and a high-pitched voice above. I move my pelvis to the left and right on each bumping noise. Someday someone is going to find this pelvis sexy or I'll never have children. I test my feet, bringing one out and then back, moving one to the side and returning it. I control my body. Hips, legs, feet, arms. I can do incredible things with this body. I can do this.

I'm between a cluster of boys and girls. I keep my eyes straight ahead so I won't make eye contact with anyone and ruin the moment. I dance—I really do. I put my neck into it. I whirl my head around, feeling my hair hit my forehead. The song says something about "1999" and I realize this is *Prince*, the person Mortin Enaw mentioned! He makes it easy. I dip down, pushing out my knees in what I think is a bitchin' dance move—

"Perry!" Sam hisses. He's with a few people from our yurt, doing the boy-group dance. "What are you *doing*?"

"Dancing?"

"No, no, hold up. Relax. You're embarrassing us!" He nods ahead and I see who I'm embarrassing him in front of: six members of Oasis Villa dancing in a circle, looking at me like I'm a large warm-blooded grasshopper. "Just move your *hips*."

"I started with my hips!"

"Stick with them! Don't be throwing your arms around—you look like you're being electrocuted!"

I stand up straight and let my hips sway to the downbeats. I nod at the girls, but none of them nod back. I migrate, in what I think is a subtle way but is probably obvious, closer to Sam and his friends.

"Nuh-uh," JB says. "You're not staying here. I don't need a spastic white boy messing up my game."

I don't say anything. Heat rises in my chest. I start to move away, but Sam tugs me back. "It's okay," he tells JB. "Perry's not so bad."

"Look at the fags," Ryu says. He steps in front of us with his henchmen. He doesn't dance; he manages to look better not dancing. "You two want to be gay for each other, do it on your own time."

"Who do you think you're talking to?" Sam asks.

"Don't make me mess you up—"

"Really? I'd like to—"

"Sam!" I grab him. "Don't worry. I'm gonna dance across the room and get some punch, okay?"

"No, you can stay here. I don't—"

"Sam. You see who's at the punch?"

He turns. She's striding up to the punch bowl in a black dress—not a bad match for me, all things considered.

"Anna? You know her?"

"She's who I dressed up for. Don't worry. I talked to her before. I'm gonna nail it this time."

54

I BRIEFLY CONSIDER TELLING ANNA EVERY-
thing—that she corresponds to the princess in the World of
the Other Normals, that her relationship with me is a matter
of universal importance. As I get closer, though, her breasts
prevent me from using words with multiple syllables.

I know, from watching talk shows, that some women get
breast-reduction surgery. This is bewildering to many men,
but the women speak of how their breasts are ponderous and
hassling; they cause too much trouble, just being out there all
the time. Seeing Anna, I believe it. Outside the nurse's office
she wasn't so imposing, but she was wearing a sweater then, and
knitting mittens, so perhaps she knitted the sweater too, and
constructed it so as not to emphasize the powerful forms that
loom before me now. She sips her punch. At the head of the
table, gender-inscrutable Miss K eyes us.

"Anna? Pe. Re. Grine. Nurse. We talk. Good?"

"What?"

Get ahold of yourself, I think. I picture Ada watching me,
telling me not to be a perv. I picture her: blue hair, long fingers, body made of wind. My eyes migrate to Anna's face.

They stay there. That's better.

"Can you talk to me like a normal person now?"

"Yeah, sorry, this music. Distracting! So, did we talk earlier today?"

"Uh . . . Perry, right?"

"Peregrine, if you don't mind."

"Whatever. You don't remember if we talked or not?"

"I think we did, I just wanted to make sure—"

"We did. I guess I left a big impression on you."

"No, no, you did! I just went through a lot of crap since then."

"Crap like amnesia?"

"Just . . . adventures."

She sips her punch. "The first day of camp *is* complicated. You have to work out your scene, try and figure who your friends are. . . ."

"Avoid celates, escape from jail . . ."

"What?"

"You two! No funny business!" Miss K says. Behind her/him, I see through the kitchen door into the dark innards of the dining hall. I imagine what it will be like tomorrow at breakfast—hissing, clanking, cooks running around. . . . My brain is working again now that I'm looking at Anna's face. I remember Ada's advice: *don't talk about Creatures & Caverns.*

"How's your knitting going? Still working on the mittens?"

"Of course! I told you it taught you patience. How would it teach you patience if I was already doing something else?"

"Sorry."

"You seriously apologize too much, Perry. Peregrine. Whatever."

"Okay, let's try something. Let's try me not apologizing to you anymore in this conversation."

"Really?"

"Yeah. If I say *sorry* again, it's over."

"Deal."

Something weighs on my mind. I have to clear it up. It violates Ada's advice, but not precisely. "Earlier, when we *were* talking, Anna, did I . . . uh . . . mention a 'role-playing game' called Creatures and Caverns? I'm not mentioning it *now*, I'm just asking if I mentioned it *then*."

"No. I'd remember that, and I probably wouldn't be talking to you now." She laughs. I make myself laugh with her.

"What did we talk about, then?"

"Knitting. The fight you were in. Ryu. Did he come after you yet?"

"We had some words."

"You better watch your back. Where you from, anyway?"

"New York. Born in Manhattan, but after my parents got divorced, I moved around a lot between there and Brooklyn."

"You rich?"

"We're—I don't know, I thought we were normal. But maybe we are rich. Rich people never say they're rich."

"Why'd your parents send you here?"

"I think it was an experiment. To see how I deal with the

real world. Help me be a man. You know."

"Not really."

This isn't what I expected. I figured I would either like Anna and find it easy to kiss her, or hate her and find kissing her repugnant. I didn't expect this middle ground, where some of what she says is okay, but some of it makes me feel like an idiot. I ask, "Where are *you* from?"

"Spring Creek. Brooklyn."

"That near Flatlands?"

"Yeah! You know it?"

"I have a friend from Flatlands. Well, kinda. He's here. He lent me these clothes."

She eyes my outfit. "I'm not sure he's your friend."

"He is! He's been acting weird, though. Avoiding me."

"People do that. What, he was your friend at home, but now he's treating you bad? Girls do that the worst."

"How do you handle it?"

"Just be straightforward about what you want. Don't waste time with knuckleheads. Say what's on your mind."

"You know what's on my mind?"

"Do I want to?"

Compliment her. "Your posture. You have great posture. How'd you get it?"

"My mother." Anna laughs. "She always told me, 'Stand up straight, you don't know when you're gonna meet the president.'"

"My mother's lawyer sent me to classes for ballroom dance once."

"Her *lawyer?*"

"Uh, her, I mean. Her."

"Uh-huh. And that's relevant because . . ."

"I just figured, I don't know, weird things our moms made us do. I didn't want to go. But the ballroom dance classes gave me increased leg strength, I now realize, which may have enabled me to survive when I was . . . anyway. Did you ever get to meet the president?"

"Not yet."

"You will. You have that look about you. You look important. You *are* important. I know that for a fact."

"You need to move away from the punch bowl so other people can get punch!" Miss K orders.

"Right, sorry." I reach out to pull Anna aside, but she's gone. She's off on the dance floor on her own.

55

"WAIT!" I DON'T KNOW WHAT THE PROBLEM is. I thought things were going well!

"No," Anna says. "You said you weren't going to apologize anymore."

"I wasn't apologizing to *you*. I was apologizing to . . . them!" I point at Miss K.

"It doesn't matter." Anna looks at her watch. "I think you're a very nice person." I get the impression she's delivered this speech before. "If we had unlimited time, I could talk to you about Caves and Creatures or whatever and posture and ballroom dance. But tonight is one of the only times that I'm going to get a chance to talk to the *men* at this camp, okay? And I want to talk to the ones who are going to act like men, as opposed to little boys."

I thought it hurt when Ryu punched me. I thought it hurt when Ada spurned me as I tried to kiss her. Nothing compares to how I feel as Anna nods bye and joins her glittering friends to dance. Then she doesn't even stay with them: she keeps going across the floor to Dale Blaswell and says hi to him, like they're old friends, and he says something that makes her laugh, and she nods at me like, *Isn't it weird to have him as a camper?* and he nods like, *Yes.*

So many times, in movies and books about growing up, I've been told that it's silly to fear rejection. Rejection is all in your head, right? You have to be brave, to act without fear, to push rejection aside; in the rare cases where it happens, it isn't ugly or debilitating so much as world-weary and funny. Right?

Not for me. First, Anna's rejection isn't only in my head—it's paramount in the World of the Other Normals, where now the princess is going to remain firmly in the clutches of Ophisa. More importantly, it's based on a false assumption: I'm not a *man*? Excuse me?

Anna has no idea about the things I've done. She doesn't know I'm practically a hero. A whirlwind of pain and action-spurring psychosis cycles through me. I know I shouldn't do what I do next, but I do it.

I clench my fists and yell, "Anna!" She turns from her conversation with Dale. She looks at me as if I'm a homeless guy trying to get money from her, and that makes me even more insane.

"I *am* a man! See?" I unbutton my pants. They drop in one swift motion; they're big enough to fall off like a robe. I tug down my tighty-whities. Anna gasps. Dale flares his nostrils. I stand ten feet from them with the disco ball shedding its square-inflected light on my lone pubic hair. "That's new today! That's for real!"

Anna covers her face with both hands. Another girl sees me

and shrieks. Another laughs. The music stops. DJ Cowboy Pete looks at me openmouthed and says into his mic, "Ah, I think one of our li'l partners is having trouble. Counselor, please?" Miss K screams, "Pull your pants up, what's wrong with you!" Ken strides toward me. The inspector counselor from the parking lot, Travis, raises his arms at me across the room like, *What?* Sam looks at a wall so he won't have to look at me. Ryu points and chortles. Dale Blaswell screams, "Put that away!"

The world, which froze for a moment to allow me to collect all these observations as my heart plummeted into my pelvis, snaps back into action. I pull up my pants and run.

56

I BARREL OUT OF THE DINING HALL AND
speed across the parking lot. My various injuries hurt, but it's
nothing compared to the shame that beats through me. I'm
truly worthless now; my life is over. I've heard people say "my
life is over" after doing something socially horrific, but they
probably didn't expose themselves in the middle of a dance
floor on the first day of summer camp. The dining-hall door
bangs open behind me. I steal a glance: Dale.

"Get back here! Peregrine! You've made a mockery of Oasis
Village! I'll kill you! You can't avoid the consequences of an
action like this!"

Like hell I can't. I know *exactly* how to avoid all the
consequences of an action *exactly* like this. In front of me are
the dark woods, which I'd have been scared of yesterday, but
now I understand that the things that really undo a person
aren't in the woods; they wear dresses and dance with their
friends.

I look back at the dining hall as I take off my shoes. Dale
runs after me; Ken appears behind him, talking to Sam, who
looks like he's trying to explain that I haven't been myself lately.

I throw my shoes at Dale. He bats them away. I take off toward the woods with bare feet.

Crack! I try to step on roots and rocks, but sometimes a branch looks like a root. I don't worry about it. I only have so much time. If Dale catches me, I'll be taken to a psychiatrist, who will order me sent home and put into special exhibitionist therapy. *Indecent exposure*—isn't that a crime? I picture myself in jail. I've already been in jail, but that doesn't make human jail any more appetizing. My ankle burns. I grit my teeth. What I did back there was wrong; what I am doing now is pure and right.

The noises of nighttime birds and bugs are overtaken by my huffing breath. South of the dining hall is the nurse's office. I get there in five minutes, although time seems to mean something different when the world consists of me and my footsteps and my breath in the forest. I find a branch that I snapped to demarcate the path back to the mushroom patch. See, Anna? See, Ada? See, everybody, *anybody*, how competent I am?

I follow the trail I left in the woods. At each tree with a broken branch, I stop and spy the next. I move with clarity and purpose, checking over my shoulder for pursuers. I hear noises—someone is clomping around after me; from the heavy tread it sounds like Dale, but whoever it is, they're far away. It doesn't take me long to find the patch of mushrooms and the Logo Spermatikoi battery.

I take off Sam's clothes and leave them daintily folded at the side of the tree. I unscrew the caps on the battery and touch the lead marked *negative*. This is like an escape hatch from a bad dream. How does it work? You go toward what you're picturing in your head. So if I picture the thakerak chamber I arrived at before, I might pop back into a room with Officer Tendrile and his men trying to kill me. Maybe I can picture a person—Ada. Wherever she is, that's where I want to be. I can explain to her what I did, and maybe she'll understand. I try my best *not* to picture her—her pointed ears and sparkling nails—so of course I do. There's still pain, but this time, while the halos move up my legs and the trees explode in light, my dominant emotion is *relief* as I speed back into

THE
WOR
OF THE
NOR

LD

OTHER

MALS

57

I REAPPEAR IN A DARK ROOM—THE ONLY
light comes from the sparking thakerak on the floor. I stumble
away as the itching roars into my body. I reach a wall. It's
curved, so if I feel along it, I should find . . . *there.* A springy
sack on a shelf.

I hold the hepatode bag to my chest. It sucks all the itching
out of me. I groan in relief, throw it aside, and grab a getma off
another shelf.

"Hello?" No one. I'm still in near-total darkness. I don't
think I'm in the same thakerak chamber as before; in addition
to there being no light, there aren't any signs of a struggle, no
splintered wood on the floor, no Ryu. . . . I feel along the wall
until I find a door. I push it open.

A bare corridor stretches in front of me, with another door
at the end. Light and voices leak through the bottom of it. The
light looks lively, chromed . . . *sunlight?* Am I above ground?
The walls are wood, not rock, so maybe. What a relief. I head
toward the door. I hope Ada's on the other side. It'd be cool
if she had been in the chamber waiting for me, but of course
she has better things to do. Maybe the way it works is that you

come out of the thakerak *closest* to the person you're picturing. I reach the end of the corridor, push the door open, and enter my first bar.

58

I THINK IT'S WHAT YOU CALL A DIVE BAR.
The windows have cracked shutters that support sedimentary
deposits of dirt. The sunlight that gets in illuminates dancing
filth that circulates up from the floor, which is covered with
sawdust. The tables and chairs are mismatched and of widely
disparate size. The clientele is a sparse and depressed-looking
collection of other normals. At some tables, ferrous ones who
look like Mortin sit next to okapicentaurs who lie on the ground
like horses, sipping from giant beer steins. At others, attenuates
who look like Ada huddle over glasses. The space is huge; the
bar that runs across the front is as long as the ticket counters
in airports. There's only one person behind it: an other normal
like Mortin, with long yellow hair and red skin, chatting with
a faun.

"Who's that?"

"Human in the bar!"

"What are you doing here?"

I stammer and gesticulate. This doesn't look good.

"Ah . . . Ada Ember?" I manage, and then the front door
slams open and Gamary rushes in.

He has Ada on his back. He has *Mortin* on his back! I'm so happy to see them that I forget everything and run to them. I fling my arms first around Gamary's hairy torso; then Ada and Mortin hop off and I hug them, too, tight, clapping their backs, crying a little because they are real and they are friends.

"Whoa, *whoa*!" Mortin says. "How'd you get here, buddy?"

"Who is he?" a faun at the bar calls out.

"Don't worry about him, he's with me, okay? He's part of a correspondence experiment fully approved by the Appointees; he has just as much right to be here as you."

"Mortin! I thought you were in jail! Where are we?"

"*Shhh.* You're in a bar called the Monard. Keep quiet." He has sweat and dirt on his face. A black eye, too, just like the one I would have gotten from Ryu if I hadn't been given an ice pack. I remember how when I came over before, I caught him putting on what I thought was sunscreen under his eye.

"Did you just *break out of prison*?"

"Yes, and if you don't keep quiet, I'm going right back in. Let's get a drink."

"Why are we getting a drink if you just—"

"Haven't you ever heard of hiding in plain sight?"

I put on a straight face. We approach the bar. The bartender with the long hair cleans out a glass with a rag and eyes us suspiciously.

"Leidan!" Mortin says. "How's it going? Can you do a round on the house for your brother?"

59

AS SOON AS HE SAYS IT, I SEE THE
resemblance. The bartender, Leidan, has the same small ears
and Hollywood button nose as Mortin. His eyes sparkle with
similar grievances, but Leidan's are hidden behind a glassy film.
He moves slowly, like he knows it's his bar and couldn't care less.
"I hear you're in trouble again," he says, wiping his mouth.

"Everything's fine."

"You mean that door *isn't* gonna fling open with officers
looking for you?"

Mortin shrugs. "That's always a possibility."

"You got a reward on you?"

"Hey, Bro." Mortin grabs Leidan's hair. "I've just been in
Granger and I come to the *one* place I think might be safe, and
you're already trying to turn me in?"

"Off the hair, please." Leidan steps back. The drinkers watch
us. One spits on the floor, and the sawdust soaks it up. I wonder
if all bars are this tense and depressing and, if so, why anybody
goes.

"Why haven't you tried to see me?" Mortin asks.

"Been working."

"Been drinking, more like."

"Least I haven't been smoking earthpebbles like you. You gonna introduce me to your new friend, or does he just like to hang back and spy on conversations?"

"Sorry, I'm . . . ah . . ."

"Don't worry. I know. You're a traveler."

I nod.

"Leidan Enaw," the bartender says. As we shake, he smiles. It's the kind of natural smile that glossy magazines like. He nods to Ada. "And who's this, your girlfriend?"

"No!" I say, like it's an accusation.

"Why not?" He leans in. I smell liquor on his breath. "Ada's a real catch. Not that I think that way."

"Of course you think that way, Leidan," she says. "You have more girlfriends than customers."

"I don't like to think in terms of numbers. Gamary, how you holding up?"

Gamary indicates the bandages around his midsection. "I've been better."

"Hey!" a centaur yells. He's sitting down the bar with a red-skinned female other normal. "Some service here?"

"Hold your horse."

Leidan slowly pours beers for Mortin and Gamary. He gives me and Ada water. After he takes the centaur's order, he concocts an alchemical mix of liquids from five bottles and tops it off with a dash of clumped white dairy product. He serves the drink in a bowl; the centaur and his date take turns lapping it up like dogs.

"So what are you doing *back*?" Ada whispers. "Did you kiss Anna?"

"He didn't kiss Anna," Mortin says. "If he kissed Anna, the princess would be free, everyone here would be celebrating, and we'd have our much-promised return to normalcy. He didn't kiss anybody."

"I tried, okay? The plan kind of backfired."

"What did you do?"

"I had a momentary lapse in judgment. I didn't have anywhere to go but here. How'd you get rescued?"

"With great difficulty. They were ready to string me up in a public hanging. Ada and Gamary created a disturbance and freed me."

"When? Just now? While I was at the dance?"

"Time gets fuzzy between our worlds. It depends on the observer. For us, it's been three days since we sent you back to camp. How long has it been for you?"

"Maybe eight hours?"

"Then you didn't do the right thing. When you act out of fear, you get left behind."

"I think it might be better if I *stayed* behind here, with you guys. I'm better suited to it."

"That's not possible, Peregrine," Ada cuts in.

"Ada, you realize you talk to me more than anybody at camp?"

Leidan comes back. "Another round?" He pours a shot for himself and slams it before I can tell what color it is. Mortin and

Gamary are still working on their beers. I haven't touched my water.

"My brother," Mortin says as Leidan shuffles away. "So much potential, wasted." He takes a swig of beer. I wonder whose potential he really thinks is wasted. I look through his upturned drink at the walls and ceiling. Things look sadder when glimpsed through alcohol.

As Mortin chugs, the centaur and his date down the bar finish their bowl, get up, and walk past us. The centaur bumps into Mortin, pitching him forward so he spills all over himself.

"Hey! What's your problem?"

The centaur stops. His lady friend eyes us from atop his back. "I do not have a problem," he says. "Do *you* have a problem?"

"Yeah, I guess I shouldn't go to mixed bars anymore. It's better to just drink with men."

"Be quiet, Mortin!" Gamary says. "It was a mistake—"

"He spilled my drink. He owes me an apology."

"*Mortin*," Ada hisses. "*Hiding in plain sight.*"

"It's hopeless! Wherever I go, the world is full of idiots trying to impress their whores." Mortin spits in the sawdust. It's an ugly word, in any world. The woman on the centaur gasps. Ada smacks Mortin's arm. The centaur pulls out a studded stone club.

"Now I will ask you to apologize to my lady friend."

"Gentlemen, please, we can't have fighting in here," Leidan says. "If you can—"

But Mortin stands and faces the centaur, just as the front door opens.

60

"MORTIN ENAW!" A VOICE CALLS. I KNOW its self-satisfaction and cruelty before I even see Officer Tendrile. He's a little dirty, but his blade and mustache are intact. "Freshly escaped, with all of your compatriots, in one convenient location! Sir with the club, you'll have to back away. Mortin is my quarry."

Behind him, fish-creature guards and octopus-man officers march into the bar. "I don't want anyone to move, and I don't want anyone to *speak*. You're all coming with me—"

Ada jumps up. Mortin darts under the centaur, who swings down at him. The club misses Mortin but catches a batracian guard who got too close. The guard lets out a horrible gurgle as he crumples to the floor. "Murderer!" Officer Tendrile yells, and the other guards start attacking everyone around them, beating the bar's patrons with spear butts. "You're all under arrest for collusion with Ophisa!" Gamary kicks a guard away—Ada grabs Leidan—docile alcoholics who were sitting at tables snarl at the police, defending themselves—a chair flies across the room—I duck—to be honest, once I see the chair, a check mark goes off in my head next to *barroom brawl*, and I know the best thing to do is get out.

"Leidan! Back door!" Mortin yells, clutching my neck as he scrambles past flying bottles and mugs and clumps of sawdust. His brother runs ahead of him and kicks open a second entrance to the Monard. Light streaks in. Outside is an alley and another building; we're in a city, aboveground.

"Stop them!" Officer Tendrile yells. Someone shoots an arrow; it lands just above the door as Gamary and Ada run out. Mortin tosses me into the alley. I squeeze my eyes in the sun. I'm between two wooden buildings with clotheslines holding laundry ruffling in the wind.

"C'mon!" Ada says, already on Gamary's back.

"Where're we going?"

Gamary leans back so I can get on. Mortin says something to Leidan in the doorway before running out in front of a volley of arrows that tear the laundry and thud into the building opposite. He jumps onto Gamary behind me; Gamary takes off down the alley.

I peek back: Leidan is climbing a pipe against the bar's exterior wall. Two tentacled officers bust out of the doorway; one tosses a spear at Leidan while the other looses an arrow at us. We speed around a corner. The arrow hisses past Mortin. I grip Gamary's rough hair, screaming in joy and terror.

"Where are we?" I yell.

"Surface Subbenia!" Ada says. "Above the market chambers where you were before!"

It's a run-down, dirty city, with wagons drawn by centaurs

and okapicentaurs with sores on their legs, beggars in the streets, fortune-tellers in ramshackle booths, and homes that look like the ones I saw when Dad dragged us to Colonial Williamsburg, but not as preserved. I look up. Cloudless—a perfect day. There isn't an extra sun or anything. I'm glad. I can only deal with so much.

"I'm sorry I did that, guys! It was like I couldn't control myself!" Mortin yells.

"Did what?" Ada asks.

"Said that to that woman!"

"It's too late now!"

The wind whistles in our ears. Gamary runs faster than I think he knew he could. People point and call for the police and yell, "Isn't that the escaped prisoner?"

"How did Tendrile know where to find us?" Mortin asks.

"I can't—*huff*—hold you three—*huff*—any longer," Gamary says. He stumbles past a well and a broken cart propped against an abandoned building. Elsewhere I see piles of burning trash and celate officers knocking on people's doors, demanding answers. *The dark shroud of violence that you've seen will continue to befall us*, Ada warned. The city has no sidewalks—Gamary gallops on swaths of dying grass. The wind kicks up the smell of waste. Gamary hightails it away from the chaotic citizenry, cresting a hill, and I look down for the first time at the spreading, peaceful countryside of

BE

NIA

61

GAMARY COLLAPSES OUTSIDE THE CITY
limits. We tumble off him onto a road. I keep running.

"Stop!" Mortin calls.

"There are people after us!"

"Nobody's coming out of Subbenia to get you! Come back
here!"

I walk back. Gamary catches his breath, and we all walk next
to him. It seems strange to move at a leisurely pace after being in
such a death-defying chase, but Mortin explains, "The law here
is very provincial. Celates in the city worry about their territory;
once you leave it, they couldn't care less."

"Even Officer Tendrile?"

"Officer Tendrile would be terrified out here," Gamary says.

"Of what?"

"Nothing; don't listen to him," Mortin says. "What's there to
be terrified of?"

He gestures toward the big deep sky and layered hills in front
of us. The countryside surrounding Subbenia requires a word
I've never used before, but I know from C&C: *heath*. Like the
moors of England, it's an open landscape of low-growing shrubs,

with wind-polished, grassy slopes as far as the eye can see. The road we're on dips out of sight and pops up again over and over as it stretches toward the horizon. Among the shrubs I see big stones and small huts. There are no trees, no animals, and no farms. A cart approaches in the distance, but other than that, the only movement is the grass bending and swishing in the breeze, throwing up mirages of reflected sheen.

"Welcome to the suburbs," Ada says.

"No Slip'N Slide?" I joke. Nobody laughs.

"Perry, what exactly happened with Anna?" Mortin presses.

I take a deep breath. "I sort of . . . exposed myself to Anna."

"*Exposed* yourself? Exposed what? Your *male parts*?"

". . . Yes."

Ada looks at me for a minute and then puffs her cheeks out and laughs. She tries to hold it in at first, but then bends over and wraps her arms around her chest—

"It's not funny! It's not funnier than my Slip'N Slide joke!"

"Oh man," Mortin says. "You flashed the princess's correspondent? Why would you do that?"

"She was saying I wasn't a man, and I wanted to show her I was! You don't get it—when I went back to Earth, I had a *hair*, okay? Ada, could you please stop laughing and cover your ears? I don't want you to hear this."

"Too bad!"

"Mortin, I must've done something here to make me hit puberty!"

"Or you might've just hit puberty."

"Well. Maybe."

"Didn't anybody ever tell you to be patient?"

"Anna did. Before I pulled my pants off."

"This is why the Appointees don't approve pants," Gamary says. "People on Earth are always taking them off and getting in trouble."

"All right, very funny. What are we gonna *do*?"

"We're on the run," Mortin says. "You may have escaped a bad situation at camp but you're not in a good one here either. Since you failed to kiss Anna and free the princess, the Appointees have expanded their powers to try and find her. Police can break into people's homes now. Celates are running wild, killing citizens in the streets. Anyone who questions what's happening is branded a traitor in league with Ophisa. Subbenia is lost. It's gone mad. I told my brother to meet us in Upekki. It's not far from here. There's a thakerak there, so we can send you back to camp and set things right with Anna. As long as the princess is in Ophisa's clutches, things will get worse."

"Upekki's too far!" Gamary says. "We'll never make it!"

"Would you rather go back and get killed?"

"We'll get killed anyway!"

"By who?" I ask. Nobody answers. "Look, you guys aren't seeing the positive here. We have an adventuring party now! We can free the princess *ourselves*! Ada, do you still have the figure?"

She hands it to me. I hold it. The princess is more tarnished than when I saw her last. I know it doesn't make sense—she's only silver—but she also seems sadder, more hopeless. Time is running out.

62

"GIVE THAT BACK TO ADA," MORTIN SAYS, "and forget about it. We're not going on any quest to kill Ophisa and rescue the princess. If anyone could do that, the Appointees already would have. The only way to free the princess is through her correspondent."

"I wish you'd stop saying that word. I don't understand about the freaking correspondents."

"Very few people on Earth do," Ada says. "We made the important discoveries ourselves, once our universes reconnected, around the time of Marco Polo in your world. Our first explorers stumbled into thakeraks. For reasons we still don't understand, the thakeraks like to take living beings, codify the position of every single atom in their bodies, and send that information into your universe, where it's reverse engineered by a corresponding mushroom patch."

"How did your 'first explorers' get back? They weren't stashing car batteries in the woods, were they?"

"They didn't get back. They were trapped. Many were killed for being demons or witches. Most were never heard from again. But some assimilated into your cultures."

"I find that hard to believe."

"Why? Earth is a big planet. Lots of hidden spaces. Lots of people who could be convinced that an other normal was a god. The ones who wanted to come back knew that travel had to do with energy, and with mushrooms. They noted where they arrived on Earth and went back to those places to attempt a return. Eventually, three hundred years ago, one traveler hooked up a lightning rod to the clump of mush-rooms he'd emerged near when he came to Earth, and got zapped back. Certain mushrooms on Earth need a little kick, and then they act just like thakeraks."

"What happened when he came back?"

"He emerged just after he left, but his life was radically different. His mother had been alive when he left; when he came back, she had died during childbirth. He was married when he left; when he came back, he'd never met his wife. He'd been dirt poor when he left; when he came back, he was rich. *Di-* just appeared in his bank account, where it hadn't been before."

"Somehow," Mortin says, "the things he did in your world had great ramifications here. The loss of information that brought our universes back together made them *cohere* in specific ways. The traveler reported his findings, but no one believed him: they remembered his life as the skewed version that he birthed. So he started doing experiments. He would head to Earth, run in a circle three times, and come back to see if anything was different. He was the first correspondence consultant. Paolo Sulice. A brave and crazy individual."

"After years of experiments, Sulice figured out the guiding principles of correspondationalism," Ada says. "Every person in your world has an other normal correspondent in ours, whether it's an ingress or a highborn. Doing things to a human affects that human's correspondent, and vice versa. Have you ever woken up with a bruise you couldn't explain?"

"I thought those were my brother."

"Nope. Something happened to your correspondent."

"Who *is* my correspondent?"

"We can't tell you. It's policy."

Mortin illustrates: "You get punched in the chest, your correspondent gets chest pains; you fall in love, your correspondent meets someone; you grow up, your correspondent gets more mature."

"Your correspondent dies, you die," Ada says.

"Paolo Sulice kept at it. He pioneered analysis techniques to determine what causes would have what effects for people willing to travel in the multiverse. He went into business with Sulice Correspondence House, my former employer."

"You could go in," Ada says, "and say that you wanted to be rich, and Sulice would run an analysis on you, determine what had to happen to your correspondent on Earth to make *them* rich, and then go and pull a 'tweak,' or small change, to make that happen."

"So that's why I'm a 'tweak'?"

"Yes. Sulice's work was an unqualified success. It got so

popular that the Appointees started regulating it, and now it's a very specialized field."

"Dangerous, too," Mortin says. "But I have a perfect record: never hurt anybody, never killed anybody, made plenty of clients at my company very happy, and no humans were ever the wiser."

"Until me."

"Mortin," Ada says, "I don't want to hear you talk yourself up when you just said that disgusting thing in the Monard."

"I said I was sorry. I snapped. I couldn't control it."

"Sure you couldn't."

"I was stressed."

"That's no excuse."

"I know," Mortin admits.

"I know too," I say.

"What?"

"Stress is no excuse to do disgusting things. It's easy to rationalize in your head, but it's wrong."

"Like how?" Ada seems very interested.

"Like you go through life with girls not liking you, with no one noticing you, with people calling you Mini Pecker, and then you get a chance to do something outrageous, and you think, *I deserve this—I suffered enough at the hands of my peers and now I'm allowed to do whatever I want.* But you're not. It's childish."

We walk in silence for a moment. Then Ada slaps my shoulder. "Maybe that hair's making you smarter."

63

WE WALK BAREFOOT DOWN THE PACKED
dirt road. The sun has warmed the taut earth; it feels great
radiating up through my soles. Maybe we're outlaws, and maybe
we're doomed, and maybe we've left behind everything normal
in our lives, but we do have the sun and the air and they're
free. I focus on my footsteps. Mortin asks Gamary about his
daughter.

"She's fine," he says. "She's better. The fever came with the
troubles but now it's gone. I just have to get back to her."

The road is sparsely traveled. A few times an hour Gamary
yells, "Cart!" and Ada hops onto his back and squints and eval-
uates someone coming toward us. She has terrific eyes and can
see for miles over the hills. She describes the approaching party
to Mortin ("two hequets with a cargo of pottery"; "a faun with
a knapsack with rugs sticking out"), and Mortin nods okay and
then for good measure we all get on the far side of Gamary
and walk past the traveler without saying a word. When people
approach from behind, Ada hears them with her long ears and
performs a similar scouting role, sitting backward on Gamary

and reporting to Mortin. In the meantime, she talks to me.

"See the grass? It lives on three inches of rain a year. The whole climate here is hot and dry. Feel." She reaches off the road to dig up some soil and lets it crumble into my open palm. It has a tangy, unpleasant smell.

"Sulfur?"

"Comes from the runoff of the Ouest Beniss Range." She nods to the mountains north of us, where Subbenia is—I can still see structures and smoke. "The grasses metabolize it."

"Cool." It actually is cool.

"So what's it like to go to school on Earth? With boys and girls in the same room?"

"It's . . . ah . . . pretty paralyzing and unpleasant."

"Would you rather have a mentor like Mortin and work with him like I do?"

"Probably."

"But no one's allowed to do that on Earth."

"No, school is like prison. You have to go."

"And camp?"

"I haven't been there that long, but it also seems like prison."

She smiles. I like watching her smile; I like watching her move. Mom and Dad would be proud of me, walking in the country and talking with a girl. Isn't this what they sent me to camp for?

64

"CAN WE SING A SONG?" I ASK MORTIN.

"Why?"

"When travelers are off on an adventure, they sing songs to pass the time. Everyone knows that."

"Maybe travelers who are interested in getting killed."

"Aw, c'mon. Do one! You've got to know one!"

"Do *you* know any songs?" Ada asks.

"I know a song from my brother's band."

"What's your brother like?"

"He's in rehab. His songs have good melodies but terrible lyrics. I can try to change the lyrics on the fly."

I look around. No one in any direction. No kids to make fun of me. I tilt my head to the sky and sing, switching to a falsetto to do a shadow of the backing vocals:

> *We are the stoners (aah-ah!)*
> *We'll hit you with large stones (aah-ah!)*
> *We'll never fight alone (ah-ahhh)*
> *On the road*

"What is that?" Mortin says. "I didn't hit anybody with a stone. Did you?"

"I'm improvising!"

"I think it's good, Peregrine," says Ada. "What are the backup parts? *Aah-ah?*"

I teach the notes to her, and then to Mortin and Gamary. We sing out variations as we walk through the hills.

> *My name is Mortin (aah-ah!)*
> *I've been cavooortin' (aah-ah!)*
> *With all these miscreants (ah-ahhh)*
> *But I look good*

> *My name's Gamary (aah-ah!)*
> *I'm really sorry (aah-ah!)*
> *For selling you out to the cops (ah-ahhh)*
> *Y'all got robbed*

> *My name is Ada (aah-ah!)*
> *I'll catch you later (aah-ah!)*
> *Unless we catch you first (ah-ahhh)*
> *In a world of—*

"Hooves!" Ada yells.

I cup my ears. Faint. It sounds like they're coming out of the hills, like something is beating the inside of the earth.

"Off the road!" Mortin orders. He runs to the left; Ada,

Gamary, and I follow onto the grass. The hooves get louder quickly; their studded beats fill the air. I trip and tumble down a hill, alternating views of sky and grass as the ground hits me over and over. I glimpse a group of centaurs passing by, done up in shining armor, their arms pumping at their sides as if they're running as men and horses at the same time.

"Who—are—?" I manage. Ada pulls me behind a rock, where I watch the cloud of dust behind the centaurs recede over the next set of hills. She points to a rolling platform that they're pulling. Tentacled figures and fish-men stand on it, gazing out. "Oh."

"Reconnaissance."

"Officer Tendrile? I thought he wouldn't leave the city!"

"Me too. If he and his troops are looking for us, we're no longer a regional issue. Maybe he got a special dispensation from the Appointees to find us."

"Like FBI-style?"

"We've got to keep off the road," Mortin says. "We'll cut across the hills."

"I'm not going off-road in the suburbs," Gamary says.

I laugh. I can't help it. He's so serious.

"What?"

"It's just . . . where I'm from, the suburbs are pretty safe."

"Hey." Gamary lifts me up. I'm glad the centaur patrol is down the road because it would be easy for them to see me kicking in the air. "Don't think your ignorance is cute, okay? You don't know what's in these hills."

"Gamary, put him down!"

"What's there to be worried about?" I nod at the grass, the clouds, and the small huts (where I hope we will be stopping soon for a meal from a kindhearted family). Gamary drops me.

"Ow! That's my bad ankle!"

"Calm down, everybody," Ada says. "Look." She pulls out something I've been hoping I would see at some point: a map.

"Amazing!" I say. "What's a Villalba?"

"That's the name of the supercontinent that makes up our world."

"So *that's* what I can call it! Not World of the Other Normals. Villalba."

"No, that's like saying China and Asia are the same thing."

"Why does it look like New Jersey?"

"It's how the geology worked out here, Peregrine, okay? Could you not argue with me?"

"I just really dig maps. They're a critical component of playing Creatures and Caverns. I wish I'd seen this sooner—"

"We're here." She points at a spot depressingly close to Subbenia. "We have to go here." She points to Upekki. That's depressingly close too. We can't go any farther in this world? "Off-road it'll take forever, but not if we cut across to the Warbledash River and travel by boat."

"Where are we going to get a boat?" Mortin asks.

"We can make a raft."

"With what wood?"

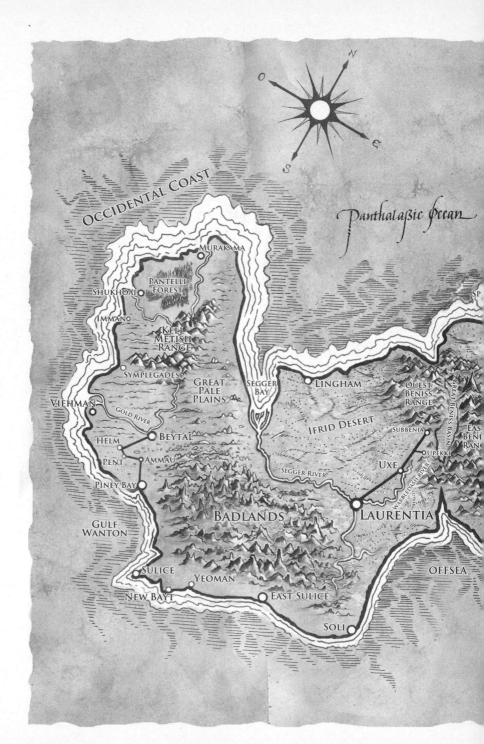

"You and I both know what's going to happen by the time we get to the Warbledash," Gamary warns.

"I've got that covered," Ada says. "We'll roll in some dirt."

"Why?"

Mortin sighs. "To hide our scents."

"Why?"

"Because the Benia suburbs are populated by cynos."

"Which ones were those? The dog-heads? So?"

"They're sort of . . . culturally different from city cynos."

"How?"

"They eat trespassers."

"It's actually legal here," Ada says. "Once you're off the road, it's legal to eat you."

I hear a howl in the distance.

65

WE ALL WORK QUICKLY ON A PATCH OF
grass, pulling it up to expose the dry, crumbling earth beneath.
Mortin presses it against himself, using spit to make it stick. He
dabs some under his eye and covers up his bruise.

"Where'd you get that, Mortin?"

"I was in prison; don't be asking me stupid questions."

"But didn't you have it before, when I first met you?"

"*Don't*, Perry."

Gamary is next; he rolls in the dirt. When he gets up, he
looks like an abused circus animal. Ada gently pats herself with
handfuls of soil; it brings out the sharp, rotten smell she showed
me before.

"Is this necessary?" I stand in front of the dirt patch. I don't
want to be smelly in front of Ada. She nods at me, and I kneel.
The soil is cool and stinky on my knees. I drop to my stomach
and roll, spitting on my hands, pressing them against my chest,
feeling the dirt cling to me. "How do I look?" I ask.

"Earthy."

"How do I smell?"

"Uncompromising. What do you say? 'Punk rock.'"

We go single file: Mortin, Ada, me, Gamary. Dirt falls from me as I walk, but enough stays on to provide the unpleasant tang. We keep silent; the sun creeps along at the same pace as us. The hills are low and manageable, but there's something strange about them—I only realize after the first hour. There aren't any bird or insect sounds. No buzzing, no squirrels running around . . . the countryside is filled with silence that eats up the sunlight and makes me think that we're in an illusion, a terrarium, being watched.

The howls come frequently, at unpredictable intervals. They echo through the hills, clear and defined in the unnatural silence, always answered. Unseen creatures are speaking over us.

Whenever we spot a hut, or a clump of rocks that looks fashioned by intelligence, we stay clear. At times, Mortin holds his hand up for us to stop and then drops to the ground to crawl up the nearest hill. At the top he licks the end of his tail and lifts it above him to determine wind direction. If the wind is blowing toward a nearby hut, he brings us around the leeward side of the hill so the breeze won't pick up our scent. It's slow, painstaking work, and soon the sun is close to the horizon behind us.

"When are we going to eat?" I ask.

"I was waiting for somebody to say it," Gamary says.

Mortin stops. "Ada, where are we?"

She pulls out the map and looks for a landmark, but besides the mountains to the north and the huts, which aren't big enough to be *on* the map, there's nothing. "Maybe here?" She points to a spot a hairbreadth off the main road.

"We have to have come farther than that," I say. "My legs are aching, seriously."

"I thought you were an adventurer who wanted to kill Ophisa. Now you have achy legs?"

"*Shhh*," Gamary whispers.

"Are you sure *all* the people who live here are cannibals?" I press. "Maybe some are, but some are nice folks who will give us food."

"You're about to get smacked," Mortin says. "We keep moving all night if we have to. If we make the Warbledash by tomorrow morning, we'll catch some fish."

"Uck. Who eats fish for breakfast?"

Everyone stares at me.

"Sorry. I mean, it would be great to have fish for breakfast."

"Hi!"

We all jump back. The voice is chipper and young; it comes from the hill next to us, but when we look at it, we see nothing, and for a moment I wonder if the *ground* spoke. Then I hear giggling and look at the hill opposite the one that seemed to talk. A small boy with a dog head sits on a rock, wearing a getma.

66

THE DOG-BOY HOPS UP AND RUNS FORWARD
on all fours, then stops and eyes us again, curious. "Fooled ya!
It's the echo. See? *Puuu*-la!"

He throws his voice against the opposite hill. It's even better
this time; I *see* his mouth move but still hear "la!" from behind
me. It makes me wonder if the howls we heard all afternoon
were really coming from where we thought they were.

"Watcha'll doing?" the boy asks. His dog head is shaggy
and brown, with drooping ears and a bright black nose and
pointy yellow teeth. He wears a simple leather collar. His boy
body is tan and wiry. "Why you all painted up in dirt?"

"We're . . . ah . . . we're playing a game," Mortin says.

"Really? I love games! You been playin' awhile! I seen you
from allaway back. Been playing my own game, following you,
practicing echoes. *Puuu*-la!"

The sound hits me from behind again.

"We're just passing through," Mortin says.

The boy's face drops. Like a dog, his expressions are exag-
gerated and easily understood. "That's no fun. Why you wanna
leave the Echoing Hills? Here you can have fun all day! Play in

the sun, make friends, what's the problem?"

"Are your parents around?"

"Why you want to get them involved, huh? You trynna get me in trouble?"

"Not at all, no. We just want to get through the Echoing Hills and finish our game."

"You from the city?"

"Yes."

"You got candy?"

"No."

"You got a fire maker?"

"A lighter? No. And I don't have any pebbles either, so don't remind me."

"*Mmmm*-kay. I'll play a game with you. If yer from the city, you like fire, right? Campfire? Place to stay for the night?"

"Yes! Definitely!"

"I'll take you to an old campfire. You just gotta find me first. Close your eyes!"

Mortin shuts his. He taps my side and I do the same. There's a lot of emotion in his tap. It says, *This is a dangerous cannibal cyno child and you must do as he says.*

Behind my eyelids, shapes dance in echoes of sunlight. "Now where am I?" the boy calls. "*Puuu*-la!"

It sounds like he's right in front of us. I can picture his floppy ears, lolling tongue, and askew head. I start to speak, but Mortin says, "Behind us!"

"Open your eyes!"

I blink. The boy is nowhere to be seen. I wheel around. There he is, on the hill opposite, squatting, eyes bright, ears up.

"Good one! Not so dumb fer city folk! Now close 'em again!"

He does it once more, calling seemingly from behind us. Mortin guesses that he's in front of us, and when we open our eyes, there he is, at the top of the next hill east. "This way!" he calls. Mortin shrugs at us like, *What else can we do?*

67

WE TAKE TWENTY MINUTES TO WALK THE
next half mile because we have to close our eyes and guess
where the dog-boy is every two minutes. If Mortin gets the
right answer too often, he says, "No fair! Yer cheating!" and
makes us do it all over.

"Where am I now?" he asks. The sun has set behind us but
some light remains.

"Polo!" I yell back.

"What? What'd he say?"

"It's a game! Marco Polo. It's faster. We'll just close our
eyes and call 'Marco,' and then you say 'Polo,' and we'll try to
follow you by your voice."

"Why 'Polo'?"

"Marco Polo, he was an explorer."

"Where?"

"Ah . . ."

"Subbenia," Mortin cuts in. "Upper Subbenia."

"Okay, try!" the boy says. "Try!"

"I'm closing my eyes! And I'm holding everybody's hand!"
I reach out for Mortin's worn one and Ada's fine soft one.

Gamary grips my shoulder. "Marco!"

"Polo!" the boy calls from behind me. He isn't very inventive when it comes to tricking us; he uses straight reverse psychology every time. I walk forward. My friends step with me.

"Marco!"

Behind me: "Polo!"

I walk forward. "Marco!"

"Open your eyes!" We've reached him. He sits at the foot of the next hill, grinning ear to ear. "I *like* this game!" He squints at me. "What are you, anyway? You're not ferrous; you're not a satty—"

"He's an attenuate, like me," Ada says.

"His ears aren't pointy."

"I know, that's just—"

"And he's not tall—"

"He's still growing—"

"Is his hair blue? I can't tell, can't see color, wouldn't know what blue is, heh!"

"He's a mutant," Ada says.

"Hey!"

She squeezes my hand. "He's a mutant friend of mine. Don't you like playing Marco Polo with him?"

"Yeah!"

"So let's keep playing then, and you lead us to that campfire."

"What's his name?"

"John Johnson," I say. "What's yours?"

"*Puuu*-la!" the boy calls, throwing another echo behind me, and I'm not sure if he's telling us his name or just going off into his semidemented dog-child world, but that's what I end up calling him.

68

IT'S DARK WHEN WE REACH THE PLACE
Pula promised: an old campfire next to a thin brook. The
brook is narrow enough for me to stand over with one leg on
either side. All of us, including Pula, drink heaping handfuls
from it.

I've never been a fan of water. When I get thirsty, I get
thirsty for soda. If I get water instead, it feels like punishment.
But this is different. This is magic. All my cells rejoice. I lie
in the grass with a full, sloshing stomach and look up at the
night sky.

"*Whoa.*"

"What?" Ada asks.

"Stars!"

"So?"

"Look at how many! So much more than Earth!"

She eyes Pula. He's conversing by the campfire with Mortin and Gamary, ignoring us. "There aren't more stars here
than on Earth. Even with six hundred million years of sepa-
ration, our stars are roughly the same. Can't you recognize
them?"

"You can't see stars in New York."

"That's horrible. How can you live without stars? What keeps you from thinking about yourself all the time?"

I think about how I think about myself too much. Do I? Of course. I think I have an *excuse* because it seems the world is out to get me and I *have* to think about myself in order to defend myself. But all egotists have this excuse.

"Stars pull reverse psychology on you, my mother always told me," Ada says. "When you look at them, you should feel terrified, because they're so big, and so far, but they comfort you instead."

"Do you see your mom still?"

"She's dead."

I almost say *I'm sorry*, but the words are too small.

"Your father?"

"He was never part of the picture. I lived with my mother until she got sick. Then I became an Appointee ward. Officially, the state is like all of our parents, so when our actual parents are gone, it takes over their responsibilities—and benefits. I was slated to work in an orchard, but Mortin saw something in me. He purchased me at auction."

"Like a car?"

"Like a father. It's tough for you to understand. The relationship between consultant and intern is time-honored. Mortin's like my boss, my business partner, my mentor— but he could trade me up if someone better came along. He never has. He's training me to work in a big house like

Sulice. In exchange, he'll get a cut of my income when I'm older."

"That seems kind of . . . wrong."

"What, you don't have that arrangement with your parents?"

"My parents are divorced, Ada."

"I know. They don't expect to be taken care of when they're older, though?"

"I never thought about it."

"Too busy thinking about yourself?"

"My parents hardly take care of me now. They leave that up to the lawyers. I don't feel responsible for them."

"Do you love them?"

"Jeez." I think about it. "In a knee-jerk way, sure. But I don't know if it counts."

"You should love them. You should love them hard."

I look at the stars. Ada's right: they force you to think in a different direction.

"What was your mother like? Mrs. Ember?"

"She wasn't Mrs. Ember. Her name was Athis Danet. She sold baskets at market. She was always picking fibers off herself."

"How'd you get 'Ada Ember,' then? Your father?"

"I picked Ember. After I started working with Mortin."

"Why?"

"Because embers turn into flames."

That's because a name has to mean something.

"Hey!" Mortin calls. "John Johnson! C'mere!"

I don't want to go, but it sounds like I'm needed. "I'm gonna . . ."

"Go." Ada nods, understanding.

69

THE CAMPFIRE PIT IS A HEAP OF ASH AND half-burned logs inside a circle of smooth stones.

"We have to make a fire from this," Mortin says. "Thought you might be able to help."

"Can't you do it?"

"My lighter's smashed, remember?"

"City folk." Pula smiles.

"It's not going to be easy," Mortin says. "We found this on top." He indicates a big rock in the grass. "We pushed it aside, but there's not much underneath. I don't see any kindling. How'd the people who made this fire even get the logs?"

"They brought themselves," Pula says. "In packs. Few days ago."

"You saw them? Who were they?"

"Travelers. Different kinds. Some with the big fishy head, one with the slime feet. Lotsa weapons. Headed back the way you came. They stayed one night and went. You got enough wood left from them if you can start it."

"Why can't *you* start it?"

"Oh, I dunno how. Only the grown-ups are 'lowed to start fires."

"We can do it if we've got a log, a stick, and a string," I say. "I mean, I've never done it, but that's how you do it in C and C."

"What's that?" Pula asks.

"Don't worry about it," Mortin says. "That's like a code word for this kid. Here's your string." He pulls a loose thread off the bottom of his getma. "And here's a log." He pulls a half-burned one from the fire pit.

I look closer at the ash. It goes deep. Was this fire used on multiple nights? And why was the rock on top of it? Did whoever built it snuff it out?

I set the log on the ground. It's split down the middle, as if by an ax, which is good for me—it means the flammable flaky wood in the center is exposed.

"I need a stick." Ada approaches. She hands me a six-inch shaft of wood.

"What's this?"

"Broke it off a spear in one of our many battles."

"Perfect. Now a knife. Anybody? Gamary? Your ax?"

Gamary shakes his head.

"Somebody has to have something! Ada, can I see the princess figure?"

She hands it to me. I inspect the ragged bottom of the princess's torso. There's one piece of metal that seems sharp enough. I try it against the spear shaft. It shaves the wood off, but only a tiny bit. This is going to be painstaking work. Luckily I can do painstaking work. I used to be in Summer Scholars.

I sit in the grass and use the princess figure to whittle Ada's spear shaft to a fine point. It takes forever. Pula slobbers as he watches; I figure he can't control that and it would be rude to mention. He scratches his ear, and I notice something odd about his hand. It's a human hand, but different somehow, like there's an extra finger. . . . It's too dark to tell. I look back at the spear shaft. The point seems sharp enough. I wrap the string around the shaft once and press the point into the log. Holding one end of the string loosely, I pull on the other. The shaft spins in the log . . . and quickly hops into the grass.

"I need another string to keep it stable."

Ada pulls a thread off her top and wraps it around the shaft, above the string that's already there. Now it's balanced, and if we pull together, maybe we can get it to spin without flying off.

"One . . . two . . . *go*," I say. Ada pulls her string as I pull mine. The shaft spins in the log, sending up a tiny bit of smoke that curls away under the stars. Once again, though, the stick jumps out beside us.

"I got an idea," Gamary says. "Put it back."

We reposition the shaft in the log. Gamary sticks the princess figure on top of it, holding it in place with her jagged nether region. "Now try."

Ada and I pull our strings at once. The stick spins but stays still, like a top, with the princess securing it. I swear the figure mouths at me, *Good job.*

"Other way!" Ada says, and we pull back, twirling the shaft in the other direction. Smoke puffs up. "Other way now! Keep going!"

"It's good!" Pula says. "Almost got it!"

Ada and I lock eyes, pulling our strings back and forth in sync, spinning the shaft in the log—

With a *piff,* a tiny flame bursts up.

"Yay!" Pula calls.

"Don't let it go out!" Mortin says.

"Move," Ada tells me, and she breathes, calm and insistent, on the nascent flame. It hesitates, blocky and orange, and then takes root in the log as she slips it into the fire pit.

"You did it!" I tell her.

"We did it," she says.

Within a minute we have a full-on fire burning bright under the stars. It's better than television. It feels so good. It looks so mesmerizing. For a moment I'm happier than I can ever remember being. Then Mortin says, "Now's a time to celebrate. Where there's fire, there's smoke. None of you have pebbles and a pipe, do you?"

We all keep quiet.

"Gamary?"

"No, Mortin."

"You're not holding out on me, are you?"

"No—"

"I *know* you are!" Mortin rushes Gamary and presses his hand against his okapi underbelly. It takes a second for me to realize that he's pushing *into* him, into a *pouch* that Gamary has at his front. Mortin pulls out a small pipe and a handful of pebbles.

"See? How did I know?"

"Mortin, that isn't for you!"

"You cheap bastard! No wonder you ended up a thaklord. Keeping it to yourself." Mortin lights up, figuratively in terms of his expression and literally with the pipe, which he stuffs with pebbles and holds over the fire with the tip of his tail. Once the rocks are steaming, he puffs and passes to Gamary.

"Fine, just to celebrate the fire." Gamary lies down like a horse. "But I'm enabling an addict."

"I don't understand," I say. "What do the pebbles do?"

"It's the quartz," Mortin answers. "It interacts with other-normal brains. Quite pleasantly."

"Can I try?"

"Won't work for you. And you've got a big enough addiction."

"What?"

"Do I have to spell it out for you? You know, John Johnson."

But I don't, really. I rack my brain thinking about it while Mortin and Gamary pass the pipe and laugh and the fire reaches into the sky. I know it isn't a good idea for them to smoke—Ada won't even look at them—but what can I say?

"I'm hungry," Gamary says finally. He and Mortin have been having an emotional chat about his daughter. "There's gotta be some fish in that stream. Can somebody spear one?"

"City dwellers done *good*," says Pula. He holds his hands to the fire. In the light of the flame, I see what's wrong with them: his *thumbs* are tiny. Underdeveloped. They have only one knuckle, and they stick out across his palms instead of away from them. He has no opposable thumbs. He couldn't start a fire if he tried. "Got the good fire going, drank some water, nice and juicy, smoking up, extra flavor, best way to have a barbecue."

"Oh crap," Mortin says. "What did he say?"

Pula rocks back and forth on his heels, talking to himself. "Ain't had a barbecue in the Echoing Hills for a week, no fires anywhere, but I knew how to save one, huh? And I got it started up again."

He turns his head to the moon and howls. The sound echoes through the hills—louder than any cry we heard in the day, and louder than any of his *puuu*-la calls.

"You little punk!" Mortin leaps across the fire at him. Pula laughs and runs toward the stream. Answering wolf calls sound off the grass.

All around us, from the top of each hill surrounding the campfire, heads appear: slavering, hairy, pointed. The heads creep forward, on top of men and women on all fours.

"Barbecue!" Pula calls, dancing by the stream. "Barbecue!"

70

A DOZEN CYNOS CIRCLE US. THEY MUST'VE been following all day, tracking my idiotic game of Marco Pula. They crawl closer, slinky and confident. Their hairy arms glisten in the moonlight. They wear getmas; the women let their breasts hang freely below them, which distracts me.

I back against the fire with Ada, Gamary, and Mortin.

"These two are smokified inside!" Pula yells. "And this one's got the girlyparts! But don't hurt him! He's my mutant friend."

"I'm your friend? Pula, if I'm your friend, let us all out of here!"

"Nuh-uh. Your friends gotta go in the barbecue; you can stay with me."

A big male dog-head comes up to him. One of his eyes is a slit with skin tags on it and tears dribbling out the side.

"You did good," he says, and then he speaks a name that vanishes in the air. Pula's real name. "This fire we gonna keep going a long time." He licks Pula's head. "But they all gotta go in the barbecue."

"No, Daddy, no!" Pula squats in front of me, throwing his arms across my legs. "Not John Johnson!"

"C'mere, you," Mortin says. In one quick motion, he grabs Pula, lifts him off the ground by his collar, and holds him to the fire. "Back off, you savages! Or you'll be having *him* for barbecue."

"Ow!" Pula struggles. "You're strangling me, you big stupid!"

The dog-heads look to Pula's father. "You got a count of three to let us out of here!" Mortin orders. His voice echoes through the hills: *here, here, here,* calling from different slopes.

"Daddy, it hurts!"

"Three!"

Three, three, three.

"That's what happens when you get too close to your food, Son."

"Two!"

Two, two, two.

"Daddy, help me!"

"One!"

Pula's father opens his mouth wide and clacks his teeth shut. The dog-heads leap and attack.

They tear Pula out of Mortin's hands. His collar comes off and Mortin stares at it, agog, as they fling Pula to the ground and rip his stomach open. He flails and gnashes his teeth as hungry dog-heads toss his innards out on the grass.

"Holy *crap!*" Mortin yells. "Gamary, c'mon!"

A dog-head jumps at Mortin. He ducks. It sails over him and narrowly avoids landing in the fire, scrambling to the side as Gamary kneels and Mortin climbs onto his back. Two dog-heads leap at Ada. She whips them with the only weapon she has—the princess figure—and tears into the ear of one and the eye of the other.

A female pounces at me; I kick at her. She watches my foot fly over her head and bites calmly into my calf. I fall. A snarling face jabs forward at me—

And Ada knocks it away, loosening several canine teeth.

"Get up!" Another one is already on me, a male, at my ankle. My bad ankle. I kick his face and reach toward the campfire to grab a log. The end of the log is on fire, and it makes a pretty comet trail as I fling it at him. It lands on his head. He howls, fur flaring up, face sizzling. He runs to the stream to put himself out. The log burns in the grass. The dog-heads take notice.

"Get it!"

"Stamp it out!"

They run to it. This makes sense. Lots of animals don't like fire. There are monsters in C&C that you get a bonus against if you have fire. I grab another log and wave it at the dog-heads, pulling it through the air like a matador, trailing flame.

"Back off!"

They snap and growl. My leg is bleeding. They seethe and spit at the heat.

"Come on!" Gamary yells. "Hurry up!" He kneels with Mortin and Ada on his back.

"I'm coming!"

Gamary takes a log and swats at the dog-heads that attack

his front, while Ada beats at the ones who circle his flanks. Mortin grabs a rock with his tail and swings it like a club *(we are the stoners!)*, fending off the creatures at his rear. One of the cynos snatches my log with his jaws. It drops to the ground. A group of them stamp it out.

"Peregrine!"

They have me now. I'm separated from my friends, with no weapons. Nothing to hit the cynos with, nothing to slash them with, nothing to light on fire and throw at them . . .

My getma.

I pull it off. I'm not wearing anything underneath. Here I am, naked with naked breasts around me, but it's all wrong. I snap the loincloth like a washcloth at the circling dog-heads. One yelps as it nicks his eye. I dip it into the fire; it catches and I have a flaming weapon again.

"I can't"—I swing—"believe"—I swing—"you made me"—I swing—"get *naked* again!"

They part for me, growling. One attacks my back, but I spin and hit him with the burning fabric; he retreats.

"All right, Perry! You crazy naked othersider! C'mon!"

Almost there. I whip my getma in the air twice more as I reach Gamary's back and hop on. The dog-heads nip at me. The flames reach my fingers, and I drop the cloth in the grass as we take off. I don't have anything to hold on to but Ada.

"I'm sorry Ada I know this is inappropriate I'm naked I hope—"

"Shut up! When we *met*, you were naked!"

Gamary gallops along the stream. The dog-heads follow, snarling and howling, Pula's slit-eyed father in the lead. They snap at the okapicentaur's flanks, which are already injured and bandaged from the fight in Subbenia. "I don't know—*huff*—how much longer—"

"Don't start talking like that." Mortin clocks a pursuing cyno. "We got you covered."

"But Mortin—*huff*—I can't breathe—*huff*—I shouldn't have smoked—"

Gamary slows. I look at his sides. The bandages are streaming off him. The moonlight is making his blood black. Cynos bite his back hooves. They can't just crawl on their hands and knees; they can *run*, with their knees acting as feet and their feet curled up behind them. When they get close, they rear up on two legs to take bites. The end of Gamary's tail is gone; it bleeds onto the grass. *They're taking us down*, I think, *like hyenas bringing down a wildebeest.*

Roaring, Pula's father leaps through the air and clamps down on Gamary's leg. With a twist of the cyno's head, Gamary's thin shinbone snaps sideways. He screams and keels over. I jump off him and roll away in the grass. Gamary hits the ground with a thud and some cracks—his ribs. Ada gets to her feet and runs toward the stream with Mortin. I go to Gamary and grab his arms as cynos bite into his hide.

"*Bigmeat!*"

"*Freshmeat!*"

I pull, like he's a friend I'm trying to get off the couch.

"Come on, Gamary. *Up!*"

"No, othersider. Go with your friends. It's too late."

"What about your daughter? You have to see her!"

"I'm going to. Don't you understand? I'm going to. . . ."

He smiles. A cyno snaps at me, but it isn't to try and eat me—it's to shoo me away from his meal. I back off, letting Gamary's hands fall to his sides. He kicks his head back, still smiling, and collapses.

I run, naked, crying. I shut my eyes against the image of steam rising from Gamary's opened flesh. Behind me, his body scrapes against the grass as the dog-heads drag him away. "Barbecue!" they call. "Barbecue!"

71

WE REGROUP BY THE STREAM. "STUPID pebbles!" Mortin gasps. "We would've been fine if I weren't smoking!" He punches the grass, wild-eyed, maddened.

"Are you okay?"

"No! Are *you* okay? What kind of stupid question is that? Don't ask any more meaningless Earth questions. In this world, when we talk, we mean what we say. My friend just got eaten alive! I'm not okay! You're not okay either! Your leg is bleeding and you have no clothes!"

"I can help with that," Ada says. She pulls a bandage off her shoulder from where the guard jabbed her back in Subbenia. Her wound is dark but not wet. She washes the bandage in the stream and hands it to me. It's the bare minimum that will cover me; I put it on like a diaper. For my calf wound, she presses grass against me until the blood dries. It looks like I'm growing a small lawn, but it feels better.

"Oh, that's cute," Mortin says. "You two get quality time while Gamary is eaten because I can't keep my head straight for forty-five seconds. If I hadn't smoked . . . if I'd been alert . . . I would've seen that trap coming a hundred helms away." Mortin takes out Gamary's pipe, which I'm sort of surprised he's held on to in all the excitement. "No more. We're burying this to remember him by. I don't even need to smoke. It's just an oral-fixation thing. Here"—he rips up a clump of grass and chews it—"just as good!"

As Mortin chews and spits, we dig a shallow pit by the stream and place the pipe inside. I notice Pula's leather collar around Mortin's shoulder. "What about that?"

"Oh, I figured we should keep it. Might need it. We don't have much!"

"We should bury it." I slip it off and place it next to the pipe.

"Why?"

"I don't know—respect?"

"That cannibal dog ragamuffin doesn't deserve any respect!"

"He tried to protect me."

"So?"

"He was just a boy," Ada says.

"So?"

"His dad had him ripped open in front of us!" I yell. "It'd be dishonorable not to bury something of his!"

"Honor? What do you care about honor? Honor gets people killed!"

I know where I've heard that before. Suddenly I have an idea who Mortin corresponds to. "At least they die for something," I say, and he doesn't protest further as we bury Gamary's pipe and Pula's collar, piling dirt on top until we have a small mound by the stream.

"You want to say anything, Peregrine?" Ada asks. "You believe in God, right?"

"Ah . . . it's complicated. This whole thing . . . I don't even know what I believe anymore. Do *you* believe in God?"

"We're not allowed to. He's not appointed."

"Oh, well . . . I guess . . ." I take a deep breath. "God rest the souls of these two creatures—"

"*Friends*," Ada corrects.

"Was Pula really our friend?"

"He said he was yours, at the end."

"Friends, then. Take them to a better place, and, ah, please lead us safely on our own journey, amen. And help Mortin with his new decision not to smoke earthpebbles. Amen. And please help me find some more clothes because this itches. Amen."

"Very good. Can you walk?"

I nod. The adrenaline that ran through me when I escaped in Subbenia is back in full force. I feel like I could walk for days.

72

THE MOON REACHES THE TOP OF THE
sky. The stream burbles and widens as it winds east; it looks
like black glass under the stars. Ada asks, "What's that?" A dark
shape lies beside the stream bank.

"It's not a body, is it?" I ask.

"If it were a body, the dog-heads would've taken it," says
Mortin. We creep closer. It's a pile of rucksacks. The moon
shines off buckles and snaps. Mortin kicks the pile. The bags
clank against one another. We dig in, tearing everything
open. I find a saucepan, a spoon, and a lighter (traditional,
not tail). Mortin finds metal sporks and sleeping bags. Ada
finds bottles of wine. That's not even counting the weapons:
a hefty broadsword, a pair of axes, a trident with spiral tips, a
few daggers, and . . . yes! A war hammer, like Pekker Cland's!
"I call the war hammer!"

"Stop," Mortin says. "Consider what happened here." He
picks up a bag and holds open a ragged hole at the bottom.
"Do they all have holes like this?" Ada and I nod. "And what's
missing from them?"

"Food!" I say, raising my hand. Partly I know the answer

just because I'm hungry.

"Exactly. This is the equipment of three members of Ophisa's rebel horde. You've got three sleeping bags but enough weapons for six. They go armed to the teeth. What else don't you see?"

"Firewood," Ada says.

"Right. They were passing through and got ambushed like us. The dog-heads made one of them take the wood to the campfire. Then: barbecue."

"What were Ophisa's followers doing here?" I ask.

"I don't know, but their loss is our gain. Let's sew up these holes and start traveling in style. Ada, can you open a wine bottle?"

"Didn't you just say you weren't smoking anymore?"

"This is drinking, it's different."

"Mortin—"

"I need something, okay?"

"Open it yourself."

As Mortin looks for a corkscrew, I check the bags and find something curious: a small leather case attached to a mirror. Inside is a two-inch comb, perfect for a mustache. There are two people I've met recently with mustaches—Officer Tendrile and Dale Blaswell. Only now do I recognize that they have the *same mustache*. Looking at the mirror, at myself, I start to think I might be putting more of this correspondence thing together.

73

I WAKE UP WITH AN UNGODLY HEADACHE on one side of my head, the side I slept on. I'm snuggled inside a sleeping bag beside the stream. I remember Ada giving me the sleeping bag around when she took away my bottle of wine. Was that my *second* bottle? What time is it? The sun assaults me. I get on my hands and knees and dry heave. "Rise and shine, buddy!" Mortin says. "I told you to drink some water before you crashed out!"

I crawl forward. It's a beautiful morning, from an objective, nonheadache perspective. Ada has started a fire with flammable items we didn't need from the rucksacks we found. "What *happened?*" I ask.

"You tried wine for the first time," she says. "You and Mortin started . . . talking."

It comes back to me. Mortin opened the first bottle, and I asked if it was any good. He told me to try some. I thought about how I didn't want to end up like my brother, but then I thought about how I'd just seen two people torn open alive and I decided this was when you were *supposed* to drink. I took a sip. The wine made my mouth shrivel and my nose wrinkle, but after I passed it to Mortin and watched him take a few manly swigs and start telling Ada about how this stream had to meet up with the Warbledash River soon, and we were going to be in Upekki any day, and his brother Leidan was going to be there, and it would all be all right, I decided I wanted more. Ada didn't drink any, and she shot me a look when I took a second sip, but some switch that controlled whether I cared about her had been flipped. I cared more about being cool with Mortin. I drank—I saw the stars behind the bottle—and then I talked, and then I forget what happened.

"It hurts . . . ," I tell Ada. I kneel by the stream gulping handfuls of water. As soon as it hits my stomach, I heave it back up again.

"That's what happens when you guzzle Jiringian wine. You better keep some of that down. You're dehydrated. Your *brain* is dehydrated."

"Really?"

"That's what a hangover is."

"What you have to do," Mortin says, "is drink twenty-one handfuls of water before you go to sleep. I tried to tell you."

"Where are . . . *ugh* . . . the dog-heads?"

"Having a party eating Gamary, or maybe passed out. We're ready for them anyway." Mortin shows off his new arsenal. He has a sword on each hip, two daggers above his crotch, and an ax strapped to his shoulders. Ada has the other ax, two more daggers, and the trident. That leaves me with—

"The war hammer," Mortin says.

I take it. "In C and C, my character makes war hammers."

"I know. In the World of the Other Normals, you get to use one. Slightly more impressive."

Ada brings up a pot from the stream. Inside are three silver, flopping fish. Ada slices them open and lays them out on a metal rack over the fire. Mortin and I stand guard (*stand guard!*) as she cooks them, their oil dripping and sizzling. I hold my stomach. "I'm hungry, but I don't think I can eat fish."

"What do you want?" Mortin asks. "McDonald's breakfast?"

"Yeah! How'd you know?"

"It's the best hangover food. I know, I've had it."

Ada hands me a fish on a metal plate, split in two, cooked in its own skin. Its eyes are dried and creased. I dive in with a spork.

"It's *good*!"

"I can cook," Ada says.

"I mean it's *really* good! I think my headache is going away!"

"You saying you want to do the dishes?"

Ten minutes later I'm washing them in the stream. I investigate my wounds: hand, head, leg, ankle. Everything looks slightly better. We mix up sulfurous mud, splat it on to hide our scents, and start off, following the water. I wear a cloak that we found in the rucksacks. "I got my prayers answered," I tell Ada. "I prayed for new clothes and here they are."

"What do you say about that? 'Amen,' right?"

"Amen."

74

WE MARCH FOR MOST OF THE DAY
without incident. The Echoing Hills even out, and we see less
of the huts that indicate cyno settlement. One of the bags I
shoulder is empty, and every time we come across a piece of
wood, I pop it in. By early afternoon we have enough for a fire;
we eat more fish. The stream is wider now and slower moving. I
feel braver than the day before. It's amazing how brave you can
feel when you're armed.

"Are we *still* not going to fight Ophisa? Because, I'm just saying, look at these weapons!"

"Perry, no. Drop it."

"I think you better get used to the idea. Because I'm not
going back to camp." No one answers. "I tried it once and it
didn't work."

"Perry—"

"Don't call me that, Mortin, okay? Why can't you be respectful like Ada? My full name is Peregrine, and by now I'm at least
a level-three warrior, master of the war hammer—"

Mortin draws a sword and brings it up to my cheek with
one swift stroke. I stop. He holds the blade flat against my skin.

"Don't get cocky, kid. You're not the master of anything except luck, and that runs out."

"Stop!" Ada says. "What's wrong with you? Are you *trying* to act like stupid boys with weapons?"

I inch my hand toward a dagger I have strapped to my thigh. Mortin whips out another sword and presses my fingers against my leg. "Eh, eh, *ehhh* . . . don't get tricky with me."

"I wasn't gonna do anything. Just . . . show you my skills."

"Your biggest skill is your honor." Mortin draws back his weapons. "So think about that when you think about not going back. People need you."

"Who?"

"Your brother, for one."

"My brother doesn't need me for anything except a sounding board when he's wasted. What's he have to do with this?"

"Don't take your brother for granted."

I'm tired of riddles. "Mortin, who's my correspondent?"

"Can't tell you that."

"Is it a frog-head? A dog-head? Is it *you*?"

He smiles. "It's not me."

"I demand to know!"

"You never meet your correspondent. The consequences are too great. You could meet him and shake his hand and go back to Earth and suddenly have been born a flipper baby."

"Do you know who *your* correspondent is? Do *you*, Ada?"

"No, and I never want to." She keeps walking, and we follow. The stream widens and joins other rills and brooks. By evening it's too big to jump across. By nightfall it's a river. As it grows, the grass around us gets thicker and longer. Tangles of vines spread across the ground. The soil, so dry in the hills, turns moist and friendly; sometimes I step in a patch and need help from Mortin and Ada to *shlooooop* out. We camp in a flat marsh landscape of whistling reeds.

"We've been going the right way all along," Mortin says. "Ever since that campfire, we've been on the darned thing." He goes to sleep without any wine or pebbles, which he makes sure we notice, and then starts snoring; he sounds like a cross between a frog and a lion.

"Is that going to attract animals?" I ask Ada.

"Might repel them."

"Do you know anything about my correspondent? Is he brave?"

"Your correspondent could be a woman, Peregrine."

"Oh no; if that were true, I'd understand women better."

She sighs. "We're *people*. I'm a *person*. Remember? Not a mystical creature out to get you."

"*Anna's* not a mystical creature. You actually are! If I were to describe you to someone, what would I say? I'd say you were a highborn attenuate other normal with pointed ears and blue hair and sparkling fingers and toes."

"You wouldn't say I was a cool girl who could catch and cook fish?"

"I guess I'd say that too."

"You're getting better," she says. She turns in her sleeping bag to face me. "When you get back, maybe you'll do just fine with Anna."

Anna isn't the one I want to do just fine with, but I don't say so. Ada has to know. How can she not? The force of need in my brain is manifesting itself physically *at this very moment.* I want to touch her tenderly but with unstoppable confidence. I understand, now: some part of me believes that if I touch Ada naked, I will connect with the infinite and be free of earthly concerns forever. The word *horny* doesn't sound like it contains these emotions, but they're in there.

"Are there constellations?" I ask, trying to change the subject. "Like, other-normal constellations? Different from ours?"

"See the Hequet?"

"Kind of . . ."

"You call it the Big Dipper. And see those three stars? That's Orion's Belt on Earth. Here that's the Sword of Hentator, the great ferrous other-normal warrior, and that star on the right is his tail."

"I see it!"

"And that one . . ."

She keeps going. The longer I look at the stars, the more depth they generate, like thakerak threads reaching underground. Her voice, too, is lovely. My brain calms and my body slackens. The last thing I see before I close my eyes is the moon, full and high, distorted in the ripples of the

WARBL

R

EDASH
IVER

75

THE WARBLEDASH RUNS SOUTH OUT OF
the Ouest Beniss Range past Upekki, which we reach the next
day. It's a small trading station populated mostly by frog-heads.
Ada shows us on the map. In two and a half days we've gone as
far as the overhang of my nail on my index finger. Speaking of
which, I bite it. Dirt is packed underneath.

"Ew," Ada says.

"This is gonna be great," Mortin declares. "No one cares
about Upekki; the authorities won't be terrorizing it the way
they are Subbenia. And hequets are laid-back." He's been in a
jolly mood since breakfast: barbecued crabs. They sizzled like
bacon in their shells. The smell nauseated me at first, but as
soon as I popped the white flesh out of the first steaming leg,
my body demanded more.

"Hequets have a reputation," Ada explains, "for being—"

"Partiers! Gamblers, smokers, and degenerates. My kind of
people."

"I thought you weren't smoking anymore," I say.

"I can still get excited, can't I? It's a lot better than getting
eaten by dog-heads. And Leidan will be there."

269

"What are we gonna do for money? Or whatever you call it—*di*-?"

"Don't worry. We've got my good name."

"I thought you had a terrible name. I thought you *owed* people money."

"Then we'll sell your war hammer, smart guy."

"No you won't!" I step away from the river and take a few swings. The war hammer is a metal bar as long as my forearm with what looks like a railroad spike mounted perpendicularly on the end. I arc it down, then flip it around and swing back up, mentally dechinifying an attacker. I love how the hammer's heavy but I can still handle it—no, that's not the word—*wield* it!

"You better watch that thing," Mortin says, "in case someone sees you and thinks you know what you're doing."

Upekki squats on the river ahead of us: a group of dingy brick buildings with creaky wooden docks sticking into the water. None of the buildings are more than three stories high. They exhibit a color range from brown to red-brown to red. It looks like Queens. It's a sleepy town; I don't see any smoke rising from chimneys or hear marketplace hubbub. But it's still morning.

A road from the west joins our riverside path. "Bartleby Way," Mortin explains. "Probably how Leidan's getting here."

"Why didn't he come with us?"

"We couldn't fit another person on Gamary. And he gets annoying in close company."

"My brother does too."

Ada sighs in relief as we merge with Bartleby Way; it's nice to walk on something devoid of thistles, slippery rocks, and muddy pits. The town grows closer. Fishing rods stick out the windows of the buildings on the river, with lazy lines trailing down. Suddenly, one of them jerks, but instead of being reeled in, it hops out the window and *ksssshes* into the water below.

"Who's holding the rods?" I ask.

Mortin draws his swords. "We should've seen somebody by now. We should be fighting off drunken frog-heads—it's almost noon."

I tap my war hammer against my palm. Ada holds her trident across her chest. My heart pounds as we edge forward. Upekki stays quiet. Surrounding it is a tall metal fence with a gate. Bartleby Way runs up to it. A guardhouse stands to the side, no bigger than a token booth in the subway, made of red brick, with barred windows. Its door swings freely, the top hinge mangled. A figure lies on the steps in front of it. His big frog head is still.

"Hey! You okay?"

Mortin runs up to him. The hequet wears a cloak with a pin around his neck like a sheriff's star. He's dead. At his side is a curved scabbard. The sword that goes in it is a few feet away in the grass. Through his forehead, from front to back, is a neat circular hole. Blood pools around him, drying.

"Careful," Mortin says, "not to touch his poison sac." He points at the frog-head's cheeks. "That's where we get hepatodes from."

"She doesn't have a poison sac, Mortin. She's a she." Ada points out the slight bulges beneath the cloak.

"That's a bullet hole," I say.

"What?"

"Right there. Entrance wound, exit wound. I don't know what caliber it is or anything, but I've seen enough cop shows."

"Bullet hole? But guns aren't approved. Nobody's got guns!"

"Someone does. Maybe Ophisa?"

Mortin squints at the hole. "I don't know. Look at that. Dead in an instant. Have you ever heard a gun? I hear they're louder than volcanoes."

"I've heard bangs near my house, but my parents always said they were trucks backfiring. They would, though. Where's the bullet? That's important evidence."

"I bet her ears were still ringing when she died," Mortin says.

We search for the bullet but can't find it. We retrieve the hequet's sword and place it in the scabbard at her side. Ada closes her eyes. "Say one of your prayers, Peregrine?"

"Ah, may God rest the soul of this hequet, and, ah, keep us safe. And thanks for all the free weapons and clothes. Amen."

"You're getting better," Mortin says.

We leave the hequet on the ground. There's no time to bury her.

"Could the Appointees have approved guns while we were on the run?" I ask. "Maybe they're allowing the cops to have them, so they can search for the princess."

"That's what I'm thinking. And it's not good. Backs together. We'll find out more in town." We form a triangle. The bags over our shoulders clank against one another as we crab-walk into Upekki.

THE TOWN IS ABANDONED. BARTLEBY WAY passes through the iron gate and becomes the main street, cutting between taverns, rooming houses, and commercial establishments that don't have any identifiable characteristics and which I therefore assume are dens of iniquity—or were. Everything is empty. A few dogs patrol the streets—when we first see one, I think it's a dog-*head* and clench my war hammer tight.

Another hequet lies shot outside a tavern, his head in the gutter. Once again there's a hole through the skull, clean, with a pool of blood and no bullet. I say one of my lame prayers.

"Some people fought back," Mortin says. "The town was attacked. The people who played along lived. The ones who fought back got shot. Otherwise there'd be a lot more bodies."

"Do you think your brother was here when it happened?"

Mortin shakes his head and starts toward a wooden storefront with a hand-painted sign.

"'Boggolove?'"

"*The* Boggolove. I've won some serious card games here."

He pushes open a pair of swinging saloon doors. I follow him into the dark. Ada grabs my hand as we move forward and squeezes it tight.

"LEIDAN?"

The Boggolove is a step up from the Monard, less of a dive and more of a Wild West brothel: the large circular tables match the chairs; the hardwood floor gleams; there are shining fancy bottles behind the polished bar. But a lot is wrong. The bottles are empty, the floor has scattered impact craters of broken glass, and a chandelier tilts crazily above us, one of its support chains severed. Mortin leads us behind the bar.

"Leidan? You here? It's me!" He crouches and pulls a lever by a barrel. A trapdoor swings open. Below, a chorus of voices croak and gibber.

"Riggit!"

"Up with the Appointees!"

"Who're you?"

"Riggity buggle!"

"Down with Ophisa!"

"Can we come up now?"

Mortin says, "Identify yourselves! Is Leidan Enaw there?"

"Mortin! You made it!"

Mortin backs away as his brother climbs out the trapdoor. His long hair is tied over his neck and his smile reaches from ear to ear. "You're not dead! I'm not dead! *Uh!*" He flings his arms around Mortin and swings him around the room.

"Put me down! I'm serious!"

"Aren't you happy?"

"Down!"

Leidan drops him. "Hello, Ada; hello, little traveler. We've had a hell of a time waiting for you—"

"What were you doing down there?"

"Hiding with us," a throaty voice says. A woman climbs out of the trapdoor. She's a hequet with vivid eye makeup wearing a white see-through gown. Her hunter-green head is puffy and grotesque, but her body is straight out of a glossy magazine. *"Criminals!"* she says, surveying the room. "They took my booze!"

"Iyatra!" Mortin bows and lightly kisses her hand. "Thank you, as always, for having me at the Boggolove. And thank you for taking care of my brother!"

"'*Celebrate* good times, *come on!*'" Leidan sings. "You got any drinks, Mortin? Iyatra says I can't deplete her emergency stores."

"No." I know that's a lie. Mortin still has the mind-melting Jiringian wine in his bag.

"Oh, that's convenient. I'm sure you've got plenty of pebbles, though."

"No, actually. I'm not smoking anymore."

"Yeah, right."

"It's true."

"You're just saying that to have one over on me."

"I made a personal decision, Leidan. I'm sticking to it."

"Who's your friend?" the frog-woman asks.

"Perry—I mean *Peregrine*—meet Iyatra, proprietor of the Boggolove."

I offer my hand. She doesn't shake it. Instead she puts out her own hand, palm down, and I kiss it. She smiles. Behind her wide teeth I see a strong, curling tongue.

"And you know Ada," Mortin continues. Ada curtsies but she looks pissed.

"Girls! It's safe! C'mon out!" A parade of frog-headed women stream up through the trapdoor, each dressed in the same sort of scantily enticing outfit as Iyatra. They aren't beautiful, on account of the heads, but I find it difficult not to stare. Their bodies are outrageous. They look around the bar and sigh and sob and hug one another and commiserate over how horrible everything is.

"It happened yesterday," Iyatra says. "I had a room full of customers, Mortin; you know how much I love that. Leidan came in and asked for me, said it was urgent. He explained that you all had to flee Subbenia on account of a legal snafu and were going to meet here. I told him it's no problem and asked if he wanted to tend a little bar, and of course he said yes, so he was behind the bar and my normal bartender had taken off when the cops stormed in! They demanded we hand over traitors loyal to Ophisa."

"They followed you," Mortin says to Leidan. "I thought

I told you to *avoid detection*. You can't follow simple instructions?"

"I tried! You don't think I tried?"

"Were you drinking?"

"Don't fight, you two. *Riggit!* The cops interrupted a big burlesque number my girls were doing. Batracians and celates, armed with spears and swords. They started pushing around all my customers. 'Name all the Appointees.' 'Do you respect and love our princess?' 'Does anyone in your family have pro-Ophisa sympathies?' I wasn't going to take it. I told them to get out. Then one of them pulled a gun."

"Oh no."

"I didn't know what to do. I'd never seen a gun before, only heard about them. You know it's not good to think about such things. *Riggit!*" She notices me staring at her. "You got a curious one there, huh? What are you going to do with him?"

"Send him back to Earth."

I don't protest because I'm trying to solve the mystery. "Who had the gun? Was it a celate? An octopus-man? With a bad mustache like from a seventies cop movie?"

"Seventies? No, no, he looked forty."

"Wait." I pull out the mustache comb I found. "Did he have a mustache he would use *this* on?"

"Yes! Yes he did!"

"Officer Tendrile."

"That's right!" Iyatra widens her eyes and clicks her big tongue. "He announced himself a few times, now that I remember. Very pompous. Officer Tendrile, on the warpath. But he didn't know how to handle the gun. As soon as he pulled it out, it went off, right into the air—see what he did to my chandelier? It was the loudest thing I ever heard. Everyone panicked. My customers jumped out of their chairs; they left their drinks on the tables, but we'll get to that. This squid-bottom Tendrile picks up the bullet, puts it in his pocket, and starts ordering people cuffed double-quick. Luckily we all know what to do. We have drills. I grab Leidan and my girls, and we stay in the safe pit as the cops take people out to the street. Then I hear *bangs*. We held one another; we were so scared. Then these brutes came back in and *took every last drop of my liquor*. Look at this. Not just from the bottles, from every glass on the table! Can you believe it? *Rilligig!*"

"You're lucky to be alive."

"I've got to get back to business. The Boggolove can't stay closed for long."

"Take a look outside," Mortin says. "Your whole town's gone."

78

WE SPEND THE REST OF THE DAY CLEANING
up the Boggolove, which is a "dance hall and leisure house"
according to Iyatra. First we wash the sulfurous mud off our
bodies. Mortin borrows some makeup from the hequets to
reconceal his black eye. I tend to my injuries. Iyatra takes an
hour to herself to weep over the loss of her town, but then she
says she never left her room without cleaning it since she was a
little girl, and she doesn't want to leave her place of business in
disarray now.

We put the chairs back. We get out a ladder to fix the chandelier. We sweep up the glass. Leidan is helpful and charming,
although he and Mortin argue. I get a chance to enter some of
the private rooms upstairs, which have sumptuous beds next to
tables with fat, worn-down candles. I'm assigned to help one
hequet and then another; they pass me around with great interest. They are dancers and "professional companions" to the male
other normals who travel through Upekki. As long as I block out
the frog-head part, they're the most attractive women I've ever
seen. Besides Ada.

"So what's it like on Earth?" one asks as I help her make a bed. Mortin and the others are downstairs talking. She wears a dress with a criminal V cut out of the middle, revealing the sides of pendulous breasts that bounce as she tucks in the sheets.

"It's . . . ah . . . it's more boring."

"But you have all these things. Televisions. Pants."

"It's all abstract. Symbols on top of symbols. You don't get adrenaline rushes like you do here."

"So you've never been in a fight?"

"Not before a few days ago. Now"—I look at myself—"I've been in a few. First in summer camp, then—"

"What's summer camp?"

"It's a place where especially cool human teenagers are sent to interact without parental supervision."

"Uh-*huh*," Ada says from the doorway. "Is that what summer camp is, Perry?" She walks in.

"I thought your name was Peregrine," the hequet says.

"What's up, Ada?"

"I'm just checking to make sure you're having a *good time*." She turns on her heel and leaves.

"Excuse me one second." I catch up with her in the hallway. "What's the matter?"

"Should I not have held your hand?"

"What?"

"When we came in here, I held your hand. Should I not have done that?"

"What—no—why?"

"Maybe you're one of those boys who needs to be treated badly in order to like somebody. I've studied a lot about humans, don't forget. I know that there are some guys who don't know what to do when a girl likes them, because deep down they think they're inadequate, and the only girls who *could* like them would have to have something wrong with them."

"Can we even do anything together?" I ask quietly. "I mean, we're different species, right?"

"*Do* anything? I'm not talking about sex. I'm talking about respect. Species boundaries don't seem to be stopping you now anyway. Why don't you go back and see if you can make your new friend's tongue curl up?"

"It's not like that," I say, but Ada's already stalking away, and it *is* like that. My Honor score is deteriorating. Maybe it's 30 now.

I return to the room to finish making the bed. I have a sudden flash of making the bottom bunk at Mom's, back when my biggest worry about mystical beings was whether I could roll the dice to defeat them in battle.

"Are you okay?" the hequet asks.

"Yeah, just . . . confused."

"That's the number one thing I hear about humans. You have all these choices, so you're confused all the time, and you think so much that you're never happy."

"Do you think a lot?"

"Only when I have to. The one you were just talking to? She thinks a lot too. When people think too much, they let out a little bit of sweat, and it has a sour smell."

"Do I have the smell?"

The hequet nods. "Worse than anybody."

79

WE COOK DINNER WITH FOOD FROM Iyatra's emergency stores. She doesn't serve any alcohol; she says she's saving it. Considering my experience with the wine the other night, I'm okay with that. We all sit in the main room under the now-fixed chandelier. I'm given a wild brown hunk of meat that makes me long for a side of mac & cheese. Ada isn't talking to me. I sort of expect that, but Mortin isn't talking to me either, and that makes me nervous. He bounces his leg under the table, like I often do.

"Stop," Leidan says, elbowing Mortin.

"What?"

"You're moving the whole table when you do that."

"We're not kids. You can't tell me what to do."

"You're making it so I can't enjoy my meal."

"You have food in your *hair*, you realize that?"

Leidan picks some meat out of his locks.

"Well," Iyatra says, like she's trying to make conversation, "I'm sure glad I expanded into floating entertainment. I learned some time ago that the Appointees were considering a 'morals' tax, you know, so I got myself a Boggolove cruise raft. If I'm in the water, I'm not on taxable land, am I? But I never expected it to be used for a quest." As she talks, Mortin shakes his head at her—*Shut up!*—but she doesn't notice.

"What quest?" I ask.

Nobody answers. Mortin shakes his leg harder.

"What *quest*?"

"We're going to the Badlands on the Boggolove cruise raft," Mortin says quickly.

"What? That's great! That's awesome! Why didn't you tell me?"

"You're not coming, Perry."

"Excuse me?"

"You're headed back to camp like we discussed."

"No I'm not." I put down my spork. Everybody uses sporks in the World of the Other Normals. "I'm *in* this now. You can't just ditch me and save the princess yourself."

"Maybe we're not saving the princess. Maybe there's no princess to save. You ever think about that?"

"What are you talking about?"

"Listen." Mortin addresses the whole table, which is actually two circular tables pressed together. The hequet dancing girls watch him. "Ever since we were born, we've heard about the princess and how she's honorable and virtuous and the pride of our world. But ever since she's been kidnapped, that world has gone to shit—pardon my English. Now everyone here is liable to get shot in the street at any time for being suspected in the princess's disappearance. Who gains?"

"The Appointees," Ada says.

"That's right. They keep giving themselves more and more power. To fight Ophisa, to save the princess . . . first they allowed the police to arrest and detain. Then they allowed them to kill. Now they've given them guns. We're turning into Earth!"

"That's why we've got to save her! So it'll all go back to normal."

"How do you know the princess even exists, Perry? Have you seen her?"

"I've seen the mini! Ada, where's that figure?"

Ada puts it on the table. I hold it up. The princess still looks beautiful and pure. Pure silver and pure something else.

"That's just a doll," Mortin says.

"This 'doll' winked at me, okay? She needs my help."

"You're seeing things," Ada says.

"It doesn't matter. Perry, if you want to save the princess so badly, stick to the original plan and kiss Anna at your camp. I did the analysis on that one. They correspond. But I'm starting to think this whole thing is a setup and the princess was never kidnapped. And I'm going to the Badlands to find out."

"And Ada's going with you."

"Yes."

"And your brother's going with you."

"I'm gonna try and dry out," Leidan says, staring at the water in front of him. He looks despondent, but then he claps Mortin on the back and perks up. "Maybe spending some time with my bro will do me good."

"They're quite serious; they've even refused professional companionship!" Iyatra says. "I said I could send one of my girls to keep the Enaws company, and they said they'd rather stay focused. Can you believe it? Mortin and Leidan, electing to keep their getmas on?"

"Mortin?" I say. "Fuck you."

I slam my chair back from the table and storm upstairs.

80

I LIE IN THE BED I MADE WITH THE HEQUET. I can't believe they want to send me back. Everyone else gets to do something important, and I get to go back to yurts and counselors and Ryu? What a joke. I should fight Mortin. I should get out my war hammer and bash his brains in and take over this quest myself. But I can't—I'm not strong enough. After everything, I'm still not.

"Perry?" Mortin pounds on the door. "Let me in!"

"Go away! It's locked!"

"You have to go back! You can't stay here!"

"I'd rather die!"

I hear whispers.

"Who's out there? Leidan? Ada? I hate *all* of you!" I know it sounds a little childish, but it's true. Even Ada, right now.

"Okay, Perry," Mortin says. "We understand you're upset. Get some rest. Can we talk about this in the morning?"

"I guess so."

"Good. Good night."

Their footsteps recede down the hall. Huh. Better than nothing. I sit up in bed. I guess this is one of those moments where I would read or play video games or mess around on the internet on Earth. It's funny how you don't miss that stuff. I think about all the arguments I can make in favor of me joining their quest: I picked Ada's handcuffs in prison; I stood up to Officer Tendrile; I never gave up against the cynos. I'm really not bad. I'm not. Someone knocks again.

"Who is it?"

"Come see."

It's a woman's voice, not Ada. The door has no peephole, so I have to open it to check. It's the hequet with the plunging V who got me in trouble before.

"What do you want?"

"Iyatra sent me to comfort you."

"Oh. That's not necessary."

"It looks necessary. May I come in?"

What the hell, I let her in. We sit on the bed. I watch her rounded bottom distort the sheets. My body reacts to hers and, even though I don't want to, even though I shouldn't for a lot of reasons, I flare up down below. I turn to the side to hide myself.

"Don't be ashamed. I saw you look at me before." She leans in. Her frog head is scary, but her breasts look so good!

"Wait! Stop! Is this like . . . are you trying to do this for *di-*?"

She shakes her head. She opens her mouth. I see her long tongue. I don't want to brag, but if I go through with this and I go back to camp, I'll have something unique to talk about. I can be like, "Hey, not only am I not a virgin, I lost my virginity to a *frog-headed exotic dancer*." Will that be something to brag about or something to be ashamed of? It's funny; that was always clear to me before.

I let my Honor drop to 0 and close my eyes and open my mouth to kiss the hequet.

Something bitter drips onto my tongue.

I snap my eyes open. The hequet is squeezing her cheek, pushing out drops of green fluid that *plat* into my mouth.

"Agh! Hepatodes!" I try to kick her away, but she holds me down. I clamp my mouth shut but I can already feel the tiny creatures spreading along my tongue and commingling with my spit.

"I thought—*ptttt*—only male hequets—"

She smiles. "First impressions." She has a much deeper voice all of a sudden, and I remember the telltale sign you're supposed to look for with men versus women: the Adam's apple. I never thought to look for an Adam's apple on an other normal!

"Are you . . ." I start. I try to say, *Are you going to kill me?* but my tongue has gone heavy and dead. It protests the whole idea of working for me and sits in my mouth like a hunk of fish. My toes clench up. My feet freeze. I try to grab the hequet to escape, but my hands won't respond.

Mortin, Ada, Leidan, and Iyatra walk into the room.

81

WHAT'RE YOU DOING? I TRY TO YELL, BUT it comes out "Hrrgrbbbb . . ."

"You got him?" Mortin says.

"Secure," the hequet says.

"Poor guy," Leidan says. "I don't blame you, little traveler. It could have happened to any of us."

"Not *me*," Ada says. "I can't believe you, Perry. I didn't think you'd go for it."

"Earth men are all animals," Iyatra says. "This one was well-behaved, to tell the truth."

Mortin slings me over his shoulder. "Perry, sorry it had to end like this, but we saw no other choice."

"Nurrr . . . ," I say. My war hammer sits useless on the bedside table.

"The hequet poison will wear off soon. You'll be fine." Mortin carries me out of the room. My eyes face the floor. I see Ada's sparkling toenails as she follows us to the stairs. I try to beat Mortin but I can't move.

"Consider yourself lucky," Ada says. "We can't do an orbitoclasty on you here, so you're going to remember all this. Most people who come never remember." Downstairs, Mortin carries me behind the bar. Leidan pulls the lever to open the trap-door. Iyatra waves good-bye with her dancing girls, and they all curtsy to me. The male, the one who poisoned me, bows.

"Don't tell anyone about us when you go back," Mortin says. "They'll just send you to the mental institution."

Below the bar, in the "safe pit," Ada lights candles on the wall. We're surrounded by bottles and barrels—Leidan looks at them longingly, but I guess he really is trying to dry out because he shakes his head and pulls aside a burlap sheet on the floor. A thakerak sparks underneath, like it expects me.

No! Let me go! I want to scream, but what comes out? "Uhhhrrrrrr . . ."

"It's okay, Perry," Ada says. "Next time just be a little more suspicious when strange women come into your bedroom."

"*Mmmmmrrrrr!*" I manage, which is the paralyzed way to say, *I'm sorry; I don't hate you; I actually might love you!*

"Check his wounds," Mortin orders. Leidan looks at my palms, my leg, my ankle.

"They'll think he just fell. It's not a very good camp, right?"

"It's a ghetto camp, Perry," Mortin says, "I want you to understand something. I owe you my life. In addition to that, I think you're a pretty cool guy and I've had a good time hanging out with you. I have a feeling we'll see each other again. But for now, you have to put all this behind you. You never should have gotten caught up in it, and it got out of hand. If I hadn't had my addiction to pebbles—and you know now I have two days clean, that's a big step—I never would have been smoking over in your world, and I never would have been caught by you, and I never would have had to bring you over here for correspondence analysis, and so on. So just think about it as a really great dream and go back to your life, and let us worry about the princess and Ophisa and all the rest. Enjoy being safe."

Dead, I want to tell him. I'm dead when I'm safe. All my life I've been dead and I didn't even know it.

"You remember how this works, right?" Ada asks. Mortin rests me on the thakerak. *"Don't* think of Camp Washiska Lake. . . ."

I try not to think of something else so that I think of something else. I try not to think of India, Australia, Antarctica, a place I can appear and instantly be killed so this will all be over. But the brain is a slippery thing. The image that comes to me instead is *me*, in the dining hall, pulling my pants down—I am going back to a world where I've just made an irretrievable fool of myself—I can't—*please*—I'd rather—

The thakerak springs to life and sends me back to

CAMP

WASH

HISKA
LAKE

82

THE ITCHING HARDLY BOTHERS ME THIS
time. I come to on the ground in the dark and as soon as I
feel it, I hit myself—a good strong punch to the face—and
it dissipates. I crawl to Sam's clothes, which I left by the tree.
Someone's messed with them. I remember leaving the pants
folded with the shirt on top; now the shirt is folded with the
pants on top. I spin around. I was followed.

"Dale?"

It has to be Dale. I think back to the acne handout I got at
the nurse's office, the one where I wrote *Ryu = Eric Chin*. I need
another paper and pencil, to write *Dale Blaswell = Officer Tendrile*. It's not just the mustache; Dale was following me when
I escaped the dance. Then, when I went to the World of the
Other Normals, Officer Tendrile was following me. That can't
be a coincidence.

But he's not here now. Maybe the light of me coming back
scared him. Or maybe Dale is biding his time because he
knows about the World of the Other Normals. Maybe that's
why he works here. Maybe he knows what a "special place"
Camp Washiska Lake really is.

Screw him. I raise my foot over the patch of mushrooms next to the Logo Spermatikoi battery. I pause—*do I want to do this?*—*yes*—I slam my foot down and squish them all, over and over, flattening them into a pale paste, cursing as I do. I know it doesn't make a lot of sense, but when you get emotional, things that make no sense make a lot of sense. I probably spend forty-five seconds stomping on the mushrooms before I realize—*how am I going to get back?*

"No no no . . . ," I say. I kneel down and touch the negative end of the battery. I put my finger in the mushroom biomass. Nothing. I'm stuck on Earth.

"No!"

I spot Mortin's tail lighter, still by the tree. I go stomp on that until it's splinters in the dirt. That makes me feel better, and I don't mind that I'm barefoot: I have soles of steel.

I put on Sam's clothes one by one—like a small boy, like an old man. I'm crying but I don't acknowledge the tears. I let them fall to the ground without wiping my face as I walk back to camp wondering what the hell I'm going to do.

83

MAYBE I SHOULD BURN DOWN CAMP.
See what kind of correspondence *that* causes for my "friends" in
the World of the Other Normals. Maybe I should tell everyone
what happened and test out some padded walls for a while. I
want to hurt Mortin; I want to hurt Ada; I want to hurt myself.
Then I realize one thing I can do: I can actually kiss Anna
Margolis.

They don't think I'm up to it—Mortin hardly even asked
me this time. They've given up on me. But I'd like Ada to know
it happened. I'd like her to *watch* me kiss Anna, actually, and
see how that feels. It's going to be challenging (because of the
whole indecent exposure thing), but I can handle a challenge;
I already have. I'd like to do it to prove to Ada that it was
wrong to trick me and send me back. Not to save the princess:
fuck the princess. I'd like to do it out of spite. I know spite is
supposed to be a terrible emotion, but it stops my tears from
falling and puts a smile on my face and gets me motivated as
I get back to the dining hall.

The music of the dance is still pumping out. The banner
is still over the door: WELCOME TO CAMP WASHISKA LAKE!

I don't see any counselors looking for me or girls comforting Anna. Did something happen to *erase* what I did? How incredible would that be? It would be like coming back from the dead!

I put my hand on the wooden banister and go up the steps. Inside, boys and girls are distributed in the same formations I left them in. The wallflowers are still on the wall; the dancers are still dancing for one another's benefit; Miss K is still at the punch bowl. I *did* it—or my correspondent did. I took it back!

I jump and click my heels; I can't think of another appropriate action. A kid sees me and snickers, and I snicker right back. What a stroke of luck. Now, where's Anna?

"Perry!" a voice calls behind me. "What're you so happy about?"

Standing at the wall—a wallflower, who knew—is my brother. He has his head bent to one side and his shoulders slung back in the kind of pose he always uses to get people to notice him.

"Jake?" I do a double take. I hug him. I haven't hugged my brother in a long time.

"Whoa, whoa! What's the matter? Everything okay?"

"How'd you get here?"

"Excuse me? I work here. C'mon, Perry, you're embarrassing me!" He hugs back reluctantly. He feels like a man. And he doesn't smell like liquor.

"Jake—I didn't expose myself to any women at this dance, right?"

"Not that I *know* of . . . Why?"

"And our parents, they're not dead, right? No bad corre-spondences?"

"What are you talking about?"

"Just come outside for two seconds." I pull him onto the dining hall porch.

84

JAKE LOOKS SO MUCH BETTER: CLEAR-eyed, open, *younger*. His hair is cut short, like mine. (Well, not quite like mine: I still have the three-quarter bowl going on because of the knife other-normal Ryu threw at me.)

"Tell me everything. Please. Pretend I know nothing. How'd you get here? What are you, a counselor?"

"I'm a counselor's assistant. You know that. I saw you, like, five minutes ago."

"You didn't go to rehab?"

"*Rehab?* That's weird—I had a *dream* about rehab. It was one of those middle-of-the-day nap dreams just before dinner. Why?"

I laugh. Inside, the crowd whoops as DJ Cowboy Pete cues up a thick summer jam. For the first time, I think it might be fun to go in and dance. Not obligatory, not part of some mission. Fun.

"Have you ever heard of a person named Mortin Enaw?"

"No. Is that a real name?"

"Have you ever been to a place called the World of the Other Normals?"

"No. Are you on drugs?"

"That's the next question. Do you do drugs?"

Jake leans in close. "That's none of your business."

"I think I know who your correspondent is."

"What?"

"I can't believe he didn't tell me. Thank God he stopped smoking pebbles. The whole time we were there, we were changing you, and now look at you—you look better!"

"What are you *talking* about?"

"I just—the universe isn't all the same, okay? There are some universes where people do different things. There's a universe where Mom and Dad are married and a universe where they never met. And I know for sure there's a universe where you're in rehab, and—"

"Perry, maybe you should go to the nurse—"

"And remember what you told me about the *Odyssey* and honor? You're right, you *can't* be honorable all the time. Heroes lie—"

"Perry." He grabs my shirt and shakes me.

"Whoa. Are you allowed to do that, as a camp employee?"

"I'm allowed to do whatever it takes to calm you down."

"I need my book. The *Other Normal Edition.* And my pewter mini. The nurse said they were in Dale's cabin. Can I get them back?"

"What are you talking about? What book?"

"Creatures and Caverns? The game I play?"

"You don't play any role-playing games. Jesus. Girls hate that stuff. C'mon, we need to go back in. This is the only coed activity for a week, you know that?"

85

I DON'T PLAY ANY ROLE-PLAYING GAMES?
How can I not play role-playing games? That would be like
coming back to Earth and suddenly being gay!

"All *right*!" DJ Cowboy Pete says into his mic. I'm back
inside; Jake is doing his counselor-assistant duties by breaking up a pair of campers who are dancing pornographically. "It
looks like everyone's having a great time, but are you ready—
are you set—for the *chicken dance*?"

The crowd groans. I approach Sam. Ryu and his henchmen
eye me—whatever crazy correspondences I've set into motion,
they still seem to hate me. I couldn't care less. "Hey, Sam, what's
the chicken dance?"

"Can't talk, man." Sam's chatting with a girl. I back off.
I guess I haven't made him any more willing to interact with
me. I try to look cool, standing with my head cocked, like my
brother did by the wall.

"Please form a square," DJ Cowboy Pete says. "This *is* a
square dance, so don't be shy. Boy-girl, boy-girl, find a partner
and give it a whirl."

The counselors start herding us into a human square. I see

that the people who aren't proactive, who don't grab someone, end up next to someone they don't know or like. I spot Anna across the room and approach.

"Hi, I'm Peregrine. Remember?"

"Uh, hi. I think when we met, you called yourself Perry."

"That works too. I'm getting more comfortable with both. You want to dance with me?"

"The *chicken* dance, you mean?"

"If that's what we're doing. It'd be a real honor."

"Have you ever *done* the chicken dance? It's not an honor."

"I haven't. Can you tell?"

Anna smiles. "You look different."

"Better?"

"Less nervous. I guess I have to admit that's better."

We get in the square as DJ Cowboy Pete announces, "Here we go!" and starts up some music that sounds like a demented local mattress commercial. "The chicken dance goes like this!" He folds one arm in front of his face and sticks his wrist over his nose so that his hand sticks out like a beak. "With a beak beak beak!"

He waves his hand up and down, imitating a chicken's beak.

"And a wing wing wing!"

He folds his arms out and sticks his hands under his armpits, flapping up and down.

"And a tail tail tail!"

He pushes his rear end out and bops it up and down.

"Bwak bwak bwak bwak!"

The music makes chicken noises in sync with the DJ. Then it repeats, "With a beak beak beak! And a wing wing wing! And a tail tail tail!" as he does the same absurd motions. Then it goes into an incongruous lilting bridge with an Italian feel. It's the dumbest piece of music I've ever heard, and there's no way anyone is going to—

I turn to my left, and there's Anna, beak-beak-beaking. I ready my hand at my nose. Around the room, everyone in the square is chicken dancing, from the hardest-edged boys to . . . well . . . *me*.

"Second time's the best! Switch to your left! Chicken Dance a-*gain*!"

I switch positions with Anna, shaking my tail-tail-tail at her while the music cavorts along. I'm dancing! Not like last time, when I was dancing in a way that was going to get me made fun of. In the chicken dance, it'd be foolish to get made fun of; it'd be tautological.

"Let's meet!" I yell at Anna over the music.

Propose that you meet in a romantic location to continue your conversation.

"What?"

"Let's meet, me and you!"

"Like a *date*?" She laughs.

"Yeah, exactly like that!"

"I'm on the other side of the lake!"

"So? It's a little trickle of water! I'll walk across!"

"What are you talking about? It's a *lake*."

"It's full?"

"Yes!"

"Huh. Then I'll sneak over in a canoe!"

"You wouldn't!"

"I would. I will!"

"One week, then!"

"One week from tonight?"

"Yeah!"

"Midnight! I'll meet you at the girls' waterfront!"

"You're crazy!"

"I know!"

"Bwak bwak bwak bwak!"

We switch partners. I face Ryu. He stands there with his arms folded. "You think you're cool?" he asks.

"Ryu! Why don't you chicken dance?"

"No, don't *touch* me, okay? I'm here to give you a message. You ever heard of White Lotus Crew?"

"Ah . . . no?"

"That's who's gonna kill you. You understand? *Kill you.*" Ryu puts his hands up to his nose and does a beak-beak-beak.

86

WE SLEEP ON THE FLOOR IN THE YURT.
I understand academically that this is how yurts work, but it's
not until I'm down there, with my feet facing the center, in
my underwear on top of my sleeping bag, that I realize what a
terrible setup it is. Jaxson, Kolby, George, JB, Ryu, Sam, and I
produce a heap of nocturnal sweat. Everyone's odors combine
to form one rank nimbus.

Even if I were in a fragrant spa, I wouldn't be able to sleep;
I'm worried about Ryu's "White Lotus Crew." I end up getting
strange snatches of half-sleep where I dream I'm fighting a gas
demon.

Breakfast is at eight in the morning, back in the dining hall.
It's bright and cavernous—all the boys from all the age groups
fit inside at once. It smells so much like breakfast food—like
eggs and bacon and those diced potatoes that you only find
in hotel buffets—that I think I might pass out. My whole
body aches. My leg feels freshly bitten. Across the room, the
kitchen door swings back and forth. Inside are the steam and
machinery needed to feed two hundred campers and counselors
three times a day. The younger boys surround us like horrible

reminders of what we used to be. They're yelling, chewing, scraping plates . . . kids are fighting over *orange juice*. Once you take soda away, it's amazing what people will fight over. Our counselor, Ken, sits with our yurt, drinking a muscle shake.

"How are you two doing today?" he asks me and Ryu. "Getting along?"

"Ask him," Ryu says.

"We're fine," I say, but Ryu gives me the death eyes and mouths, *White Lotus Crew*. I edge toward Ken. "Is there any chance I can change yurts?"

"Just let me enjoy my protein. Don't you want some food?"

I look at what my yurtmates are eating: thin soggy waffles doused with syrup and flecked with hard butter on bright pastel plates with cloudy plastic cups of water and juice. I want fresh fish. I want crab.

"This is the stuff right here," JB says, grabbing the syrup dispenser, whose sides are caked in layers of hardened syrup, and dumping it on his eggs. I never understood how people can do that.

"I'm going to talk to my friends in yurt three," Ryu says, standing up.

"No you're not—get—*Ryu!*"

He walks off without a look back. Ken sighs and refocuses on his shake. Ryu goes two tables away to confer with his henchmen, kicking a thumb at me.

"Is that the White Lotus Crew?" I ask JB.

"That's right, son. Big one they call Tiny; the other one they call the Silver Eel. You shouldn't have messed with Ryu."

"I still did? What did I do? Beat him up?"

"Yeah. You don't know about White Lotus?"

"What are they, a gang?"

"Yeah. They stabbed a taxi driver."

"*What?*"

"Initiation rite. Put him in the hospital for three weeks. Aren't you from New York? Everyone knows White Lotus."

"I go to kind of a—"

"White school?"

"Well—yeah. What do you mean, *stabbed* a taxi driver? Was he in on it?"

"Excuse me?"

"Was it like part of a performance-art piece?"

"Nuh-uh. He got *stabbed.*"

I watch Ryu discuss some plan with Tiny and the Silver Eel—his *fellow gang members.* He outlines a scheme on his palm like a football player.

"Have you ever stabbed anybody?" I ask JB.

"*Pfff.* Have *you?*"

"What if I have? Would you respect me?"

"I don't know what you'd have to do to get me to respect you. Probably talk less."

I don't say anything.

"It's the quiet people who get respect. You don't know that? How come I'm even talking to you right now? Here I am giving out free advice. It's because *I* like to talk. Don't get it twisted."

"I don't understand. I beat Ryu in a fight. Doesn't that mean he's supposed to respect *me* now? Isn't that how it happens—you defeat the bully and then he's nice to you?"

"That only works with people who *aren't* in gangs," Sam says.

"Sam! You're talking to me! Thank you!" I nudge Sam's shoulder, but he shakes his head and goes back to eating his eggs. My body sags. I finish eating breakfast without another word, trying to earn people's respect.

87

AS DALE BLASWELL CHAIRS ANOTHER
Hideaway Village powwow, I examine him for signs that he
corresponds to Officer Tendrile. Besides his mustache and
general imperious attitude, I don't get any clues. He explains
that we need to fill out sheets to select *electives* for the next
week: camp activities like canoeing, nature studies, archery. . . .
Clearly the best is archery. They don't have sword fighting or
hand-to-hand combat, so I put *archery, archery,* and *archery* as
my choices.

"You're not getting archery," my brother says, collecting my
sheet. "They're still mad at you about the fight. You're gonna
get nature studies for sure."

"Can you help me?"

"I'll try."

I get nature studies. It's the worst: a thin woman with red
hair brings me and ten other campers into a sweltering cabin
by Lake Henderson, which is, like Anna said, now filled with
water. (I wonder why—did I do something in the World of the
Other Normals to change it? Maybe it was seeing that small
creek turn into the Warbledash River.) While other kids swim

and frolic in the lake, we stay in the cabin looking at books of lizards and frogs. A week ago I would have been thrilled to study lizards and frogs, I really would, but now I don't want to read about them; I want to capture them, free them, feel them. And I want them to be on human bodies and have weapons and be able to talk.

Next to me is Sam, who got relegated to nature studies too, but every time I open my mouth to speak to him, he shies away or finds something interesting to look at on his hands. He talks to Jaxson and Kolby, and when he catches me looking at them, he turns in, closing off their circle.

After nature studies I check out the canoe shed by Lake Henderson. This is where I'm going to steal a canoe in six days to travel to Anna. It's a six-foot-tall wooden shack, long enough to keep ten canoes stacked on one another, next to a short pebbled beach in front of the lake. A rusty padlock holds the shed's door shut. I remember Ada, in jail: *These local locks, cheap.*

I grab a paper and pen from nature studies. In our yurt after lunch, lying on the floor between Jaxson and George, I write out my best guesses as to what's happening.

1) Mortin Enaw = Jake

They both have substance-abuse problems that they now seem to be overcoming; they both have chaotic, seesawing issues with authority; they both think they're intelligent. The thing is, if Mortin's my brother, who does that make Leidan? *Me?* That's not possible, because Mortin told me that if I met my correspondent, everything would go haywire for me. Also,

Jake is seventeen; Mortin seems forty-five. But the fact is, Mortin changed and then Jake changed. They have to match. I just hope the change lasts.

2) X = you

Somebody corresponds to me, and I have to have caused some big changes in that person's life, because I erased my actions with Anna and apparently made it so I don't play Creatures & Caverns anymore, *and* I have another hair. I can't think what I did, or what was done to my correspondent, but the answer feels like it's at the tip of my brain. It's maddening.

3) Where are the book and the miniature?

If I don't play Creatures & Caverns now, did I ever play it? And are the *Other Normal Edition* and Pekker Cland mini disappeared, or are they still in Dale's cabin? Something tells me there's a clue there—especially since Mortin was a special consultant on the book. . . .

"Mail!" Ken says, tossing a letter at me.

"Already?"

"Guess somebody loves you."

"*Pussy*," says JB.

The envelope is addressed in Dad's blocky script.

Dear Perry,

I write you from home, having left you and your brother at camp. Thank you for spending time with him these past few months. I don't know what you did, but when Jake said that he wanted to be a counselor's assistant, that was a big turn-around, and I know it had something to do with you.

Love,
Dad

PS If you can, get a picture of yourself with a girl and send it, please, so that your mother will get off my back about you doing well at camp.

I fold the letter up and put it in my pocket. If Dad wants a picture, he'll get one.

88

KEN RUNS THE CANOEING ELECTIVE, which I wheedle my way into by the end of the week. I've never been in a canoe before, but Ken makes it easy: he shows us bow (sitting in the front of the canoe) and stern (sitting in the back, where you have to steer); he explains port for left and starboard for right; he demonstrates back strokes, J-strokes, and sweeps. The main thing he emphasizes is that canoeing is a two-person activity. "It's deadly to canoe alone unless you have lots of experience," he warns.

Well. That's where Sam is going to come in.

Canoeing takes place on Lake Henderson at two p.m. every day. At the end of each session, as we boys watch the girls across the lake swim and wave and call out and be unattainable, Ken always asks for someone to help him put away the life preservers; I always volunteer. The other kids make fun of me for being a kiss-ass (a "white kiss-ass," specifically), but this is what allows me to further reconnoiter the shed where the canoes and life preservers are stored. The rusty lock opens with a key that Ken keeps on a chain of official camp keys, including keys to magical places like the storage room in the dining hall (where soda is reportedly stashed) and the female counselors' cabins on the other side of the lake.

On day eight (12.5 percent of my full sentence at camp), after putting away the life preservers and locking the door, I slip the key off and pocket it. Ken doesn't notice when I give him back the key chain. It's the first time I've used any of my RPG skills at camp, and it feels good; I grin all the way through dinner with the stolen key in my pocket. When I'm done with my plan, I figure, I'll leave the key in the lock, wiping it for fingerprints, and someone'll find it the next morning.

I'm not going to steal a canoe. I'm just going to borrow one. I can barely get through the day, I'm so excited. I want to explode and tell everyone what I'm up to. I'll have to settle for telling the one person who I hope will get it. Time passes slowly at camp; the sun lounges in the sky, and clocks in cabins (old, cookie-cutter clocks with dust on top like at school) take breaks to go backward when you aren't looking. It's the sort of pacing adults say they love, but I can't stand it. I prefer slowed-down adrenaline time.

Finally, night covers Camp Washiska Lake a week after the square dance, and we all go to our yurts to sleep.

89

I WAIT UNTIL NINE. MY YURTMATES AND I lie on the floor in our sleeping bags. This is when you're allowed to read, but nobody in our group reads. Maybe I'll be reading, soon, if I get my *Other Normal Edition* back, but the funny thing is I don't miss it. Anytime I want to read *Creatures & Caverns,* I think back to the real creatures and caverns I've fought in and escaped from. My memories are crystal clear—Ada was right; they did me a favor by not giving me an "orbitoclasty"—and they make me smile to myself with a kind of satisfaction I haven't felt before. Even if no one knows what I've done, they can't take away that I've done it.

I try to do mind-over-matter to deal with the developing boy-sweat smell. Ken is off at a counselor meeting with Dale; he'll come in later. I have my clothes on inside my sleeping bag, but no shoes.

The plan is simple: the other kids in my yurt might be cooler than me, and better with the lyrics to rap songs, and more knowledgeable about New York City gangs, but they haven't encountered creatures like I have. I'm going to bet on their fear of creatures.

"Yo, that's what I'm sayin'," Kolby says. "When we gonna have another dance?"

"Next week, I heard." Jaxson.

"I liked that one girl I was talking to, remember?" JB. I know all the voices now. "She's got what you call the ass *shelf.* You could put a Dr Pepper on that shelf."

Quietly, carefully, I reach out of my sleeping bag and run a fingernail across the floor. *Skkkkkkkkkkkritch!*

"What's that?" JB sits up in his sleeping bag. Moonlight comes through the screen door and illuminates his chest, which is strangely concave. "You hear that?"

"What?" George asks.

Wait for it . . . wait for it . . . *skkkkkkkkkkratch.*

"That's a raccoon! Right Jaxson?"

"I dunno!"

"Don't they got rabies?"

I lie very still, controlling my breath to keep from laughing.

"It's not a raccoon," Ryu says.

Skkkratch. Skritchskritch.

"Yes it is! Damn! It's coming in here to bite us! We gotta get it! Sam, you awake? Wake up Perry-bitch. Call Ken. This is an animal attack!"

Sam looks at me. I wink. It's a dangerous move. He could switch right then and report me. He avoided me all week. I didn't bother him, and he didn't bother me. I have to rely on the wink to bring back memories from home, from when we were lost in our own world by the fire stairs, because I know those memories and I can't believe they've been entirely erased.

Sam shakes me lightly. "I can't wake him up," he says. "You really think it's a raccoon? What are you gonna do?"

"Kill it! C'mon!" JB rounds up Jaxson, Kolby, George, and Ryu. "Get sticks. We gotta kill it before it gives us AIDS!"

"I don't hear it anymore," Ryu says.

Skkkkkrrrrratch.

"That's it!"

All the campers besides Sam put on their clothes and head out of the yurt. "I'll stay here and protect our stuff," Sam says.

"Yeah, and if he wakes up, tell him he's missing out. We're gonna kill something!"

When the last of them is out the door, Sam grabs me. "What are you doing?"

"*Shh.*" I unzip my sleeping bag. "Put your clothes on and get your backpack. We're going."

"Where?"

"On an adventure. Unless—am I not cool enough for you?"

"Well, you just did one of the coolest things I've ever seen."

Outside, JB yells, "There it is! Get it!" We hear the thud of sticks pounding the forest floor as we escape the yurt and head around the edge of Hideaway Village.

90

"ARE WE GOING ON A RAID?" SAM ASKS.
His backpack slaps against him as we hustle through the trees.
I showed him how to step on roots and rocks.

"What's a raid?"

"A raid's when you sneak into one of the other yurts at night
and trash everything. Usually you wait until they're doing a
campout. And sometimes you do it to the girls. It's a Washiska
Lake tradition."

"That's horrible!"

"I'm not saying we should do it. I'm asking you. Or maybe
we're going the dining hall to steal soda? I heard they got soda
in the storage room. Cigarettes, too."

"No. We're going to Dale's cabin."

"Why?"

"Sam." I stop. He pushes his glasses up his nose. The night
is calm and warm around us; crickets buzz. Through the trees,
I see the bathroom and the clearing with the picnic benches.
"Did we ever play Creatures and Caverns together?"

Sam seems worried that spies in the trees will report his
answer. "Yes. We used to. You don't remember?"

"Remind me."

"You stopped when we came to camp. You said you didn't need it anymore. We used to play near the fire exit at your school."

"Yes!" I hug him. He isn't quick enough to resist. I squeeze him tight and feel his cheek against my hair.

"What's wrong with you? You know we used to play that!"

"Hold on, I'm not done. How come you treat me like crap at camp all the time?"

"What do you mean? I don't—"

"Yes you do. Maybe I'm just your home friend and not your camp friend, but what's the deal? It's confusing."

Sam sighs. "You're kind of . . ."

"Weird?"

"Yeah, Perry. You've always been like that. I don't mind—I *like* it—but around other people you could just, you know . . . hold back a little."

"Dial it down."

"Yeah."

"Okay. I'll dial it down if you stop treating me like crap."

"Deal."

We shake. "Now come with me; we're going to get my *Rule Book* and my Pekker Cland miniature."

"*That's* dialing it down?"

"Wait until you see what I have planned for the rest of the night!"

91

WE SNEAK AROUND THE BATHROOM toward Dale's cabin, which is not a yurt. The camp director doesn't sleep in a yurt. He gets a place that looks like a stylized house drawn by a preschooler: single door, two windows to either side, slanted roof. It's quiet; the lights are off.

"We could get in a lot of trouble for this," Sam says. "The dining hall is one thing. You're talking about the guy who runs the whole camp."

"Don't worry about it. I've done more dangerous things."

"Yeah? When?"

I smile at him. "In another universe."

"Excuse me?"

"I went to another world." I can't not tell him. I have to let it out. "It's better than Creatures and Caverns. I think it's why I stopped playing, because it's *like* Creatures and Caverns, but real."

"Don't mess with me, Perry."

"It's true. If you stick with me, I'll tell you all about it. After we get my stuff, though, we've got to go down to the lake and get a canoe."

"What?"

"You know how to canoe, right?"

"I can be bow, not stern."

"No problem. We're going across the lake to meet Anna Margolis."

"No! You and her?"

"Yes. We arranged a date."

"What am I gonna do while you're macking it to her?"

"'Macking it'?"

"You know what I mean."

"I don't know, stand guard? I'm not gonna hook up hardcore with her. I just want to kiss her. That would be a personal victory for me."

We creep closer to Dale's cabin. There's no movement inside. Sam chuckles. "You and Anna hooking up is harder to believe than you going to another universe."

"Very funny. I already talked to her. I would've told you about it, but you were being a dick. If you want out, tell me; I'll canoe over by myself."

"No, no. You'll drown."

Inside the cabin, through the window, we see a tidy bed and a fold-out table holding milk crates full of confiscated goods. "I bet they got my comics from last year," Sam says.

"Don't get distracted. We're looking for my backpack."

Sam picks up a rock and rears back—

"Stop!" I grab his arm.

"What? How we gonna get in?"

"I can pick locks." I go to the door, shaking my head. If Sam's going to be the impulsive crazy adventurer, I have to be the smart leader. This lock is my first test. I don't have any tools like last time with Ada, but I'm counting on all the movies I've seen where people pick locks with credit cards. Step one: stick a credit card in the seam of a door. Step two: slide it up and down. *Click.* The universal metaphor again.

"You have your library card, Sam?"

He hands it to me. It's green and worn; it's definitely been through the wash.

"Don't tell anybody I carry that around."

"You know I won't."

"How'd you know I brought it to camp?"

"Because I've never seen you happier than when you're telling me about some book on Egypt."

I stick the card in the side of the door. I slide it down to the doorknob; it meets resistance. I wiggle it. I can feel the piece of metal that sticks from the door into the door frame; I just need to get around it—

"Move," Sam says. He grabs the card, closes his eyes, and sticks out his tongue. He slides the card up and down, wedges it to the side, and . . . *click.*

"Nice!"

"My mom locks me out sometimes."

92

I DON'T DARE TURN THE LIGHT ON. We let moonlight and light from the Hideaway Village bathroom illuminate Dale's cabin. I check for spike traps and trip wires. The world is back to being difficult and exciting.

Sam points two fingers at his eyes and then across the room, at the table with the confiscated goods. We tiptoe to it. One of the crates holds comic books. Sam separates out the ones he claims are his. I search for my backpack. Sam opens a shoe box.

"Look!"

Knives. Dozens of pocketknives, probably the result of many years of confiscations.

"Pick out the best ones. I've got a gang threatening me, remember."

Sam goes to work. In the corner I spot a pile of backpacks and dig in. Mine is near the top: a black L.L. Bean bag with a white splotch from a Wite-Out incident last year (part of why I prefer mechanical pencils). I unzip it. The *Creatures & Caverns Rule Book: Other Normal Edition* stares back at me, with the genie over the pirate ship on the cover. The amount of time I spent in there—insane . . .

"Here, take these," Sam says, handing me two of the choicest knives from the box. "And check this."

He pulls out a Polaroid camera from a milk crate of electronics. "Vintage." He stuffs it into his backpack. My own bag feels comforting on my back, like armor. "You see your mini anywhere?"

I shake my head.

"Is that it?" Sam points to a small table next to Dale's bed. There he is: shiny pewter, kneeling over a forge with his war hammer.

"Perfect! Let's go." I put him in my pocket.

"Let me check something." Sam opens another shoe box.

Cigarettes. Menthols, lights, reds . . . glistening, vibrant packs.

"No, Sam. You don't need those."

"Speak for yourself."

"You *don't*. I know why you smoke—you're nervous. But there's gotta be a better way to handle it."

"They've got Special Blend, though!"

"Look!" I dash outside and pull up some grass. "Put *this* in your mouth. It's an oral-fixation thing. See?" I chew some blades like Mortin Enaw did. Maybe *Sam* is who he corresponds to. "*Mmm* . . . tastes like . . . chlorophyll."

Sam laughs. I hand him some grass. He nibbles it. "Could use a bit of Worcestershire," he says in an English accent.

"Seriously, Sam . . . it's not good for you. I have a friend who smoked, and it really messed him up."

"Who?"

"You don't know him."

"I'll take the Special Blend. That's it. You never know when you're gonna have to bargain with cigarettes prison-style."

Sam zips his bag shut. We close Dale's door and head into the woods. I stop, as soon as I feel we're safe, and look at the Pekker Cland figure.

"What's wrong?"

"I think this looks like me."

93

THE FOREST MURMURS AND SNAPS AS
we go to Lake Henderson; we follow the road a little way off
to avoid any counselors or other kids on raids. On the water,
the moon looks like a shimmering spotlight. I inspect Pekker
Cland; there's no question: he has my facial features now.
Big eyebrows, full lips, wide nose, *bowl haircut*—he's more
Peregrine Eckert–like than before.

"I don't get it," Sam says. "What does that mean? Is it
magic?"

"There's no such thing as magic, according to Ada. Maybe
Mortin can explain."

"Who?"

I sigh. "It's a long story. You ready?"

We sit on the pebbled beach. I put Pekker Cland in my
backpack and tell Sam everything. I begin with Mortin and
the car battery in the woods, and then Ada, Officer Tendrile,
Leidan, the dog-heads, the death of Gamary, the transsexual
hequet, and my ignominious return. (I don't say anything about
the indecent-exposure interlude in the middle, since now that
hasn't happened.) It feels good to talk. Sam starts out calling

me a liar every few minutes, but as I fill in the details, he comes around, asking questions that make me think.

"So when you go through a thakerak, you can't bring anything with you?"

"Your clothes vanish. I assume not."

"Because if we could bring pebbles over there, we'd be rich as shit! And where did Mortin get the lighter that he has on Earth?"

"I don't know, maybe one of those head shops."

"Probably. Like one of the crazy ones. And what do they use for money?"

"Gold coins. But the word for money is one of those words you can't understand. It's like *di-*."

"Well, you don't have to *say* money to *get* money. Did you like it over there?"

I look at the stars, above stringy clouds. "I miss it."

"You could be having a florid hallucination, you know. An extended psychotic break."

"Do you think I am?"

"Nah. You remember my policy on pyramids, right?"

"'Until someone explains the pyramids, how'm I going to take life serious'?"

"That's right. Maybe the other normals *built* the pyramids."

94

FOR A HORRIBLE SINKING MOMENT I can't find the key in my pocket; then I feel it at the very bottom. I unlock the rusty padlock on the canoe shed. The chain unwinds and slides to the pebbles below. I open the door. Three bats fly out and cavort over the lake.

"That's bad luck right there," Sam says.

"We don't have time for bad luck. Help me with this?"

I know just which canoe to take. I've been scoping them out for days, noting the ones that leak, the ones that house gigantic water spiders, the ones that are dented and chipped. The one I select is a sleek aluminum beast, unexpectedly light and maneuverable. We pull it out and ease it halfway into the lake. Shallow ripples—you can't really call them waves—lap against the boat and suck it this way and that. Sam climbs in and keeps his center of gravity low as he goes to the front. I lock the shed and hand him two paddles and our backpacks. I push the canoe into the water, getting my feet wet before hopping into the stern.

"You're not wearing shoes!"

"I got used to it. They're not approved over there."

"Screw that. If I go, I'm showing them how to make shoes."
He gives me a paddle. "Hot shoes." I shove us off the beach;
with a scraping *sluck* we enter the domain of the lake.

Sam paddles on the port side; I handle starboard and steer.
In the woods on the opposite shore we see scattered lights—the
girls' restrooms and maintenance facilities. The ladies of Oasis
Villa are there somewhere, asleep (in bras? *do they sleep in bras?*)
or maybe up and about like we are, causing trouble.

"You see Anna?" Sam asks. "Maybe she's standing you up."

"Don't say that. And don't talk loud; if we get caught, we'll
get this stuff reconfiscated."

"If we get caught we're going *home*, what're you talking
about?"

"What's really bad is I forgot life preservers."

"Life *jackets*, not life preservers. Nobody says *life preservers*
except counselors. And who cares?"

"It's not safe."

"Raids aren't safe. Are you gonna tip the canoe?"

"No."

"You think I'm gonna tip the canoe?"

"No."

"Is some creature from the other-normal world gonna tip
the canoe?"

"I hope not!"

"Then keep paddling. You look better without a life jacket.
Like Indiana Jones."

"I don't look like Indiana Jones."

"If you had different hair, you might look like Indiana Jones. I'm trying to help you out here."

We settle into a quiet rhythm, our paddles cutting the black water and leaving arcing wakes of drips between strokes. It becomes hypnotic, blissful, and when we cross the halfway point of the lake, I make a point of looking all the way from one end to the other. I think about how small this lake really is, how it's not even on a map of New Jersey, how it's part of a nameless green splotch. I think of a globe, where this whole state is smaller than the nail on my pinkie, and then of that globe splitting in two, and of those globes dividing, and of innumerable globes filling a cosmic bag—and the lake still feels *big*. Tiny places have all the drama and beauty necessary for a universe.

I spot Anna on a dock. Her feet hang over the water. She's working on her mittens. I see the glint of her knitting needles and her bare legs.

"She's there!" Sam whispers. "How is she there?"

"Quiet, don't scare her. I didn't tell her you were coming."

"What? You idiot, what's she going to think?"

We paddle up. She puts her knitting down. Her dress goes to her knees. Her black hair is as reflective as the lake.

"You made it! Who's he? And where are your life preservers?"

I steer us aground next to the dock. The beach on the girls' side is sandy, not pebbly. I wade to shore as suavely as possible. "Meet my friend Sam Josephs," I say.

"I know you. You've been here for a few years."

"So have you."

"You never talk to me. You too good for me?"

"Nah. You might be too good for this one, though—"

"All right, *okay*. Anna, it's good to see you."

She leans in for a hug. I almost try to sneak in a kiss but I don't want to do anything drastic. If I come this far and then mess up, it'll kill me. The hug is nice anyway.

"You came across the lake for me. Nobody's done that before."

"Yeah," Sam says. "When he got me, I figured he was going to the dining hall to steal soda, but he's dead set—"

"Soda? Your dining hall has *soda*?"

"They got it stashed away," Sam explains. "Only the counselors can get to it. Doesn't yours have soda?"

"Some girls raided ours and took all the soda! The counselors caught them and poured it down the toilets in front of everyone. It's all anybody's talking about. Can you guys seriously get soda?"

"No," I say.

"Yeah!" Sam grins. "We already busted into the camp director's cabin."

"Sam!"

"You went into *Dale's* cabin?" Anna asks, like she's concerned for his welfare.

"Yeah, is that a problem? Do you know him?"

"No!" She waves her hand like, *No way.* "Just . . . you

know . . . I've been coming to camp for a while so I know him from events." She grins. "That's *badass* that you busted into his cabin. Let's keep it up. Let's steal some soda."

"I don't . . . really . . . how will you get back here?"

"You can bring me back after it's over. Worse comes to worse, you walk me around the lake. We have like five hours until it's light. Let me get my knitting. And a life preserver. And if we get caught, this was your guys' idea."

95

WE CANOE TO THE BOYS' SIDE IN STYLE
and ease. Sam and I have a level of coordination that makes
Anna, sitting in the middle, ask if we've done this before. "I
think we did it in a game once—" I start, but Sam slaps the side
of the canoe with his paddle.

"Water snake," he explains. "Coming up the side of the
boat."

"No it wasn't! Perry, it wasn't a water snake, was it? What
game were you talking about?"

"Nothing. Water snake."

On the shore, I help Anna out first, Sam second. Once our
bags are safe and she has her life preserver off, Sam and I haul
the canoe out of the water and stash it upside down in the
shed. I've done this many times before, but it feels different
with a girl watching. Better. Provable in court.

I lock the shed and leave the key in the lock, wiping off
my fingerprints. We walk on the side of the road, jumping into the trees at the slightest hint of a shoe crunch or
vehicular rumble. At one point a Jeep drives by and I think I
see Dale at the wheel, furious. I reach my hand out for Anna's

a few times but always draw back. It seems wrong somehow; it makes me think of the sparkling fingernails on the last hand that held mine. In ten minutes we arrive at the dining hall.

96

IN THE DEAD OF NIGHT, ABANDONED, the dining hall is like a fort. Under the porch that runs the length of it, smooth stones outline a slope down to its foundation, where huge beams rear up out of concrete. I can imagine snakes and giant insects living there, waiting for an interloper to trip and roll to the center. I clench the knives in my pocket. I haven't told Anna about them. All we're going to do is kiss, hopefully, so I really shouldn't need knives, but the knives make me calmer. I wonder if any wars have ever been started by nervousness over girls. Not like the Trojan War, where the Greeks went to *free* a woman; like the king wanted to talk to a girl, but he was scared, so he started a war instead.

"What do we do?" Anna asks.

"Sam can handle the lock, right, Sam?"

"Sure."

"So let's, ah . . . hang over here while he busts in." I see a big rock a ways off, like the ones in Central Park where people play guitar and smoke. "We'll stand guard."

"'Guard'?" Sam raises his eyebrows at me. "You got five minutes. I'll be back with the soda." He slaps my hand—an authentic New York *smack*—and bounds up the steps. Anna and I go to the rock.

"You're not gonna explain the barefoot thing?"

"I just find it more comfortable. You're not gonna explain the knitting?" She still has the needles by her side; the half-finished mittens hang off them.

"I don't like wasted time. With this around, I'm always doing something."

"That's cool."

"You ever hold a girl's hand before?"

I stop.

"It's okay. I saw you almost try back there. You ever done it? You can tell me."

"I . . . uh . . ." I don't want to lie about Ada. I feel like she'll know. What motivated me to do this again? Spite, that's right. "Yes. Yes I have."

"Was she nice?"

I stall. I know the answer (*yes yes yes*), but my brain relishes the opportunity to relive the memory. The soft length of Ada's fingers and the way they stopped time. It was different from adrenaline; it was like adrenaline but with peace added. Once I start thinking about Ada's hands, I think about her versus Anna, and then my brain messes with me, sparking up an internal dialogue that leaves me speechless for a moment, which may make Anna think I'm deep and mysterious.

What's wrong with you, Perry, you don't like actual *girls from* Earth?

Ada showed me constellations! She saved my life! It's perfectly normal for me to miss her!

What are you, some kind of fantasy elf pervert?

"You okay, Perry?"

"Nothing! Yeah! Fine!"

"What'd you bring in your backpack?"

"Nothing."

"That's a girl's trick. You ask them something and they say 'nothing' when it's really super important. You can't pull that on me. I'm gonna find out." Anna smiles. The mechanical pencils inside my backpack rattle. I shouldn't have left Sam. What if this goes wrong? I don't know how it could go wrong, but . . . who am I kidding? It already *has* gone wrong! We're not even supposed to be here!

Anna takes my hand. Hers is plump and light. She twines her fingers around mine. As soon as she touches me, we stop talking. Communication parameters sublimate into tiny variances in the grain of her skin against mine. I become instantly hard. I don't want to be, but there it is. I try to squelch it with my thighs. I'm suddenly certain—I know it's bad that this coincides with the erection, but I'm just being honest—that Anna *does* correspond to the princess. We sit on the rock. "What's that shaking?"

My knee twitches up and down, like a butterfly. "I'll stop."

"Are you nervous?"

"It's complicated. You might not realize it, but you're very significant."

"I realize it."

"Not the way I do."

"Let me see your bag." She grabs it before I can stop her and unzips it. She sees something inside, and her face twists. "Are you serious?"

"What?"

"*Creatures and Caverns Rule Book: Other Normal Edition?*" She pulls it out. The genie stares at me from over the pirate ship.

"What? What's the problem?"

"You're one of *those* people?"

I squint at her. "Don't."

"What?"

"Don't say that." I take my bag back.

"I'm just saying. Can't you take a joke?"

"I've never been good at taking jokes."

"You're from the city; you should be able to take a joke."

Anna laughs. She has beautiful teeth. They make me forget her words. She creeps her fingers onto my hand and puts her wrist in my palm. I wrap my hand around it. It's like when I talked to her back at the dance: I hate her but I want her, too. I think about doing things to her on this rock, about being fluid and hot and unstoppable . . . *manhood*! This is it! I'm about to hook up with a girl I don't even like!

"Shut your eyes," she says. I move my face toward her face. I hear bugs circling us. Bugs don't care that we're about to kiss—they just sense two warm bodies that they want to bother. Bugs know the truth. One *baps* into my closed eyelid. I snap my eyes open. I see Anna's lips and then her feet. She has open-toed sandals. Her nails are dark. My heart jumps.

"I can't do this."

"What?"

"I can't kiss you."

"Why not?"

"I just . . . I like somebody else."

"Ex*cuse* me? Who?"

"You don't know her."

"You're not allowed to *like anybody else.* I made a bet."

"What?"

"I bet my friends—don't worry about it. What do you mean, you're not going to kiss me? I came out to meet you!"

"I'm a *bet*?"

She sighs, like it's annoying to explain. "After I told my friends about meeting you at the nurse's office, they dared me to get with you. You're the only white boy in camp, and you're like the dorkiest one anybody's ever seen. They said they'd take me shopping if I hooked up with you."

"Screw you!"

"What? It's not like you have a lot of options. Where are you going?"

"Some princess you are! A *bet*? Seriously?"

"Girls bet on these kinds of things all the time. Come back!"

"Good-bye, Anna!"

"What's wrong with you? Are you gay? I'm gonna tell people you're gay!"

"*Tell* them I'm gay!"

"I *will*!"

I stomp back to the dining hall. My face is hot and my stupid penis is still hard. I slap it down, but that just makes it rowdy. "Sam!" I call.

"Over here!" His voice sounds strained. I peek around the corner and he's there, in the parking lot, but his neck is held back and a knife is pressed against his throat. Ryu holds him tight. Tiny and the Silver Eel flank him. Sam stays taut, eyes wet.

"You," Ryu says, sneering at me. "White Lotus never forgets."

97

"DID YOU REALLY STAB A CAB DRIVER?"
I manage.

"Shut up!" Sam hisses. "Do what he says! He took my
knife!"

"If you want to fight, Ryu, you messed with the wrong guy."
I pull out my *two* knives. It takes a moment to open the hinged
blades. "Stupid . . . things . . . hold on—"

"No!" Ryu spits. "Drop those or he gets cut!"

I lay the knives on the ground, blades out.

"That's good." Ryu lets Sam go. He runs to me, feeling his
neck, making sure it's still unperforated. Ryu steps forward
with the White Lotus Crew. "I don't even want him. I want
you," he says. "I know what you are."

"You do?"

"You're one of those bitches always needs to have the last
word."

"That's not true—"

"Shut up!"

Behind him, Tiny rubs his fists. The Silver Eel tugs on the
stringy hairs that hang over his eyes. "I've seen it since I first

saw you. You think it's funny to try and make other kids think there's a raccoon outside the yurt?"

"No, I—"

"Who the *fuck* are you? You think because you're smart you're better than everybody else?"

"No," I say, but that's not entirely true. I do think I'm better than the White Lotus Crew.

"You don't mess with White Lotus. It's good for you to learn this now: you don't mess with *any* crews. Some people in this world got friends who have their *back*, understand, and some are little bitches who sit by themselves and think that makes them better than everybody else. You know which one you are."

I glance at Sam. Can we coordinate a counterattack with just our eyes, like killer monkeys? Sam mouths, *Run!* I shake him off.

"I'll fight you, Ryu, if that's what you want."

"You don't fight me." He picks up my knives and gives one to each henchman. "You fight *us*." They step forward.

"Tiny? The Silver Eel? That's not fair! You have knives!"

"Who you calling Tiny?" Tiny asks.

"Sorry, I thought that was your name."

"Silver Eel? That's racist."

"No it's not! How's an eel racist?"

"Because I'm Asian."

"I'm not making this up! A guy told me at breakfast—"

Ryu slashes at me. For the briefest piece of a second, I can't believe it's happening, but then the part of my brain that knows how to handle the World of the Other Normals takes over. I jump backward in a half leap, half trip. Ryu's blade zips past where my stomach was. I hit the ground on my rear end.

"Stop!" I fling a rock at Ryu's leg. It misses his shin by an inch. He advances. I back away, my hands scrambling for more rocks, anything to throw—

He steps on my bad ankle.

"Agh!"

I struggle with my other leg but I'm pinned. Ryu draws back the knife. I reach for another rock but all that's around me is dust—I taste something in the back of my throat, fear or blood—

"Yaaaaaaaaaagh!" Sam speeds in like a cannonball.

He knocks Ryu over. Ryu's knife falls to the ground. The two of them roll on top of each other like dogs, snarling and biting. I get up and see a hefty stick a few feet away. I grab it and limp toward Ryu. The Silver Eel steps in front of me.

"I'll throw this right in your face," he says, holding his knife like a dart.

"Go for it. Free shot."

"Perry! Help!" Sam yells. Ryu has him pinned: one hand on his neck, one holding his wrists behind his head.

The Silver Eel throws his knife at me. I swing my stick. Total reflex action, a shot in the dark. *Ping*—the knife ricochets under the dining hall. The Silver Eel goes to retrieve it. "What's wrong with you?" Ryu yells. "Get him!"

Tiny charges me. I hurl the stick at him. It sails end over

end and cracks him right in the face. His feet kick up while his upper body jerks back. He lands hard on his spine. His knife skids away.

"What are you *doing*?" Ryu yells. Sam takes advantage of his distraction to head-butt him in the cheek. Considering his bald dome, it's the right move; something *pops* in Ryu's face and he rolls off, writhing in the dirt.

"Yoo difluffcated muh *juh*!" he screams. Sam rushes over to me.

"Had enough?" I ask Ryu. He sits up, grabs his chin, and pushes his jawbone back into place. *Snap!*

"Jesus."

"Not gonna help you now." Ryu takes Tiny's knife and throws it at me, but he doesn't throw it like a dart the way the Silver Eel did. He tosses it professionally, in a tight spin, and it makes a few complete circles before burying itself in my shoulder.

"Aaaaagh!"

I stagger back. I look at the knife sticking out of me. It looks wrong—not just painful, *logically incorrect*. Hot blood spreads into my shirt. It burns more than it hurts.

I pull the knife out. *Now* it hurts. I double over, holding the blade. "You made one . . . mistake . . . ," I say. "Now I've got a knife."

"So do I." Ryu picks up the one that Sam knocked out of his hand.

"Stop!"

Anna runs out in front of the dining hall. She has her knitting needles in one hand and her mittens in the other. She really must love those mittens.

"Ryu! Perry! What are you doing? You have *knives*? This is *camp*!"

"Quiet, woman, this doesn't concern you."

"I'm getting the counselors. I'm calling the *cops*!"

"With what phone?"

Anna holds her hands up like a crossing guard, mittens facing Ryu, needles facing me. "Put the knives *down*."

"You really should go," Sam says from the side, holding his head. "You don't want to get hurt."

"You're sweet," Anna says, "but I'm sure these two will—"

"Duck!"

Ryu throws his knife at me.

Anna crouches to avoid it. The knife spins; I watch, detached. It's coming right at my face. Sam picked this knife up from Dale's cabin; prior to that it belonged to some camper who had it confiscated. Prior to that it was purchased at a hobby or hunting shop; prior to that it was shipped from the manufacturer; prior to that it was made, probably in China. Now, after everything it's been through, after everything *I've* been through, it's going to end my life. I have a perfect view as it pirouettes toward my head—it looks one-dimensional, a point in space. I shut my eyes—

"Yoink!"

Mortin Enaw stands in front of me, knife wrapped in the

tip of his tail. Wearing sweatpants.

"You broke my lighter *and* you didn't leave me any clothes?" He grins, and then Ada Ember steps forward, wearing corduroys and a T-shirt that I passed over in the Lost and Found.

The White Lotus Crew is thus forced to reevaluate its idea of reality.

98

"WHAT THE—" TINY SAYS. HE'S STILL ON the ground, but suddenly he isn't so hurt.

"Who are—" the Silver Eel starts. He abandons his knife search and looks left and right as if ninjas are about to attack him.

"Get them!" Ryu yells. His henchmen stay put.

"Excuse me," Ada says, grabbing the knitting needles out of Anna's hand. Anna stays crouched on the ground, shielding her eyes as if from an explosion, saying, "This isn't real this isn't real this isn't real." Ada bounds away from her, tackles Ryu, and jabs the needles into his neck. He screams—

"No!" I yell. "Don't kill him!"

And then I see that she didn't stab his neck; she stabbed the ground *next to* his neck, the metal spikes so close they pinch his skin. The needles stick up like bolts in Frankenstein's monster. Ada pins Ryu's arms and puts her knee on his chest.

"Good to see you again, Ryu."

"Who are you, you crazy bitch? How does he have a tail—"

"Shut up!" Sam says. "Don't let him move!" He kicks Ryu in the side. "That's for breaking my glasses!" He pushes his glasses up his nose; one of the lenses is spiderwebbed. "And *that's* for messing with my friend!" He turns. "Hello. You must be Ada Ember. And you're Mortin Enaw. I'm Sam Josephs."

"You *told* people about us?" Mortin shakes his head. "Never mind." He rips the pocket out of his sweatpants and presses it against my shoulder wound. "We got big problems."

"You're right you got big problems!" Ryu shouts. "You're all—*mmm!*"

Ada covers his mouth. "Anna, do you mind passing me those mittens you've been working on?"

Anna peeks through her hands. "Who are you?"

"Just hand them over, dear."

Anna complies. Ada ties the mittens around Ryu's mouth. "Perfect."

"Mmm! Mmm guh kuh uhh, Puhh!"

I don't say anything. I figure I'll let him have the last word.

"Are you . . . monsters?" Anna asks. "How do you know my name?"

"You need to go back around the lake and stay there, okay?" Mortin says. "Don't tell anyone what happened here."

"Are you demons?"

"We're other normals. And we're just as scared as you."

"Of what?"

"Yeah, Mortin, of what?" I tap my shoulder. The lining of the pocket makes a decent bandage. Everything seems over to me. Blood adheres to my skin. I make a fist; that's the first thing I test. I can do it. I'll be okay.

"Things took a turn for the worse back home," Mortin explains.

A groaning crack comes from the woods behind us. Then a crash.

"Mortin, what is that?"

"An old friend, a new enemy, and someone I didn't think would fit through a thakerak."

A tree trunk moans as it falls and splinters fifty feet away. Whatever it is, it's coming closer. I hear a sharp, evil *hsssssssss* that ends with a rapid *clickclickclick*, like a combination snake-cockroach. Then the smell hits me. I've never smelled rotting flesh, but I know in my gut that this is what it smells like: huge, dead, *slick*, wafting out of the trees in a sweet wave.

"*Ophisa?*" I ask. "You brought Ophisa to my *summer camp?*"

"Not just him. How's your shoulder feel? You have a full range of motion?"

"Mortin! *What did you do?*"

Tiny slowly raises his arm and points, mumbling incoherent interrogatives. Ryu stops yelling into his mittens, goes quiet, and stares. The Silver Eel streaks away toward the road.

"I'm sorry," Mortin says.

From out of the woods, a gigantic praying mantis claw jabs into the earth. It rears up—it has a barbed tip, like a scorpion tail—and plunges down again as a second claw steps forward. It takes me a moment to realize that these are *legs*, and they're connected to a huge, segmented *body*, armored like a bug's or rhinoceros's, and the body is connected to a slender reptilian *neck*, with scales that shine in the moonlight, and on top of the neck, as tall as the trees, is a nest of fangs and eyes that form a nightmare *face*.

That's not all. Two creatures sit on Ophisa like they're riding a dinosaur. The first I'm not surprised to see: Officer Tendrile. His tentacles wrap around the monster's reptile neck. Behind him, though, is someone unexpected.

I recognize her immediately. Ada's silver figure was a perfect likeness. She has long straight hair and shining eyes and bounteous beautiful breasts. The princess. She looks royal and regal, right down to her waist—but then it all goes wrong. Where the figure ended in jagged metal, she has tentacles just like Officer Tendrile's, wound around Ophisa.

99

"OH, THIS IS VERY BAD," I MUMBLE. OPHISA steps forward. Ooze drips from his eyes onto his fangs. His sixth leg cantilevers into the parking lot as a small tree crashes in front of Tiny. Tiny hustles away faster than I thought he could move. Ophisa stares at me and hisses, *"Mini Pecker!"*

"H-how do you—?"

His eyes twitch. Inside each is a bulbous black pupil. *"I know all your sssecrets, boymeat."*

"That's right!" Officer Tendrile says. "There's your boymeat, for the taking! The one who caused all this trouble."

"Princess!" I call. "Why are you doing this?"

She stares straight ahead like she doesn't hear. Ophisa scans Mortin and Ada. *"You who helped will die ssslow . . . inssside me."*

Anna bolts. Ophisa swings his tail at her, crowned with bony spikes. He's about to decapitate her, but the princess orders, *"No!"* and he stops. Anna reaches the road and flees to safety.

"Good boy. We don't hurt her," the princess says, patting his neck. Ophisa purrs, a horrible leaking sound.

Ada pulls the knitting needles away from Ryu, who wastes no time running under the dining hall. Ophisa pulls back the flaps of his facial muscles and spits at me. I dive out of the way. The spittle hits the ground, bringing up foul-smelling steam.

"Into the dining hall!" Mortin yells. Ophisa whips his head around and stomps forward as Mortin, Ada, Sam, and I run under the banner—WELCOME TO CAMP WASHISKA LAKE!

100

"SAM, DID YOU PICK THE LOCK?"

"It didn't work!" He smashes the door with a rock. Ada turns around and throws one of the knitting needles at Ophisa's face. It lands in the dark flesh around his fangs—and then the eyeballs above it secrete a mucus that drips down and sizzles the needle out of existence.

"You can't stop us!" Officer Tendrile yells. "If you give up now, I'll kill you myself, and quickly!"

"Screw you!" I call back. We hop gingerly through the shattered glass. Seeing the damage makes me think of practicalities: at some point *counselors* are going to appear, and they're going to want to know what the hell is going on.

Inside, the dining hall is put away for the night. The chairs are stacked and the floor is squeaky clean. We dash under a table, all talking at once.

"What is that thing—"

"The princess is a *celate*?"

"Do we have any weapons—"

"The knives are outside—"

"Shut up!" Mortin says. "Maybe we're safe here. I don't think he can get in."

"No, but I can."

Officer Tendrile walks through the broken door. Behind him, Ophisa's shadow lies over the porch and parking lot. He must be twenty feet tall with his neck stretched up. I don't see the princess; maybe she's enjoying the show.

"You have caused me entirely too much trouble, Mr. Eckert." Tendrile approaches calmly. "If the rest of you would like to leave the boy to me, you'll find I reward you quite handsomely."

"You talk a big game for a guy with no sword," I say.

"I don't need a sword to kill a little boy."

"Excuse me?"

"Little boys I can kill with my tentacles. Care to try?" He wiggles them playfully.

I rush him from under the table.

101

"PERRY, NO!"

But I'm already doing it, and for the full effect I'm yelling, *"Dieeeeee!"* I am going to tackle Officer Tendrile like a football player and beat him with my fists; that's as foresighted as my plan gets. I can't help it. After everything I've done—everything I've done to *him*—he doesn't have the decency to refer to me as a *guy*, or a *man*, or an *adversary*, instead of a *boy*? All the same emotions that made me take down my pants in front of Anna stream through me, but now they are a guided missile of violence and hate, and besides, I can't stand his stupid mustache—

He whips a tentacle at me. It wraps around my head and slips into my mouth. I *mmmmph* against it as it slides past my tongue like the worst kiss in the world. It presses into my throat. My neck puffs up. The tongue enters my esophagus. Oh *no*. More tentacles surround me, grabbing my arms and legs. What was I thinking? I look up. Officer Tendrile is much taller than me, and he's smiling, satisfied. I feel his suckers bite into my gullet, cutting me from the inside out—and the *taste*, the taste is—

You know what, the taste isn't that bad.

I chomp down as hard as I can. His tentacle is already halfway down my throat, so the part my teeth bite into is meaty and resistant and coiled, but once I break his slimy flesh and dig in, it tears into strings under my incisors. He screams and his other tentacles twitch, allowing me to pull my hands free so I can hold the one in my mouth and *really* give it a good bite, feeling my teeth hit my teeth, and then I pull the wriggling thing out of my throat and slap him with it. It's a foot long and alive and moving and covered with my blood and his blood, and I whip him in his stupid face with it.

"Leave me *alone!*"

His severed tentacle bleeds dark red on the dining-hall floor. His other tentacles seethe against one another like they're getting mixed signals from his brain. I realize I've never seen him *hurt* before. He stares at his new stump in disbelief, and I get it: he's a coward. He did what he did with swords and guns because he could never fight with his bare hands, or his tentacles, and he got his position of power because he needed it, because he was useless otherwise. I see all this as he turns and runs out of the dining hall, stumbling on seven legs.

"Welcome to Camp Washiska Lake, motherfucker!"

102

"PERRY, YOU DID IT!" ADA RUNS UP TO ME.
"Are you okay?"

I drop the tentacle and move my jaw around and pat my
Adam's apple. "I feel a bit violated, but I'll be all right."

"Fool!" we hear outside. Ophisa turns his titanic body. The
princess leaps off his neck to confront Tendrile in the parking
lot. "Go back in there! Kill them all!"

"I can't, mistress. Look what he did to me!"

She wraps a tentacle of her own around his stump to examine it. She seems genuinely concerned about his welfare. She
speaks quietly to him—comfortingly—and then kisses him,
hard, on the lips, pressing into his body while their tentacles
commingle.

"Ew," I say.

"No kidding," Ada says. Mortin and Sam join us. We all
watch, flabbergasted, as the princess walks Officer Tendrile
across the parking lot toward the trees.

"Did you know?"

"We knew they were working together," Mortin says. "We
tracked Tendrile on the Boggolove cruise raft and found him

with Ophisa and the princess, outside Upekki. All the hequets who were missing from the town? They were feeding them—live—to the monster. But we didn't know they were . . . lovers."

Ophisa lumbers after the couple on his huge barbed legs.

"No!" the princess orders. "You, my pet! *You* must kill them! Find your way into that structure! Make them die . . . like food."

"*Yessss,*" says Ophisa. As Tendrile and the princess disappear into the woods, he turns to charge.

103

"BACK UNDER THE TABLE!" SAM SUGGESTS, but before we can get there, Ophisa roars and spits a great glob of venomous fluid through the broken door. Mortin shoves Sam aside. Ada and I dive to the ground. The spittle hits one of the table legs. It bubbles and steams. The table collapses.

"Stay down!" Mortin says. Ophisa swings his tail through the door, obliterating it. Then he swings again through the maw of the building to send stacks of chairs flying; I interlock my hands over the back of my skull and hear a scream and a dense *whap*. I look up: a chair caught Sam in the mouth. He wipes his wrist against his lips and leaves a dark streak. He stares at me like this is my fault. I have to admit it is.

"*Come and play with me, Mini Pecker!*" Ophisa calls. "*I can sssee what you want with your blue-haired friend. I will help you. I ssseee how you want her partsss. . . .*"

"Don't listen to him, Ada! I don't think about you that way!" How is he getting into my head?

He can see into the thoughts of anyone he turns his hundred-and-ten-eye gaze on.

Ophisa shoves his mouth through the door and unleashes a spray of fluid. It lands on my legs and eats through my jeans, burning my flesh where the dog-head bit me, eating ragged holes into my skin. I scream and flick the goop off and wipe my leg on the floor. I have small bloody craters on my calves. The pain is so huge that I laugh at it.

"Leave me, guys! Save yourselves!"

"Not a chance," Ada says. She pulls me back toward the kitchen. Ophisa paces outside like he's trying to figure out a way in. Even with the door destroyed, he's too big, and carpet bombing us with phlegm will only get him so far.

"How do we kill that thing?" Sam asks. We huddle against the kitchen door. Outside, Ophisa stands still. We all watch for clues to his behavior. He swings his head—with a great mound of acidic goop on it—toward one of his front legs. He brushes his fangs against the leg where it meets his body. It sizzles and steams and snaps off. His body lurches forward, on five legs now instead of six.

"What's he doing?"

Mortin gulps. "Figuring out a way in."

He repeats the process with his second front leg, sizzling it into the parking lot. When it falls, though, and he lurches forward, he catches himself—*with a new front leg in place of his old one.* The new leg is segmented and barbed like the original, but only a few feet long.

"Regeneration? Are you *kidding* me?"

"He's making smaller limbs," Ada says. "With two-foot

limbs, he can crawl right in."

"That's not fair!"

"To the kitchen! Hurry!" Sam pushes open the swinging door, and we all tumble in and flip on the lights.

104

STOVES. REFRIGERATORS. GIANT COOLERS
running under cutting boards. The kitchen has been put away
with great care. Pots and pans hang over electric ranges. Boxes
that say GOVERNMENT CHEESE are stacked in the far corner,
next to an industrial-sized canister of bleach. On one side of
the room, a conveyor belt leads to a huge stainless steel dish-
washing machine labeled HOBART.

"Why are we in here?" I ask.

"There!" Sam points to a magnetic strip above one of the
stoves. A set of knives hangs from it, in a spectrum from the
smallest paring knife to the largest meat cleaver.

"I'm okay," Ada says, holding up her remaining knitting
needle.

"Like that'll do any good," Mortin says. He takes a meat
cleaver.

"It *might*. Leave me alone."

"I call chef's knife," Sam says, grabbing a ten-inch blade. It
works for him. I picture Peter Powers, fifteenth-level barbarian,
swinging it in the snow.

"We'll wait here"—I stand by the kitchen entrance—"and

get him as he comes in. What do we aim for, anyway?"

"Eyes. Try to destroy all the eyes you can. What are you using for a weapon?"

I pull off my backpack and fill it with knives—everything left on the magnetic strip. Steak knives, bread knives, barbecue forks . . . I'm turning my backpack into an instrument of death. "You came in the nick of time," I tell Ada. "How'd you know we were in trouble?"

"Mortin felt you."

"How?"

"In my heart," Mortin says. "I felt my heart jump and I knew my correspondent was in danger."

I blinked. "*I'm* your correspondent?"

"Perry. I was giving you credit! You didn't figure it out?"

"Yeah," Sam says, "I don't even know how this all works and I figured that part out."

"But, I—Mortin—you're *old*!"

"Smoking pebbles makes you old. I've been coming here on my own time and doing it for years. I was born the same day as you."

"But I asked you point-blank if you were my correspondent!"

"So?"

"You told me *no*! You *lied*!"

"Some people think that life is about lying all the time, and some think it's about being truthful all the time, but really it's a very mundane matter of knowing when to do which."

"You lied and you had me paralyzed!"

"Would you two *shut up?*" Sam asks. "Two Perrys. What a nightmare."

Of course, it makes sense. Mortin and Leidan correspond to me and Jake. Which reminds me: "What happened to Leidan?"

"Don't worry about him," Mortin says, but he himself looks worried. I wonder if Leidan started drinking again, and what that means for Jake's drinking. Connections are coming into focus. Mortin had been covering up a black eye since I met him . . . *and I was hit in the eye by Ryu.* Mortin quit smoking pebbles . . . *and I quit playing Creatures & Caverns.*

"I'm not really sure how to do this," I say. "Pleased to meet you, correspondent." I stick out my hand.

"You do it like this," Mortin says. He hugs me and wraps his tail around my head. "Pleased to meet you too."

I retake my position at the door.

"Why did your heart jump?" Ada asks quietly. "If Mortin's jumped, yours must have."

"I almost kissed Anna."

"But you didn't?"

"No."

"Why not?"

"C'mon."

"C'mon what?"

"C'mon, you know."

"Pretend I don't. Tell me. *Humor* me."

"I didn't kiss her because I was thinking of you."

Ada smiles. "No kidding. Were you thinking of me as a mystical creature from another world, or a cool girl who can cook fish?"

"Both," I say. Then, without asking, like I'm supposed to, I lean in and kiss her. Ideally it would be a slow kiss, I know, with a romantic buildup, but Ada and I don't have that kind of relationship—we tend to always be in mortal danger. So it's a quick, scared, excited, flying leap of a kiss, my lips dashing to hers and pressing against them with nothing and everything to lose. I get her upper lip between my upper and lower lips and hold her like that, not opening my mouth, just feeling how soft she is, knowing that now, if I die, I'll have a beautiful memory instead of a burning regret. I drink her in through my closed lips.

"Peregrine!" She pulls back, shocked, but she can't hide her smile. "Listen!"

Tables and chairs crash outside. Clicking footsteps get louder on the linoleum.

"Boymeat! I sssmell your dessire, sssuckling!"

105

OPHISA'S FAST, BUT NOT FAST ENOUGH.
As soon as his head appears in the doorway—as big as my chest
and dripping eye venom—we all attack. I swing my backpack
at him; Sam stabs him; Ada jabs her needle at his neck; Mortin
hacks him with his meat cleaver.

Fail!

Sam's knife tears into Ophisa's mouth and rips off a hunk of
flesh, but then promptly dissolves. Ada's knitting needle can't
break his scaly neck hide. Mortin's cleaver slices off a crop of
eyes, but then Mortin drops it. My backpack turns out to be
the best choice—it doesn't do much as a weapon, but it acts
as a buffer during Ophisa's counterattack, when he knocks
into us, trying to smear acid on us with his fangs the way he
did his own legs. The bag sizzles on the floor as we're thrown
across the room—inside its eaten-away main pocket, the cover
of the *Other Normal Edition* disintegrates. Ada lands on one of
the stoves; Sam hits a fridge; Mortin hits the wall under the
empty magnetic knife strip. I find myself next to the HOBART
machine. I see a red switch underneath the conveyor belt and
press it. I may not play Creatures & Caverns anymore, but that

book was awesome, and I am pissed. Maybe the machine will confuse the monster.

An electronic roar starts up. The HOBART is as long as the room, full of jets of water and chunking metal. The conveyor belt leading to it starts rolling; inside, rows of brushes go after plates that aren't there.

"He's coming!" Mortin yells.

Beside the doorway, to either side of Ophisa's swaying neck, cracks spread and paint chips flutter to the ground. He's pressing his massive body against the walls, pushing his way into the kitchen.

"Hello, meatymeats!"

With a terrific crash of wood and plaster, he busts in. Dust rains over him. He works his fangs around one another. Steam from the HOBART starts to obscure him, but not before he spots the clump of eyeballs that Mortin lopped off him. He bends down and eats them.

We're trapped.

106

OPHISA'S LEGS ARE ONE FOURTH THE size they were outside, but his body is still huge. He dominates the room like a giant scorpion. He has his pick of us. He turns to Sam and disdainfully spits a small sizzle at his shoulder. *"I sssupposse I'll try the darkmeat first."*

"Sam!"

Ophisa raises one of his front legs. The plating on it is fresh and pink, unlike the rest of his body, which the kitchen light reveals to be freckled, swampy green. He jabs down—and sticks Sam in the thigh.

"Aaaaagh!" Sam grabs his leg. Ophisa digs in, pumping fluid through a translucent vein and into Sam's body. Sam's thigh swells. Just today, in nature studies, we learned that many arthropods paralyze their prey with neurotoxins before eating them alive.

"Somebody, distract him!"

"Hey!" Ada jumps on a stove, dancing between the burners. She waves her arms above her head. "Hey, ugly!" Ophisa turns from Sam and pulls his leg out of Sam's. Sam slumps over, eyes open and unblinking.

"Would you like to be violated by my fangsss, wench?"

I look at Ada.

"I don't know what he's talking about. I don't want that at all—"

Ophisa dives toward her. She vaults over his festoon of eyes and lands with her feet pointed like daggers into the top of his head. She screams as acid touches her toes, but Ophisa gets it worse. His face hits the stove—and Ada has turned it on.

Four electric burners crackle at once. A dozen eyes blow off Ophisa's head, spraying pungent white fluid on the walls and ceiling. A pupil lands next to me—a flat iridescent disc. Ada rolls into a corner and moans as she wipes her feet off with a rag that subsequently steams up and disintegrates.

"Mortin! Knives!" I hook my finger into my backpack and slide it across the floor to him. Inside, the book shielded a bunch of knives from getting eaten by acid. I suddenly have an idea. "Throw these in HOBART!"

"What?"

"The dishwasher!"

He pours the knives into the rumbling, clanking machine. I climb onto the conveyor belt. The acid pits in my legs make it so I can hardly stand. The room is getting hot and smells like death. I only have one chance.

"Here! Ophisa! Try me, I'm delicious!"

"Mini Pecker? You dare to taunt me?" He's hurt. He turns his singed head my way. I see his burned eyeballs and hanging fangs. I almost feel sorry for him, but then I see Sam, dead to

the world in front of a fridge, and I don't feel sorry at all.

Ophisa swings his tail at me. It arcs through the room, knocking aside pots and pitchers. It's so massive that it sends wind in front of it. The spikes at the end are like something from a dinosaur, and I absurdly recall which one—*stegosaurus*—as I dive off the conveyor belt. . . .

And Ophisa's tail plunges into HOBART.

"Yes!"

He hisses and clicks. Now he's arranged like a giant C—body at the front of the kitchen, tail stuck in the machine, head swaying back and forth, spitting wildly as he's pulled backward.

"Cheat! Traitor! Boymeat waste!"

"Help me stuff him in here!" I push at the base of his massive tail. Mortin joins me from the other side; Ada comes over despite her injured feet and adds to the effort. Inside HOBART, jets of water toss around the knives. Ophisa's neck might be impervious to knitting needles, but the knives do a good job on his tail, making him shut up (finally) and start screaming, a shrill, desperate keen that splits the steamy room.

"Almost got it! It's just like sex! Shove him in there!"

"This *isn't* like sex!" Ada yells. "If you're ever having sex and you think, 'Wow, this is like with Ophisa,' that's bad sex!"

We push together. Ophisa's tail fills the machine. He tries to swing his head at us, but his body is in the way. He tries to spit at us, but he seems to be running out of poison—it has burned off on the stove or dripped to the ground, useless.

"Make sure his legs get in!" I hoist the backmost one. It's like picking up a giant chicken leg. I see the huge vein for delivering poison and the tender joints where the leg regenerated. I heave it onto my back and, with Ada's help, shove it into HOBART. "Clear back!" Ophisa's tail and leg catch inside the machinery. His flesh rends as the conveyor belt hiccups.

"Mortin! Bleach!"

Mortin uncaps the huge bottle and pours it into the intake pipe. Ophisa convulses and shrieks and waves his head through the kitchen, crashing into chrome cabinets, hanging utensils, and tubs of oatmeal. Ada has stuffed a second leg into the dishwasher, so now he's fully stuck, the conveyor belt churning him in, knives and bleach assaulting him.

The chrome shell of the dishwasher bends outward. *Clang!* It distends to accommodate something inside. "Yes!" It happens on the other side. "It's his legs! He's getting injured and regenerating!"

Clang! The new legs that spring from Ophisa's body surge out against the metal but have nowhere to go. As they grow, they get damaged by bleach, so his body tries to make more, but those get damaged too, keeping the cycle moving . . . he's metastasizing limbs. At this rate, he'll end up firmly trapped in the machine, and we'll all get out of here—

I remember Sam. He's still by the fridge, paralyzed or dead. Ophisa slides his dazed head across the kitchen at him. His complicated mouthparts gyrate hungrily in the air. I reach Sam and put my arm under his shoulder. I try to lift him; he's a lot heavier than he looks. Ophisa's nightmare head—charred and wet and hissing—lunges toward us. His mouth, which I finally see under all the eyes and teeth, is open wide, revealing a straight red gullet. I feel like I can see all the way through to another world. There's no way to move Sam in time. I hold up my hands in a hopeless defense—

And Ophisa's head jerks forward and crashes to the ground.

The fangs close on his rotten mouth. His body stiffens up. His remaining eyes stare at nothing. His head lies like the stamen of a flower. I look at Mortin and Ada. They have taken one of his regenerating legs, poking out of HOBART, and steered its barb into a seam in his body. The leg jabbed him with his own poison. The metal shell of the dishwasher clangs outward. His legs are still growing in there. Mortin shuts off the conveyor belt.

"Is he dead?"

"Not yet." Mortin points to where Ophisa's middle legs meet his thorax. "If we stab here, we'll get his heart. Ada?"

"Peregrine?"

"I don't want to do it. I'm . . . I'm burned out."

"I'm not saying, kill him. I'm saying, say one of your prayers."

"Oh! Right. Lord, thank you so much for letting us not get killed and eaten, and please rest this creature's soul, even though he seemed pretty evil, and if Sam's just paralyzed, I hope we can get him back. Amen."

"Amen," Mortin says, and then Ada hands him a barbecue fork.

He sticks it into Ophisa's body. He turns away and holds his nose as he works the fork inside the creature, squelching this way and that, moving through paralyzed meat . . . and then he finds something vital. He shoves the fork all the way in, making it disappear. Brown blood gouts onto the floor. Ophisa's body sags and collapses. The eyes on his limp head lose their iridescence.

107

"WHAT ABOUT SAM?" I ASK. HE'S STILL frozen, eyes open, teeth clenched.

"We have to take him back to help him," Mortin says. "Only a precise set of other-normal herbs will reverse Ophisa's poison."

The steam from the dishwasher is clearing out. The side of the kitchen that we entered through is just rubble now, but the clock that was there, which somehow still operates, says 4:23. I can't believe that no counselors have come to see the commotion. This really *is* a ghetto camp.

"What do we do about this?" I ask.

"By 'this' you mean . . ."

"This!" I point to the rubble. *"This!"* I point to the huge monster carcass.

"Oh. We burn it."

"We can't burn down the dining hall!"

"Why? You need a new dining hall anyway. Get Sam out of here. I'll handle it."

I'm about to protest—but Ada lifts Sam's body, and I want to help. We sandwich him between our shoulders and stagger out the back entrance to the kitchen, emerging on the porch in the warm summer night. The air hits me and I breathe it in more thankfully than I've ever breathed anything. I never once stepped out of Mom's house or Dad's house and sniffed the air and thought, *I'm glad to be alive.*

"How are your toes?" I ask Ada.

"They'll live." She shows them to me. The flesh has been eaten off the tips of each one. Her sparkling nails are now just raw skin.

"But . . . how can you walk? Aren't you in serious pain?"

"Aren't *you* in serious pain where that acid hit your legs?"

"I can't tell. It's too exciting."

"That's how it works. *Tomorrow* is when we're gonna hurt."

Mortin runs out after us. "Go!" He tips Sam back and holds his shoulders as Ada and I each take an ankle. We move as fast as we can down the porch. A blast of heat hits us from behind. I turn to see fat orange flames leaping out of the dining hall.

"Go! Go! Go!"

We stagger over the WELCOME TO CAMP WASHISKA LAKE! banner; it lies on the steps in a heap. Ophisa must have knocked it down. As soon as we reach the parking lot, a thunderous boom sounds behind us. We lay Sam down and shield our faces as twisted chrome blows out of the dining hall and into nearby trees.

"And *that* was the furnace," Mortin says, satisfied. Underneath the building, huddled in the rocks, a shaking figure stands.

"Ryu! You're still here? Go! It's all gonna burn!"

He shakes his head. He's taken the mittens out of his mouth and unraveled the yarn. He twirls it in his fingers.

"I'm serious! Go!"

He shakes his head in small, tight motions.

"He's gone," Mortin says. "Some people can't handle the unexpected."

108

WE MOVE INTO THE WOODS, PAST THE
rock where Anna and I had our failed kiss. Behind us, the
dining hall's roof caves in; a yawning pit of flame opens up; ash
and smoke pour into the sky.

"So you guys are taking Sam back to cure him. . . . What
about me?" I picture myself touching the battery and mushrooms again—and then I realize: "How did you even *get* here?
I destroyed the mushroom patch!"

"How long has it been since you did that?"

"A week!"

"Mushrooms grow fast," Mortin says, "and no, we're not
taking you back. We've uncovered a worldwide conspiracy. The
Appointees are evil and they've got to be deposed in favor of
a real government. Maybe not like yours, but . . . *something*
decent. We're revolutionaries now."

"So take me! I can help!"

"Of course you can. But we need you here to give a story
to the counselors about why Sam's missing. Say you were out
exploring and Ryu attacked you and all of a sudden the building lit on fire and you don't know where Sam went. Then, when

his family gets called, reassure them that everything's going to be okay. Otherwise there's going to be a lot of needless worry. Plus it'd be nice to have a pair of eyes here. I've got some suspicions about correspondences at Camp Washiska Lake."

"Like Dale Blaswell and Officer Tendrile? And the princess and Anna Margolis? And Leidan and my brother?"

"You're catching on."

We move through the woods. I spot one of the branches I snapped on my way back from the mushroom patch. Of course it's hard to notice now, with all the destruction Ophisa has caused. "How am I going to explain this damage?"

Ada answers, "You ever hear of the Tunguska event, Peregrine?"

I shake my head.

"In 1908, over Siberia, an explosion took place in the sky that knocked over eighty million trees. Scientists eventually decided that it was a comet that blew up in the atmosphere."

"So? Was that it really?"

"Doesn't matter. After a few years of speculation, a nice scientific consensus emerged. Something boring, nonthreatening. That's what will happen here. Humans are really good at it. Maybe they'll say it was a freak lightning storm. A homegrown militia game gone wrong. It's not your concern."

"When will you bring Sam back?"

"Let's get to the battery first."

We hustle through the woods to the Logo Spermatikoi. When we get there, Leidan Enaw is sitting pretty next to the princess and Officer Tendrile, who lie bound on the ground. Their tentacles are tied together with extension cords; Tendrile's severed one bleeds lightly. Their arms are secured with belts; their mouths are gagged with underwear. They struggle weakly.

"How—"

"All from the Lost and Found," Leidan says. "After Mortin and Ada grabbed some clothes and went to save you, they sent me here to guard the battery. These two showed up an hour later trying to sneak back home. I bashed them with this"—he holds up a baseball bat—"and secured them." He swings the bat. "Also from the Lost and Found."

Tendrile moans. He rocks his head back and forth. He spots me. *"Mmmmph!"* He tries to sit up. Leidan pushes him down with the bat. "Looks like he's got something to say. You want to hear it?"

I genuinely consider the possibility. "No," I say. "No, I don't think I need to hear him at all."

109

ADA CHECKS ON THE FRESHLY GROWN mushrooms next to the tree. Leidan keeps an eye on Tendrile and the princess, who just stares up, an empty beautiful shell with a nightmare groin. Mortin reaches into his sweatpants and pulls out my Pekker Cland miniature. It's untouched by Ophisa's acid; it still looks like me.

"What? How?"

"It was still in your backpack. I got it before I set the fire. This isn't just a pewter figure anymore, Perry. It's a *beacon*. You'll find it quite hard to destroy. It's become charged with correspondational energy. Its unique importance to you as you went through your journey has given it abilities."

"Magic?"

"Just keep it on you. It's tied to you now, and you're tied to us. If you see it glow, that means we need you."

I put it in my pocket and realize that this is good-bye.

"What am I going to do without you guys? I have so many questions! How do I handle Dale? How do I handle Anna? How do I handle . . . everything?"

"You figure it out," says Ada. "That's what you do,

Peregrine: you figure things out."

She starts prepping the battery for transit. I turn Sam over—he's breathing steadily at least—and remove his back-pack. I know he has to be naked to go to the World of the Other Normals. "I'm not taking your clothes off," I tell his unconscious body. "Mortin can do that. But I am taking one thing."

I pull out the Polaroid that he took from Dale's cabin.

"Guys? Picture?"

110

TWO DAYS LATER, I LIE ON THE FLOOR OF my yurt after lunch and compose a letter to my parents. I haven't written them . . . well, *ever*, but when I force myself to sit down and start, I find it flows quickly. No television or phones interrupt my letter. It's like having their undivided attention for once.

Dear Mom and Dad,

I assume one of you will read this and pass it to the other, maybe through your lawyers, but I encourage you to read it together like the old days. How are you? I am fine. Camp is great. Jake is doing an excellent job as a CA and I see him every day. Some big things happened since I got your first letter (thanks, Dad) and I wanted to fill you in.

First of all, our dining hall burned down. This may seem like a bad thing but the camp had it insured and they're starting work on a new one as soon as possible for next year. In the meantime we're all cooking our meals at campfires! It's a lot more of a "camp experience," I think. I'm good at it, too. I can make fires, tend them, and cook everything from hot dogs to fresh fish and crab. It's made me more popular with my yurtmates.

Also, my friend Sam unexpectedly disappeared, but I have a feeling he's going to be back any day. Like I told his mom, I know he's safe. I can't explain why but I do. You know how sometimes kids are abducted by cult members and then they go missing for years, but when they come back, everything is cool? I have a feeling that's happening to Sam right now, but without the cult—and it'll take another day, maybe, not years.

You'll be happy to know that I've been keeping away from Creatures & Caverns. Actually, my book was being stored in the dining hall and it burned in the fire. But that's okay! I've been doing some of my own writing, about my camp experience, and trying to make friends with the other kids. After a few missteps with this guy Ryu, things are looking better. Ryu's out of the picture, anyway; they found him outside the dining hall after it burned and he's a prime suspect because he once stabbed a cab driver. He keeps telling the police this crazy story about a monster that attacked the building, and they think he's trying to cop a fake insanity plea.

Guys, you know how you wanted me to meet girls at camp? I met one. She has an unusual name (I'm keeping it under wraps for now), but I kind of have an unusual name too. Enclosed please find a picture of us. It's a little weird because we took it on a coed night hike (and we are slightly bruised—camp fun!), but I think it gets the point across. I really like this girl! She lives kind of far away, and we're taking things slow for now, because we have a lot of differences we're still learning about. But I think you'd like her too. Note her blue hair. This is because she is "punk rock." I hope to be seeing more of her.

Over the last two weeks, by the way, I've been thinking about my name. I always hated "Perry Eckert," because it got turned into "Mini Pecker," but I thought "Peregrine" was worse. I figured it out now. I'm going to stay Perry, because it's my name and it's who I am, no matter what, but I'm going to let the girl call me Peregrine. She told me what it means! Mom—I don't know how you could give me a cool name like Peregrine without telling me what it means. Maybe you never knew yourself? It's from Latin. It means "traveler."

Love,
Perry
aka Peregrine
aka Pekker Cland
aka Mortin Enaw

NED VIZZINI

is the author of the acclaimed teen books *It's Kind of a Funny Story* (which became a major motion picture), *Be More Chill*, and *Teen Angst? Naaah . . .* Ned has written for the *New York Times, Salon,* and *L Magazine.* He has spoken at more than two hundred schools, universities, libraries, and organizations around the world about writing and mental health. And his work has been translated into seven languages. Currently he is writing for ABC. You can visit Ned online at www.nedvizzini.com.